A PINEVILLE LIFE
COACHING MYSTERY

COACHING CAN *KILL*

KRISTEN DOUGHERTY

To my coaches and teachers for helping me continue to grow.
And to my family for your love and support.

CHAPTER 1

"I'm going to get fired!" The woman sitting in the chair across from me blurted this out when I asked what she wanted my help with today. Her name was Maggie, and she was a first-time client, in Pineville on vacation. She had come to the yoga studio for a class the day before and signed up for a free twenty-minute gift coaching session. She was on the verge of tears, and we were only ten seconds in.

"Okay, take a step back and tell me what happened. You didn't actually get fired, right?" I kept my voice steady to give her a sense of calm. This was a safe space.

"Well no, not yet," she said. "But I got a really bad review, so it's only a matter of time. I don't know why I thought I could do this job. I knew it was a mistake when they hired me. I'm just not cut out for it. It's too hard, too much pressure, and I'm not good enough to handle it all. Maybe I should quit before they let me go?" She looked at me expectantly, that last phrase a question.

I could feel the anxiety oozing off her. She was looking to have me tell her exactly what to do. As a life coach, though, my job isn't to tell people what to do, but to help them look at situations in a different way and give them the tools they can use to figure things out on their own.

"Before you make any decisions, tell me a little more about your review. What was bad about it?" I asked.

Maggie took a deep breath. "They told me I have to do a better job building client relationships, that I'm great with the internal team but I need to connect more with the client. Higher-level positions are all about relationship building, and I can't rely on my analysis and recommendations to grow the business."

"So, you're doing well with your team relationships, but you need to work on your client relationships in order to achieve a higher-level position. Is that right?" I repeated back what she told me but emphasized the positive feedback in addition to the critical feedback.

Maggie nodded in agreement.

"What other feedback did you get?" I asked.

"They told me that I need to improve my messaging skills, that my presentations could be clearer and more streamlined, and that there is too much information and too much detail. I need to focus on the bigger picture." Maggie started to explain the feedback but quickly transitioned to sharing her concern about it. "I don't have any idea how I'd even go about changing this. I feel like I'm doing the best job I can now and I'm working so hard as it is!"

"So, it sounds like when it comes to your presentations, it's a matter of working on how the information is packaged up and presented back to the client and turning your focus from the details to a broader perspective, which is probably what the clients are looking for. Does that sound right?"

"Yes, I think so." Maggie started to calm down.

"What else?" I asked.

"I guess that was really it. Those were the two big things they told me I have to work on over the next year if I want to be considered for the next level. And this is an up-or-out agency, so if I don't improve, I really will be fired. And my rating was a 7 out of 10, which is like a C–, which is like the worst grade I've ever gotten in my entire life. I've never been such a failure at anything!" Maggie started tearing up again.

I offered her the box of tissues I keep on my desk, and she took one.

As she wiped her tears, I started to share a perspective on the situation that I believed would help her. "I know you're really upset about the review, but the first thing I'd like you to consider is that the review itself isn't the problem." For clients I haven't worked with before, this is usually the first area that we spend time on. It's a concept that most people aren't aware of and learning it can open them up to seeing the world in an entirely new way.

"I'm not sure what you mean." Maggie looked perplexed but interested.

"There is the feedback you got in the review, the words themselves, the information provided to you, the suggestions for things to work on or to change." I paused for emphasis, and Maggie nodded slightly. I could tell she was with me. "And then there is what you're making it mean. And it sounds like you're making it mean that you're not good enough, or that you're destined to fail. So of course, that must feel terrible."

Maggie's expression held still. I could see she was processing what I had to say. After a moment of silence, realization hit, and her eyes grew wide. "It does feel terrible! Why am I doing that to myself?"

I smiled and reassured her, "It's totally normal. It's just what the brain does. It's trying to protect you. Having a review, hearing feedback, that's scary stuff for the brain. And the easiest way to avoid that scary stuff is to quit. If you quit, then you won't have to face the review. You won't have to work on changing things or doing them in a new way. You also won't have to face the next review. Do you really want to quit?"

"No, I love my job!" Maggie responded immediately, and I felt the truth in her statement. "I just want to feel like I'm doing it well."

"Then the way to approach this is to look at it in pieces. First, do you agree that as a company they have a way that they want things done, and it's a good thing for them to provide their employees feedback and direction on how to work the way they feel is most successful for them?"

Maggie nodded her head. "Yes, intellectually I agree, but it just feels terrible."

I corrected her gently. "You're making it feel terrible because you're interpreting the feedback you got as a message that you, as a person, aren't good enough. That isn't true. Let that sink in." I paused for a few seconds before continuing. "There is who you are as a person, and there is what you do in your job. Those two things are not at all related to each other. This job feedback has nothing to do with who you are as a person. It isn't about you at all. It's about what you do at this job, and they are just asking you to do things a little differently."

Tears streamed down Maggie's face as she allowed my words to sink in. After a good ten seconds, she wiped her cheeks with the same tissue she still held in her hand. Then she took in a big breath of air and let it out. Her voice was soft when she finally spoke. "So, what do I do? How do I stop making it mean something about me?"

"What we can do right now is take another look at that feedback and see if we can think about it in a way that will serve you. Does that sound okay?" I offered.

Maggie nodded but didn't say anything.

I glanced down at the notepad on my desk where I had jotted down the general aspects of the review, but I wanted to hear the words directly from Maggie again. It's best for the client to be engaged without me feeding information back to them. "Let's talk about the feedback on your presentations. What were the exact words in your review?"

"They said the presentations could be clearer and more streamlined and that they're too detailed. I need to focus on the bigger picture." Maggie's voice quavered slightly as she spoke the words. There was still emotion charging her statement.

"They are just words, Maggie. They can't hurt you, and in fact they're intended to help you. They want to help you succeed in your job. Can you see that might be true?" I could hear the soft sounds of music coming from the yoga studio just on the other side of my office door. It was a soothing addition to the background of our conversation. It also meant that the class was nearly over.

"I think so." Maggie said.

"So instead of taking these words and making them mean you're not good enough, what else could you make them mean?" I asked.

There was another pause as she thought about my question and then answered hesitantly, "Um, I guess they could mean that I just need to work on changing my presentations a bit?"

I smiled broadly as I responded, "Exactly! What if these words are just feedback to help you move toward that next position? What if you could take them as goals for how to grow your capabilities within this job at this company? What if the feedback wasn't emotional at all?"

"It could really be that way?" she asked uncertainly.

I nodded. "If you decide that's how you want to see it, then sure, it could be. It's a choice that you can make. You don't have control over the feedback they gave you or what they ultimately decide to do. What you do have control over is what you make the feedback mean and what you do with it now that you have it."

"But what about the fact that I don't have any idea how to do what they want me to do? I don't know how to think about the big picture. What does 'too detailed' even mean?" Maggie threw her hands in the air as she spoke.

I could tell she was starting to spin in a direction that wouldn't be productive. "Let me stop you," I said. "You do know what to do. Let's say you take this feedback, and you decide to think about it as a challenge, a way to become an even better employee than you are right now. And a way to set yourself up for that next level, that future promotion. You're going to make presentations that have a big picture message for the clients with just the right level of detail. If you thought about it that way, how would that make you feel?"

Maggie shrugged her shoulders slightly. "Motivated, I guess. Or maybe empowered…"

"Either one. They're both strong, 'positive' emotions. If you're feeling motivated or empowered, what would you do?"

I could see the wheels turning in her mind for a few seconds. Finally, the ideas started to come, and Maggie said, "I could take time to review some of the old presentations they have available, use them as examples for what to do in the future. And I could ask my manager to spend some time with me as I'm creating my presentation outline, to go over it with her to make sure what I'm doing is the right balance between high level and detail. And I do have a mentor at work, a Senior Manager, who is supposed to help me, someone I can go to beyond just my manager. I could ask him for advice or suggestions."

My smile met hers. "Any and all of those things are actions you could take, and I'm sure there are more. The amazing thing is that you can decide to think about what you heard in the review in whatever way you want to. And the way you decide to think about it will determine how you feel, what you do and ultimately your results. You could take the feedback and make it mean you're not good enough, feel terrible and spend time and energy on whether you should quit your job or worry that you might be fired. Or you could take the feedback and look at it for what it is—just words and suggestions for how you could do things in a different way, a way that might make you even more successful at your job. Then get to work on using that feedback to grow."

The tightness in Maggie's face disappeared and her shoulders relaxed. The change in her energy was palpable and came across in her words. "Wow, Kary this was amazing! Thank you! Seriously, thank you! I've been here in Pineville since Wednesday night, trying to enjoy my mini vacation, but I got my review right before I left the city. I have been miserable and wallowing and distracted ever since.

'The last two days have been a blur, and you made me feel better in like fifteen minutes!"

"Well, I didn't make you feel better. I just helped show you that you can make yourself feel better. And you did that by thinking about the feedback in a different way. That's the power of what you can do for yourself by managing your thoughts."

"It's amazing!" Maggie beamed and started to stand up.

"Before you go, I just want to share a few things," I said.

She sat back down.

I explained, "I know you're feeling better now, but I have to warn you that it's not going to last. Those thoughts you were having before will come back. That's normal and to be expected. My recommendation is to try to be aware of them when they come; catch yourself in the act of thinking them. Then you can decide if you want to change those thoughts to something like the ones we worked on together here. Most people find that it takes time to transition from thinking their old thoughts to thinking their new ones. Practicing the new ones helps. Some people write them down over and over, post them in places they see throughout the day or even put them as reminders in their cell phones. You'll have to figure out what works best for you. How long will you be here in town?"

"Just until Sunday," she said.

I reached into my desk drawer and pulled out a business card that read "Kary Flynn – Certified Coach." I handed it to her. "Here's my card with my email address and phone number. Send me an email if you'd like to schedule another session. We can do it by phone or video call, whatever works best for you. This stuff seems simple, and it is, but that doesn't mean it's easy to implement. Training your brain to pick up new patterns of thinking takes time and working with a coach is helpful for many people."

Maggie put my card in her bag as she stood back up to leave. She thanked me again and said, "I will definitely be in touch."

"Good. I look forward to talking to you again," I responded.

She left my office, closing the door behind her. I heard the music from the yoga studio stop, followed by the soft murmur of voices. The class was over. I decided to wait a few minutes for the attendees to clear out before going out to chat with my best friend, Zuri. She would be happy to hear that the session with my perspective client had gone well.

It was because of Zuri that I was here in Pineville, Pennsylvania, my hometown, trying to build my coaching business. I had been here for a year, after moving back from Boston. While things were slow for the first few months, it finally felt like I was starting to gain some momentum. I had a few consistent clients, and I was getting more walk-ins. With the summer here, Pineville would be filled with tourists, taking advantage of water sports and fishing in Pine Lake and hiking and camping in the surrounding mountains. The influx of people should help with foot traffic here in the town center and in the yoga studio specifically.

Besides the increase in clients and the potential for more of them, I was also feeling more confident in my coaching abilities. Each session was an opportunity for me to improve my coaching skills, and I was spending my free time learning and reading as much as I could about different philosophies and approaches to living a good life. I knew I had knowledge, tools and processes to help other people, no matter what problem they wanted to address. I knew that because I had been one of those people who hadn't been living a good life. I still couldn't believe how much my life had changed in such a short period of time.

Just two years ago, I was living in Boston and working as a management consultant. I had moved there right after business school and had dreams of a fulfilling career and enjoying city living. Neither was exactly what I had expected. While the job did allow me to work with Fortune 500 companies on high-stakes business issues, it required a lot of travel and exhaustive hours of work. I was barely ever in Boston, and when I was there, I felt too tired to enjoy it. After a few months, I started having panic attacks, mostly on Sunday nights, before heading into the workweek. I believed my anxiety was caused by my job, and I didn't think I could do anything about it. I suffered in silence without telling anyone or seeking professional help. I was embarrassed that I couldn't handle what many of my business school classmates had referred to as a "dream job" after graduation. I thought there had to be something wrong with me.

After a few years, I had an opportunity to justify quitting. I was assigned to an engagement that required me to put together a cost-cutting analysis. I dug into the financials of the company and was able to identify some changes that would save a few million dollars. The client loved it, and I got the promotion I had been hoping for. However, it also resulted in a few hundred people losing their jobs. I knew the financials were important for any business and someone had to evaluate them and ask the hard questions. I decided, though, that someone didn't need to be me. I resigned a few days later, with no plans for my next step. It was one of the craziest things I'd ever done, but I felt justified in walking away from what I had grown to believe was heartless capitalism. I didn't want to be a part of it.

After the initial high of quitting and feeling the relief of work pressures literally disappear, I fell into what I can only describe as a case of mild depression. I felt strongly that I had made the right decision by quitting, but I was confused about what my next step would be. I spent six months wallowing in confusion and a bit of despair until I had a chance meeting with a life coach that changed my life. It was a brief discussion on a bench in the Boston Public Garden, and from that discussion everything became clear. The woman, named Maureen, struck up a conversation. She asked if I was okay. I had been holding my thoughts and feelings in for so long, trying my best to hide them. I realized at that moment that I wasn't hiding them very well. For some reason having a stranger ask me if I was okay opened the floodgates. Maureen let me spew everything out, about my terrible job and how horrible it made me feel and how proud I was of quitting but that now I was confused by what to do next. I was stuck. I rambled on and on and she let me go on without interrupting.

Then when I was finished, she said some words that changed my entire life. She asked what I would do if I wasn't confused about my next step? What if any path I chose would work out? What if the actual next step didn't really matter? What would I do then?

The shift happened instantly. I realized the confusion itself was keeping me stuck, and I was putting way too much pressure on my next move being the "right one." Whatever I decided to do would be fine, and it didn't have to be a forever decision. I just needed to decide something and move forward. I felt the weight of confusion and powerlessness lift and decided to move toward something instead of staying where I was. I decided then and there to focus on life coaching. It would be a way for me to help myself feel better, live my best life, and then help other people do it too. I chose a direction and a purpose to move toward, and then I went to work.

Fast forward six months. I had learned and grown so much with my own self-coaching practice, along with guidance and coaching from Maureen, who I had hired to be my personal coach. I also had completed a life coach certification program that gave me a foundation of tools to use. My next step was launching my new business and getting some clients. That's where Zuri came in. She had been encouraging me to move back to Pineville since I left my consulting job. I didn't have serious ties to Boston, and I knew I could launch my coaching business from anywhere. Zuri had a proposition for me; I could use one of the rooms at her studio, "Just Be Yoga," for my client sessions and advertise at her business. There likely would be some crossover between practicing yoga and working with a life coach for people who were interested in their mental, emotional and physical health. As a bonus, we would get to see each other every day, which hadn't been the case since high school, nearly fifteen years ago. After struggling for several years in Boston on my own, being closer to my family and oldest friends felt comforting. I headed back to my hometown to see what kind of future I could create for myself. So far, things were going well.

I noticed the voices dying down in the studio, packed up my bag and headed out to find Zuri. There were still a handful of women chatting at the front of the room. I gave a short hello to them as I walked past. I found my best friend at the far end of the studio straightening up the equipment closet. She was short and thin but muscular from hours and hours of yoga. Her most distinguishing feature was her pitch-black hair, cut in a short pixie bob now. Over the years she played with the length of her hair, going from long flowing locks to this extreme opposite. The current length gave off a playful vibe, almost fairy-like, which aligned with her personality. It was what drew people to her yoga classes. She had a playful approach to life that she brought to her teaching. She turned when she heard me approaching and asked, "Good session?"

"Yep, really good. It was a nice way to end the day. I feel like things are finally coming together," I said.

"It sounds like they are," she said, turning back to straighten up a few more yoga mats and blocks. As she worked with her back to me, she continued. "So now that things are coming together—in your own words—it's probably time for you to start dating again."

I felt my face flush, embarrassed by just the topic of dating. "We've discussed this," I said. "I'm working on my business right now, so I don't have time to worry about dating anybody. Besides, dating is a lot of work and stress."

Zuri turned back to face me as she responded. "If you think about it that way, it will be a lot of work and stress. Isn't that what you would tell a client? Kary, when you moved back here, we talked about you doing three things." She held up her fingers as she spoke. "The first was getting settled back here in Pineville. The second was getting your business established. And the third was starting to date. You've been here for a year. I know you're settled, and you just said things were coming together in the business. Now it's time to have a little fun!"

"Hey, who's the coach here?" I asked jokingly, and we both laughed. "Let me think about it, okay? You know I have a history of choosing the wrong men, which has made dating somewhat miserable. And yes, I know that's a story I'm telling myself and I could change that story if I wanted to. I'm just choosing to continue to think about it that way. Now that the business is feeling more solid, I will reconsider the whole dating thing. I promise."

"And I promise I'll keep reminding you that you promised to reconsider. It's my job. I just want you to be happy."

"I am happy," I said.

"I know you are, Kary. But there are parts of life that you aren't experiencing right now, and I think you might enjoy them. That's all I'm saying." She gave me a quick hug and then turned back to straightening up the equipment closet.

I didn't say anything, but I knew there was truth to her words. I was scared to put myself out there. I was scared to lose myself in a relationship. I was scared to be hurt again.

Zuri cut my thoughts short. "Let me finish straightening this stuff up, and then I'll be ready to go. I just got a text from Dean. He's already at the bar."

Dean was Zuri's longtime live-in boyfriend. As a ski instructor in the winter and a water-sport boat captain in the summer, his approach to life was the perfect match to Zuri's. They met five years ago at a summer music festival and moved in together the following month. They had been together ever since.

"Okay, sounds good," I said.

Zuri then added as she faced me again, "Oh, and Ben is going to meet us there too."

I rolled my eyes. "Of course, now the dating comment makes perfect sense. You are so predictable."

Ben Ferguson was a friend of ours from high school. He did have a crush on me back then, but I always had a boyfriend. We had lost touch over the years but reconnected when I moved back to town. Ben owned an antique shop a few doors down from the studio, so I often ran into him. Recently, Zuri had started inviting him to our Friday night happy hours with Dean. This would be the third week in a row that he was joining us. I knew she was trying to play matchmaker. I didn't know if he still liked me in that way, and I also didn't know how I felt about him. When I decided not to date after moving here, I had blocked all thoughts of romance from my mind, regardless of the guy. I wasn't sure I was ready to unblock those thoughts. My dating life had been consumed by drama in the past: very high highs, but equally low lows. I wasn't sure I was ready to jump back into that. Ben was a nice guy, though, and I was enjoying getting to know him now as adults. It was also nice to not feel like the third wheel with Zuri and Dean for a change.

"Kary, he's such a nice guy and he's so adorable. Besides, you know he's been in love with you since like tenth grade," Zuri teased.

"Love is a strong word. I know he had a crush on me in school, but that doesn't mean he has a crush on me now. It also doesn't mean I want him to have a crush on me now. Just don't make things weird tonight, okay?" I pleaded.

"Me? Make things weird? I would never do that." She smirked, knowing that is exactly what she would do if she had the chance.

"Seriously, Zuri, just be patient with me. I need more time."

"Okay, I understand. I'll be patient, for now," she said.

"Thank you. I know you're just trying to help." I smiled gratefully before continuing, "I'll leave you to it so we can head out. I'm getting hungry, and I hear an order of mozzarella sticks calling my name."

"You and your mozzarella sticks." She shook her head and got back to organizing the closet.

I turned around and started walking toward the front of the studio. I would wait outside. Now that it was almost June, the days were warming up. It would be nice to soak in some sun.

The three women were still chatting right inside the doorway. As I was halfway across the room, the door to the studio swung open, and a woman came barging in. She pushed through their small circle without apology and marched straight toward me.

There were no classes scheduled after five o'clock on Friday nights. I was about to let the woman know we were closing when I realized I recognized her. She was one of my regular clients.

"Veronica, I didn't think we were scheduled to meet again until next week," I said, before noticing that her face was red, her expression dark. Something was off. She stomped toward me and stopped a few inches from my face.

"You bitch. You ruined my life!"

CHAPTER 2

I stood there stunned for a moment, not quite understanding what was happening. Veronica Calhoun was a client I had been working with weekly for the last three months. She was working on relationships and money issues. I thought she was making progress. She seemed happy with the realizations that were coming up for her and the changes she said she was making in her life. She kept booking sessions, so I assumed things were going well. The fact that she was currently staring me down and calling me a bitch would tend to argue otherwise.

I took a deep breath before speaking. "Veronica, why don't we head into the office so we can talk privately." I motioned toward the office area.

She stood completely still. "I don't care if anyone else hears what I have to say. It could save them the trouble of being manipulated and backstabbed by you. My life is ruined, and it's your fault. I wouldn't be here if you hadn't gotten into my head with that bullshit thinking. And then I find out you're blabbing about my life!"

I had never seen such a beautiful woman look so ugly. Her rage was palpable, and it was directed at me. I had no idea what she was talking about. "Veronica, just tell me what happened…"

She cut me off. "You know what causes my feelings? My husband deciding to leave me with no money. Zero money! Zero dollars! After everything he put me through, I have nothing to show for it. Nothing!"

I had compassion that she was going through a difficult time. "I'm so sorry to hear about your marriage."

My words went unacknowledged as she continued. "He found out, you know—about the affair. After all this time, the sneaking around, the lies, I open myself up to you and somehow the secret gets back to my husband. You can't tell me it's a coincidence. You told someone and it got back to Thomas. I wasn't ready for him to know. I wasn't ready to leave. Now I don't have a choice."

"Veronica, I didn't tell a soul. Nothing we discussed in our sessions goes any further than that room. I would never do something like that. If your husband found out, he did so in a different way. It wasn't from me." I tried to keep my voice calm and controlled, but I could feel my body starting to shake as I attempted to defend myself.

She practically spat in my face. "I don't believe you and I'm going to tell everyone. Say goodbye to your little coaching business. I'm going to make sure you don't ruin any more lives in this town!" With that she spun around, her blond ponytail grazing my face, and stomped out the door.

I stood frozen in place, unable to move, still processing what had happened. I had never been in a confrontation before. I wasn't a confrontational person. I didn't have enemies. Thoughts swirled around my head. I could hear the beat of my heart. It was loud and speeding up. It felt like it might jump right out of my chest. Heat seared through my body. I realized I might be starting to have a panic attack. I brought my thoughts back to the present by repeating the phrase in my mind, "Right here, right now, I am okay. Right here, right now, I am okay. Right here, right now, I am okay." I slowed my breathing down and my heartbeat slowed down as well. I could feel the heat starting to subside.

I suddenly became aware that Zuri was standing in front of me. She was saying something, but I couldn't hear the words. I focused on her face and the sound of her voice finally came. "You know she can't do that. It's defamation. She'll never get away with it." Zuri paused as her expression grew more concerned. "Kary? Kary, are you okay? Come with me. You need to sit down."

I allowed her to lead me to the office. We passed the three women who were still standing just inside the doorway. They looked shocked but didn't say anything.

As we entered the office, I felt the coziness of the space wrap around me, and my heartbeat dropped further. The room was in the front of Just Be Yoga, with a single window running along its back wall. It provided a picture-perfect view of Pine Avenue, the main street in town. During client sessions, I had a curtain I pulled closed to give us privacy, but when I was in there myself, I liked to let the sun stream in and watch the pedestrians stroll by. Some were residents who I recognized. Most were vacationers, enjoying the atmosphere our little town offered. I had grown to love this cozy office and my space here on Pine Avenue. My life had started to feel like it was coming together just a few minutes earlier, and now I worried that it could be ruined.

I plopped into my armchair and Zuri took the seat usually reserved for my clients. I had a fleeting thought that we should change places. I was the one who needed coaching now. She handed me a bottle of water, which she must have grabbed on the way in without me noticing. She always kept a few bottles near the entrance for clients to take as they came into or left the yoga studio.

"First things first. Drink some water and take a few deep breaths," Zuri ordered, and I complied.

I could feel the anxiety in my body fading away, and I knew the chance of having a full panic attack had passed. I was relieved. That was a part of my past, one I liked to believe I left back in Boston when I left my management consulting job. Of course, deep down, I knew it wasn't tied to the job at all. It was tied to my thoughts and my anxiety. I just was able to better control those these days with my self-coaching.

"I think I'm okay now," I assured her. "Thank you for helping me calm down."

"You're welcome." Zuri smiled softly and then her expression turned serious. "Now, what are we going to do about that woman?"

"Zuri, you're supposed to be kind and supportive and all Zen-like. Shouldn't you be telling me to send out good vibes and the universe will work it all out?" I asked.

She nodded, "Yes, of course. Good vibes, positive feelings and all of that will help, but that doesn't mean you should sit back and do nothing. A woman like Veronica has a lot of influence and her lies could seriously hurt your business. You have to get out in front of this."

Besides being one of my regular clients, Veronica was married to one of the richest men in Pineville, Thomas Calhoun. He ran an investment-banking firm in New York City, which is where he made his millions. He spent most weekdays in his city penthouse while Veronica lived fulltime at the main house, a mini mansion, here in Pineville. Thomas came home on the weekends. It was one of the things Veronica had mentioned during our sessions. She felt lonely and that, in turn, had led to an affair. The affair had been going on for quite some time. She was considering leaving her husband, but there was money at stake. I didn't have all the details. I didn't need them. Our sessions focused on working through the thoughts she was having about the situation and getting to a point where she could decide what to do. During our last session, it seemed like she was almost there, almost ready to make a choice. I didn't know what that choice would be, and it wasn't my place to ask. I never proposed or recommended courses of actions to my clients. That wasn't my job as a coach. And I certainly never told anyone about what I had learned in my sessions with her. I wasn't a therapist, but I did have ethics and keeping the privacy of my clients was something I took seriously.

"So, you think this could be bad," I said, more of a statement than a question.

"I think it could be, but only if you don't do something about it," Zuri said.

"What should I do?" I asked.

"We'll figure something out," she promised. "Let's get out of here and go meet Dean. We can talk through it together over drinks."

I rolled my eyes as I said, "Because alcohol will certainly help me make good, responsible decisions."

"Hey, I didn't say we were going to get sloshed. I just said we can grab a drink and chat." Zuri responded seriously to my obviously sarcastic comment.

I felt exhausted but knew I didn't want to be alone. "Alright, let's get out of here before someone else barges in and accuses me of something else I didn't do."

"Now you're being dramatic," Zuri said accusingly.

"I think I'm allowed to be at least a little dramatic." I pinched my fingers together and held them up as I spoke.

"Okay, I'll give you that." She chuckled. "Let me go lock up the equipment room. I'll meet you out front." Zuri left the office to finish her closing duties.

I slumped back in my chair and took a few more deep breaths. I closed my eyes for a minute and tried to clear the thoughts from my mind, but I couldn't stop them from coming. Veronica had money and a lot of influence in Pineville. If she decided to move forward on her threat, it really could be a catastrophic blow to my business. This could end up badly. Of course, I understood these thoughts were not at all helpful or productive, but I was too stressed out and tired to try to redirect them or to coach myself into a better headspace. My whole body felt tense as I stood up to leave. I grabbed my bag and left the office, closing the door behind me.

I noticed the women that had witnessed my encounter with Veronica were no longer standing by the doorway. They must have left. Hopefully it didn't scare them away from the studio in the future. I was sure witnessing a dramatic confrontation wasn't quite what they were looking for when they signed up to take a yoga class. I already felt sorry for possibly affecting Zuri's business.

I stepped outside and felt the warmth of the sun. It was a beautiful evening, and the sidewalk was crowded. With Memorial Day behind us, we had officially started our summer season, the most popular time of the year in Pineville. I turned toward the end of Pine Avenue to take in the breathtaking view of Pine Lake. It was still a little too chilly to swim, but even at after 5 p.m., there were some boaters enjoying the water. The sun wouldn't go down for a few more hours.

Zuri joined me a few minutes later, locked up the studio and we headed a block down to the Bluegill Grill. It was our favorite bar and restaurant. We started doing Friday night happy hours last fall and it quickly became a weekly tradition. I always looked forward to relaxing with my friends and enjoying the local musicians that offered entertainment on weekend nights. They also had a rotating list of local wines that I was working my way through. With heavy tourist season starting, the bar was more crowded than it usually was, and I was glad Dean had been able to get here earlier. He waved to us from a table near the back, close to the stage where the musicians would be setting up. The music usually started around 7 p.m.

Dean was tall and lean, with light brown hair, green eyes and a year-round tan on his face due to the time he spent on the water and the ski slopes. He had a playful, laidback demeanor that was in perfect alignment with my best friend's personality. I was happy they had found each other, and I was grateful to have people in my life that helped me take things less seriously. Their perspectives were usually different from my own. I had been raised to work hard above everything else and to focus on setting and achieving goals. It was a lot of pressure, and it was never as rewarding as it seemed it should be. I was realizing now that there was a different approach to life, one that was lighter and way more enjoyable. It didn't mean that I didn't set and achieve goals, but I didn't have to do it in a way that felt like a grind. I could focus on doing things I loved, and success would eventually follow. I didn't quite believe that yet, but I was working on living into that belief. Both Dean and Zuri seemed to live that way easily.

"Hey babe, thanks for grabbing us a table." Zuri gave Dean a light kiss on the lips as she sat down in the chair next to him.

"Hey babe," he replied, draping his arm across the back of her chair. Then he turned his attention to me, "Hey, Kary."

"Hi, Dean," I said as I took the seat across from him. I noticed a glass of red wine sitting in front of me. "What's this?"

"Well, Zuri called ahead and mentioned it might be good to have a little something ready for you when you got here," he explained.

I looked at my best friend accusingly. "Zuri, I left you alone for like five minutes and you're already telling the whole world what happened!"

Dean cut in. "I have no idea what happened. Honest. All I was told was you needed a drink and so there is your drink. I got Zuri one, too," he said as he motioned to the glass of wine in front of me and the bottle of beer in front of Zuri.

"See, I'm not telling the whole world. I'm not even telling Dean. I'm just making sure you have a little liquid relief ready to go. Besides, he's about to hear all about it anyway," Zuri defended herself jokingly.

"Hear all about what?" Ben asked as he approached our table and sat down in the seat right next to me.

"Ben, hi!" I greeted him. Dean and Zuri did the same. His smile was warm and kind. He pushed his glasses up on his nose as he settled in at the table. He really was cute, in a nerdy kind of way. I was glad he was here with us, but I wasn't sure if I was I-want-to-date-him glad. I refocused and started to respond to his question, "It's nothing…"

Zuri cut me off. "It's something, Kary. I think it would be good to tell the guys what happened. Get it out. Then we can start to figure out what to do about it. Let us help you."

I wasn't used to asking others for help. It wasn't something that came naturally to me. "Okay, you're right. I think I could use some help on this. Besides, you all own your own businesses, and this is related to my business. So, who better to ask?"

Ben looked over and offered, "Anything you need. I'm here for you."

"Me too," added Dean.

"Thanks guys." I took a sip of wine and then launched into a description of my confrontation with Veronica. They listened intently. The only interruption was a quick one when our server came to the table to get Ben's drink order. It only took a few minutes to tell the story, but when I finished, I collapsed back in my chair, feeling exhausted just from recounting what happened.

"Damn, I can't believe she threatened your business. She must be in a bad place right now. Maybe she'll come to her senses eventually," Dean said.

"She sounds crazy. You can't let her talk about you like that!" Ben said. Creases appeared across his forehead as he scowled with concern.

"I told Kary it would be defamation if she even tries to spread that lie around town. There has to be something we can do to stop her," Zuri added.

"Guys, I appreciate your support, but at this point, I really don't think there's anything I can do. I can't stop her from saying what she wants to say to whoever she wants to say it. I just hope people won't believe her, or at least some people won't believe her. I know the truth. I know I'm trustworthy. I would never share anything I learned in a session with others. I'll prove myself by my actions." I had gained some perspective over the past hour after calming down, and I was trying to believe the words I was saying.

"I think you're being too passive about this." Ben turned his head to look at me directly. "This is a moment when you have to stand up for yourself. Zuri is right. This could be defamation, but why let it get to that point? By then, she may have already ruined your business. You shouldn't let someone like that push you around."

"I hear you, and you might be right, but it's just not the way I want to handle things. I want to wait and see what happens. Like Dean said, maybe she'll come to her senses." I sounded more hopeful about this possibility than I felt about it inside. Veronica wasn't the kind of woman to come to her senses. I could tell that from our very first session together. Maybe I would have to be more selective when choosing who to work with in the future. That is, if I even had a chance to work with more clients in the future in this town.

"Are you sure we can't try to come up with something?" Zuri questioned.

I shook my head, "I'm sure. What I want to do now is forget about this whole thing and have a relaxing night out with my friends." I noticed their serious expressions and tried to lighten the mood by raising my nearly empty glass and adding, "Oh and wine, I want lots of wine."

Ben reached his arm across my shoulders and gave me a quick squeeze. "Just let me know if you change your mind. I'm here for you, seriously."

I believed him. "I will," I said. I turned my focus to the whole table. "Thank you, guys. Really, I don't know what I'd do without you."

Dean gave me a mischievous look. "Well, I know for sure you wouldn't be doing shots without us."

"Not shots," I pleaded.

"Yes, shots," Dean said. "I'm getting a round of fireball shots for the whole table. You'll love them." He stood up and headed over to the bar.

I didn't usually do shots, because I didn't like feeling out of control. On a normal Friday night, I would have two glasses of wine. I loved the taste of wine, and it did help me feel calmer, something I had been working on managing with a combination of meditation and thought work. I still had feelings of anxiety at times, but it was far better than it had been in the past.

I glanced over at the bar and watched as Dean ordered and paid for the round. As I watched, I decided that being a little out of control didn't feel like a terrible thing right now, after what happened earlier. I would do just one shot. One shot and two glasses of wine. Yep, good plan.

And like all good plans, there are times when they get thrown to the wayside. This night was one of those times. One shot turned into two, and two into three. I followed those with a vodka tonic, a drink I would never normally choose, but it tasted surprisingly good. The live band played mostly covers from the 1990s, taking us back to our high school days. It was exactly what I needed as an escape from what happened earlier, and I was grateful to have people in my life that cared about me. I felt a surge of joy and love for my friends and for my life overall. I didn't want things to change. Maybe this just-sit-and-wait approach wasn't the way to go after all. My head felt hazy, and I knew I would have to decide what to do tomorrow. Despite my intoxication, I knew I wasn't in a state now to make any decisions—not good ones anyway.

Before I knew it, the night had gotten away from me, and I found myself sitting in the passenger seat of Ben's truck. It was clear to everyone, including me, that there was no way I could drive myself home. Zuri and Dean had offered me the couch in their apartment. They lived right above Just Be Yoga, which was convenient to walk to from the bar. I didn't want to impose, though. Besides, I loved sleeping in my own bed and waking up in my own space. Based on how I was feeling, I wanted comfort even more than usual. Ben, who had apparently just been sipping beers the whole night, offered to take me home. I gratefully accepted. It was just a short drive to the far side of Pine Lake. We were there in less than ten minutes.

"Thanks for the ride. I really appreciate it." I grabbed my bag and got ready to hop out.

Ben turned toward me with a serious expression. "Of course, Kary. Anytime. You know I'm here if you need me, right?"

"I do know." I grabbed the handle of the car door and then paused as a new thought popped into my head. The alcohol was making me feel warm and fuzzy all over my body. I loved everything about my life here, especially my friends. "Ben, I am so glad we reconnected these last few months. It's nice to have you in my life again. A lot has changed since high school, but you haven't. You're still you, and I love that."

Ben's face lit up as he responded, "I feel the same way. Actually, I've been meaning to broach the subject of us for a while now. I just wasn't sure how to approach it. You have no idea how much I've enjoyed these last few months. I love spending time with you. I was hoping, maybe at some point, you might consider me as more than just a friend."

Thoughts swirled around in my head. I wasn't sure what I wanted. I wasn't sure how I felt. Instead of responding with words, I leaned over and kissed him lightly on the lips. "Let's see how things go, okay?" I said.

I didn't give him time to respond. I hopped out of the truck and stumbled my way inside, closing the door behind me.

CHAPTER 3

I awoke to a pounding headache the next morning and spent the first ten minutes of my day expelling everything I had left in my stomach. I hadn't felt this physically awful in a long time. I reminded myself why I generally chose drinking in moderation, and that reminder brought back the memories of the previous day, the ones that led me to choose to drink excessively in the first place: the confrontation with Veronica, the worry about my business, the bar, the music, the dancing, the kiss…that sloppy kiss with Ben when he dropped me off. I felt regret about the entire night. If only I could rewind and do the whole thing over. Of course, that wasn't how the world worked. I would have to face the consequences of my decisions. I owned my actions, and I accepted that ownership.

I peeled myself off the bathroom floor and shuffled out to the combined living-kitchen space. I turned my focus to the back of my little cottage and stared out through the floor-to-ceiling windows. Pine Lake was just outside. It was early, so a soft mist hovered over the water, and I could see the sun rising in the distance on the other side of the mountain. For a moment I forgot about my situation and allowed myself to take in the view. My view. I felt a surge of appreciation for the safe haven I created for myself here.

When I moved back last year, I decided to use a good portion of the money I had saved from my consulting job to buy this small, A-frame house on the far side of the lake. The lot itself was expensive, and I was sure if someone else had purchased it, the old A-frame would have been torn down to make room for a bigger vacation house. For me, though, the old A-frame was exactly what I was looking for. The cottage was small, just big enough for me. It was open concept with the only separate room a tiny bathroom located right inside the front door. The rest of the space was completely open, and the back wall was made up of windows as tall as the space itself, offering a full view of the lake. A loft held my bed and a similar view of the water. My cottage was cozy and peaceful and full of character. I loved the space. I couldn't believe how lucky I was to call it home.

It was another reason I needed to figure out how to mitigate this Veronica situation. I couldn't allow her to impact my life, and my life here relied on the success of my coaching business. I had a decent amount of savings when I quit my job, but most of it went into purchasing this house and for living expenses that first year when I wasn't working. Even now, my business wasn't earning enough to cover all my monthly expenses. It was close some months, but I was still having to dip into what was left of my savings. Soon that account would be all dried up. I didn't want to have to take a part-time job, because I thought it would distract me from building my business. Things had been on an upward trend the last two to three months and I had convinced myself a part-time job wasn't necessary. Now with Veronica's threat, I wasn't so sure.

I shuffled over to the kitchen area and turned on the Keurig. I guzzled downed a glass of water while I waited for my coffee to brew. With the intake of liquid, I could feel the effects of dehydration starting to melt away. When the coffee was done brewing, I grabbed my "Life Is Good" mug and pulled a few mini powdered donuts out of the pantry. I hoped their cake-like consistently would help settle my stomach. I relaxed back on my favorite recliner and took a few deep breaths before popping the donuts into my mouth and using the coffee to wash them down. The mixture of caffeine and sugar surged through my system and after a few minutes, I did feel a little better.

Once the donuts were gone, I turned my attention to my phone and checked my calendar for the day ahead. I had to figure out how to handle the Veronica situation, but I also had to stick to my schedule for the day. I had two client sessions this morning, one at 9 a.m. and one at 10 a.m., and then a third session at 1 p.m. in the afternoon. I generally tried not to book sessions on Saturday afternoons, but I had made an exception for this client. She couldn't make it during her usual weekday appointment, and she didn't want to miss a week. I loved coaching and could do it all day every day if I chose to, but I also had a life, and I was trying to carve out free time for myself. I knew it wasn't healthy to work too much. I had fallen into that trap with my previous job, and I was trying to create a balance, while also trying to make enough money to live on.

As I was mentally planning out my day, I remembered I didn't have my Jeep. It was still parked in town, a casualty of my decision to overdrink the night before. I would have to find another way to get myself to the studio. I could call someone to pick me up, but I decided I wasn't in the mood to socialize. I was still feeling a little embarrassed about the night before. Last summer, I rode my bike to town most days, but once fall arrived, it was too cold to keep riding. I told myself that once the weather warmed up, I would start riding again. Now that it was nearly June, I couldn't deny that it was warm enough. I had been making excuses, putting it off for several weeks. I wasn't sure why, maybe just laziness. With no Jeep and no desire to ask someone to give me a ride, I was left with only two options—riding my bike or walking. That made it an easy choice. I would ride my bike. I checked my phone. It was about 7 a.m., so I had some time before I needed to head to the studio. I planned to leave about an hour before my first session to give myself plenty of time to get there.

An hour later, I was showered and dressed and still feeling terrible. I drank as much water as I could while getting ready, and that had helped, but I knew what I really needed was sleep. Unfortunately, sleep wouldn't be possible for quite a few hours. I stood and looked at myself in the mirror in the bathroom before heading out. My eyes were bloodshot with dark circles underneath, and my complexion was pale, almost colorless. On a normal day, I generally felt positive about my appearance. I was attractive, about five-foot-five, with a thin build, long wavy light brown hair, hazel eyes and full lips. This was not a normal day, though, and these bloodshot eyes and pale complexion were not my best look. I sighed out loud and mentally prepared myself to face the day. I would have to pull it together to serve my clients.

As I was about to open the front door, my phone pinged, indicating a text message. I pulled it out of my bag. It was from Ben: *Feeling okay today? Want help picking your Jeep up this morning?*

I felt embarrassed, which was ridiculous. I was a thirty-two-year-old single woman who kissed a friend while she was drunk. End of story. I had no good reason to feel embarrassed by the situation, except that I knew Ben had feelings for me. It wasn't fair to lead him on, unless I knew for sure I felt the same way. Did I feel the same way? I kept asking myself that question, and I kept leaving it unanswered. I didn't know how I felt. What I did know is I didn't feel like facing any of it, especially not now, so I sent a quick response: *I'm okay. I have the Jeep situation handled. Thanks for the offer, though. Happy Saturday!*

I saw bubbles pop up, indicating he was typing a text back to me. Then the bubbles disappeared. They popped up again and disappeared a second time. Finally, a single word response came through: *OK.*

I put my phone back into my bag. I felt relieved I wouldn't have to face Ben this morning. I needed some time to work through my feelings and that wouldn't be possible until I got over this hangover. I walked outside to grab my bike. Time to face the day.

I managed to make it through my two morning sessions, helping both of my clients with the problems they were working on. The bike ride, the fresh air and the time spent focusing on something other than my horrible hangover had done me good. I was feeling much better than I had earlier in the morning, and by the time 11 a.m. rolled around, I was starving. I knew getting more sustenance in my system would help. I waved to Zuri as I walked out of the studio. She was just starting to teach a class, so I would catch up with her later.

I walked a few blocks down to my favorite lunch spot, Stews & Brews. The name was a play on their signature offerings of soups (stews) and coffee beans. As I walked through the door, the aroma of baked goods wafted over me. My stomach rumbled and I took a spot in line. There was one couple in front of me. I waited patiently and stepped up to the counter when it was my turn. The owner of the café, Misty Brant, gave me a warm smile. She had run Stews & Brews for nearly thirty years, opening it with her first husband and then running it with her oldest daughter after he passed away several years ago. If she didn't know a customer when they walked in the door, she would know them by the time they walked out of it. Misty had a way of making strangers feel welcomed. For locals, like me, she had a bit of a grandmother vibe—caring and kind but with a no-nonsense attitude.

"Kary, I'm guessing you could use some comfort food right now." Misty still had the slight tinge of a southern accent, despite being in the Northeast for years.

I was caught off-guard by her comment. "I'm not sure I know what you mean."

She shook her head as she spoke. "Oh, that nasty business with Veronica. I was hoping you'd stop in today so I could see how you were doing. That woman can be vindictive if you get on her bad side."

"How did you hear about that? It wasn't even twenty-four hours ago," I said, exasperated by how quickly gossip made it around town.

Misty explained. "Well, Lucy MacDonald and Susan Stapleton stopped by here after their yoga class yesterday. I guess they witnessed the whole thing, couldn't talk about anything else. How are you doing Sweetie? Are you okay?"

I felt deflated. I had been secretly hoping no one else would hear about what happened, at least not until I could figure out how I was going to respond. If those women were talking about it here yesterday, there was no guessing how far the news had traveled by now. There was also no guessing what detail of that news was being shared. "I'm not okay," I admitted. The heaviness of the previous day's events settled back on my chest, and I could feel a low level of anxiety accompany it.

"You will be," Misty assured me. "Word spreads fast in this town, but people know what's what. I doubt anyone who knows you would believe a word that woman says."

"But what about the people who don't know me?" I asked.

"Most people believe in the good of others, and they'll give you a chance. You'll prove to them who you really are. This is just a slight bump in the road. You'll get through it." She sounded so matter of fact that I almost believed her.

I wanted to believe her. "I really hope you're right, Misty."

"I am. You'll see." She smiled broadly and then continued. "Now seems like an appropriate time to mention the healing effects of sugar and caffeine. What'll it be?" She gave me a quick wink and motioned to the treats under the display on the counter.

I ordered a turkey and cheese sandwich and a large mocha with extra whipped cream. Both did wonders for my hangover. After I was done with my early lunch, I took a walk around town to get some clarity on my next steps. I decided I needed to take control of the situation, in whatever way possible. I would reach out to Veronica directly. If we could talk when she was less heated and less emotional, I could try to get to the bottom of what had happened. I knew for sure I hadn't told a soul about her affair. I didn't even have the information written down for someone to come across it accidentally. There had to be an alternative explanation. I knew there was a chance Veronica wouldn't talk to me, but I had to at least try. I had to take some steps to clear this up, to protect my business and myself.

I got back to the studio and prepared to coach my afternoon client. Her name was Clara, and I had been helping her eliminate some habits she felt were unproductive for her life. When we started working together a few weeks ago, the main habit she was trying to break was excessively checking the calendar app on her phone. She found herself checking the calendar multiple times a day, looking not just at the current date but looking ahead to remind herself of things planned in the future. It had become a compulsive response during any free moment, like standing in line at the grocery store, waiting in her car at a traffic light and waking up in bed in the middle of the night.

Working together, we uncovered thoughts Clara had about the future. She had a belief that the future was going to be "better" than the current moment. Whether it was tomorrow, next week, next month or next year, she was using the calendar to look forward to events that would occur at a time that was "better" than today. She daydreamed about those events, but of course when they arrived, she was focusing on the next set of future events, never fully embracing and enjoying the current moment. She was racing toward a "better" future that would never arrive.

Our work focused on having her build thoughts about how her life was good right now. There is no such thing as a "better" future. It is just a different moment than today, and the only time we have is now. I was trying to keep her present-focused and mindful, to enjoy the current moment as much as possible. In addition to our weekly sessions, I suggested she start daily meditation and appreciation journaling practices. These activities were helping her focus on the here and now, and she was checking her calendar much less frequently. She was building new ways of thinking and creating new habits that were leading to a more enjoyable life.

I worked with people on all kinds of habits, and I had learned that the habit itself, the behavior, was never the core of the problem.

It was just a response to a set of thoughts and feelings. Those thoughts and feelings were the root cause. Identifying the root cause meant that in time we could control that behavior in whatever way the client desired—start it, stop it, adjust it—by focusing on changing those thoughts and feelings. I hadn't come across a client doing obsessive calendar checking before, but I had worked with people who were avoiding the here and now in many other ways. Each of their behaviors was different, but the root cause was their thoughts and feelings. Clara left after our forty-five minutes together feeling positive about her progress, and I reminded myself how precious the present moment is. I had lost sight of that yesterday.

I heard a quiet knock on the door a few minutes after Clara left. I wasn't expecting anyone, and the yoga studio never had classes on Saturday afternoons. Occasionally there were special events, but I knew there was nothing scheduled today. There was only one person it could be.

"Come in," I responded to the knock.

Zuri opened the door and greeted me, "Hey girl." She walked in and sat down on the chair across from me.

"What are you doing here?" I asked.

"I came to see you," she said. "How are you feeling?"

"Honestly, much better. I was such a mess last night," I admitted, feeling my embarrassment rise to the surface again. "I'm sorry for anything I might have said or done in my drunken haze."

"You don't have to be sorry. We've all been there. Besides, you didn't say or do anything to be sorry about," she offered.

"Well, I don't know if that's entirely true…" I paused for a beat before sharing the truth. "I think I kissed Ben. No, I know I kissed him."

"Kary! Why didn't you call me right away? When did this happen? How did this happen? Did he finally make the move? Was it good? Was it awkward?" Zuri hit me with question after question, not pausing to let me answer any of them. It was something she did when she got excited.

I waited until she was done before explaining, "It happened when I was getting out of the car after he drove me home. It was really nothing. It happened so fast, and it was just a peck. I'm still not sure how I feel about him, and I don't want to lead him on. He sent me a text this morning offering to help me pick up my car, but I told him I didn't need his help. Honestly, I just wasn't sure what to say to him." I felt my shoulders slump slightly.

"Kary, I'm sure a little peck never hurt anyone. Ben's a big boy. He can handle whatever happens, and it's obvious that he likes you. This is so exciting!" She clapped her hands together.

"Slow down, okay? Don't get too excited yet. Like I said, I'm not sure how I feel, and I don't know where this is going. Please don't pressure me," I said.

Zuri straightened herself up in the chair and tried unsuccessfully to hide her smile. "No pressure. I promise. I know you're going to go at your own pace, which is fine."

"Thanks for your permission!" I joked.

"You're welcome." She smiled mischievously.

We both laughed and I changed the subject. "Who knows, maybe this whole Ben thing will become something, but right now, I have to focus on the Veronica situation."

"That makes perfect sense. What's going on with that?" she asked, suddenly becoming serious.

"I thought a lot about it. I decided I'm going to reach out to her directly, see if I can do anything to change her mind. I know I didn't tell anyone about what she disclosed during our sessions. There must be another explanation. I know it's unlikely I'll get her to change her mind, but I have to try."

Zuri gave a nod of approval. "Good for you! So, when are you going to call her?"

I shrugged. "I might as well do it now, get it over with."

"I agree. Do you want me to leave you alone while you call?" she asked.

"Could you stay? I wouldn't mind having you as my silent support system."

"Of course, I'll stay." Zuri positioned herself more comfortably in the chair.

"Thanks," I said, grateful to have my best friend here with me. I pulled my cell phone out of my bag. I knew I would feel a thousand times better once I made the call, and if there was any chance of clearing this misunderstanding up, the sooner the better. I felt my hand shaking, though, as found Veronica's name under my contacts and hit the call button. It rang four times before going to voicemail.

"You've reached Veronica Calhoun. Leave a message."

The beep caught me a little off-guard. I had been preparing myself to speak to her directly. I paused briefly and then said, "Veronica, hi. It's Kary Flynn. I'd like to talk to you about what happened yesterday. I'd appreciate it if you could call me back." I hit the end button to disconnect and slumped back in my chair. I looked up at Zuri. "So, how'd I do?"

"That was great, short and sweet," she assured me. "What are you going to say if she calls back?"

"I'm going to ask her why she thinks I was the one who made her husband aware of the affair. I want to know if it's a complete assumption or if there's some reason for her to believe I was the one who told him," I explained, and then continued, "I hope she's cooled down a bit. I know I've heard she can be irrational but truly there is no rational reason why I would tell her husband. It literally makes no sense for me to do something like that. What would I gain? Nothing."

"And what if she doesn't call back?" Zuri asked.

"If she doesn't call back, then I'll try to call again. I'm not going to think too far ahead about this. It will just stress me out," I admitted.

"You've got this, Kary. I know you don't like confrontations, but you can handle Veronica. You're stronger than you think you are," she said.

"I hope you're right about that," I sighed.

"I am," she said, nodding reassuringly.

I took a deep breath. "Phew, heavy stuff." I paused to allow the anxiety I felt during the call to dissipate further. I noticed my hands were no longer shaking and I was feeling more grounded. "Okay, enough about me. What are you doing the rest of the day? Is Dean working?"

"Yeah, he has the boat out for the afternoon with some tourists," Zuri explained. "I think they'll be done around five, so I'm free for a few hours if you want to do something."

"I think I need to just go home and crash. I didn't get good sleep last night and I'm feeling a little emotionally drained. Okay if we just touch base tomorrow?" I asked.

"Works for me. I'll give you a call in the morning," she said.

"Okay, thanks for understanding," I said.

I gathered my things and followed Zuri out of the office, closing the door behind me. As we stepped into the main studio, the front door opened, and two men walked in. They were dressed in jeans with suit jackets and had an air of authority about them. I wondered if they had mistakenly walked into the wrong storefront. They clearly weren't here for yoga classes or coaching.

The shorter one removed his sunglasses and turned toward us. "Is either one of you Kary Flynn?" he asked.

I was taken aback. "I am. What can I do for you?"

"Ms. Flynn, I'm Detective Andrews, and this is my partner, Detective Williams." He gestured to the man standing next to him. "We're here to talk to you about Veronica Calhoun. We believe she's a client of yours?"

"Veronica? Yes, she's a client. Or well, she was a client previously," I stumbled over my words. My thoughts were racing. Did Veronica file a complaint against me? Was I being accused of a crime? She had threatened to ruin my business, but I never expected that would mean she would go to the police.

"Ms. Flynn is there somewhere we can go to talk privately?" he asked.

"Can you just tell me what this is about?" I glanced at Zuri and she looked as concerned as I felt.

The detective then said something completely unexpected. "We regret to inform you that Mrs. Calhoun was found dead this morning. We have reason to believe she was murdered."

CHAPTER 4

It felt like I had been punched in the stomach. I started to feel light-headed.

"Easy there, Ms. Flynn." Detective Andrews reached out and lightly grabbed my shoulder to steady me. His touch was light but firm.

"I think I need to sit down," I said.

"That sounds like a good idea," he agreed.

"Let's go to the back where there's some seating," Zuri suggested, and then added, "enough for all of us." She made it clear she wasn't going to leave me alone with the detectives and I was grateful.

Zuri led us to the smaller studio, which was off the back of the main room. She held special events and meditation classes in it, anything that was for a smaller number of people and that lent itself to a more private setting. I guess this would meet both of those requirements.

I felt like I was having an out-of-body experience, watching myself move through the studio, watching myself help Zuri set up four folding chairs, watching myself take a seat across from the detectives. Sound was muffled and I heard a light ringing in my ears. I reached into my bag and pulled out a bottle of water, taking a gulp. That helped bring me back to the present. I focused on the detectives.

Detective Andrews spoke first. "We didn't mean to upset you, Ms. Flynn."

"You can call me Kary," I said, not directly responding to his comment. Words were not coming easily. I felt numb.

"And I'm Zuri Clark," my friend jumped in. "I own Just Be Yoga and I'm Kary's best friend. I also knew Veronica. She's taken yoga classes here the last few years. I can't believe she's dead! We just saw her last night. She was here."

"That's exactly why we're here now," Detective Andrews said, turning his attention from Zuri back to me. "Kary, we understand there was some kind of altercation between you and Mrs. Calhoun here in the studio last night."

I swallowed hard. It felt like a lump had formed in my throat. After an awkward pause, I forced out a response. "I don't know if I'd call it an altercation, but yes, there was a bit of a disagreement."

"Can you tell us what happened?" he prodded for more information.

"Veronica went crazy on Kary! That's what happened," Zuri blurted out. "She stormed in here and started yelling at Kary, accusing her of things she didn't do. It was aggressive and unnecessary."

"Thank you, Ms. Clark, but we'd like to hear about it directly from Kary. It might be best if you stepped out of the room," Detective Andrews glanced over and caught his partner's eye.

Detective Williams spoke for the first time, his voice surprisingly deep, "Ms. Clark, maybe you and I can have a separate chat in the main studio."

Zuri and I looked at each other and I sent her a silent message, pleading her not to leave me alone. The message was received. She stayed seated and responded to the suggestion respectfully but firmly. "I'm not going anywhere. I'm going to stay right here with my friend, but I promise to stay quiet. I'm just here for support."

The detectives shared their own silent communication but seemed to accept this. They didn't push the issue further.

A rush of warmth filled my heart. I was relieved, grateful and inspired. Zuri was so strong and self-assured. I needed to gather my own strength now. I have nothing to be afraid of. I haven't done anything wrong. These detectives are just doing their job. I felt the fear inside slightly loosen its grip as I focused on thoughts that had a calming effect.

Detective Andrews got back to the business at hand. "Kary, can you tell us what happened last night in your own words?"

I took a deep breath and then began. "Around 5 p.m., Veronica came into the studio. She was visibly upset. She claimed I shared something private that she had shared with me in one of our coaching sessions. That information got back to her husband and because of it, he was leaving her. I tried to calm her down. I tried to explain that I would never do something like that, but she wouldn't let me get a word in." I spoke slowly, trying to stay focused on the facts.

"And what happened after she confronted you?" Detective Andrews prompted me to continue.

"She left and that was the last time I saw her," I said.

"Did she say anything else?" he asked.

"I don't think so." I shook my head.

"Did she make some kind of threat?" he prompted.

That question caught me off-guard. The detectives obviously had information about what happened from another source. I hadn't realized I left that part out, not consciously anyway. I quickly divulged the rest of the story. "Yes, she did make a threat to hurt my business, to convince people not to hire me in the future."

"So, Mrs. Calhoun made a direct threat to hurt your business," he restated my response, waiting for further validation.

I felt like I was admitting to some kind of wrongdoing, but I had to tell the truth. "Yes, she did say words that led me to believe she might try to hurt my business."

He nodded and I noticed for the first time that the other detective was taking copious notes.

I knew the truth didn't look good, so without prompting I tried to explain further. "But what she thought happened absolutely didn't happen. I never told anyone anything about what she shared with me. My sessions are completely private and confidential. I have no idea why she thought anything her husband learned had come from me. I've never even met the man."

"So, I'm guessing that made you pretty upset, Mrs. Calhoun believing something you claim is untrue and then threatening your livelihood because of it?" He posed it as a question, but it sounded like a statement.

Zuri jumped in before I could say anything. "Hold on a minute. It sounds like you're accusing Kary of something."

"Ms. Clark, I thought we agreed you were going to observe without speaking," Detective Andrews stated firmly.

Detective Williams stopped taking notes and started to stand up. I assumed he was going to escort Zuri from the room. I decided that wouldn't be necessary. Zuri was right. I could see where this was headed, and it wasn't anywhere good. I had to be strong and take control of the situation.

"Actually, I think we're basically done here." I looked Detective Andrews right in the eyes and mustered all the courage I could. "Yes, Veronica was upset with me for something I didn't do. Yes, she did come speak to me last night and infer that she was going to try to share that misconception with others. Yes, I was upset but not angry. After she left, I went to the Bluegill Grill, which is right down the street, and I was there with friends, Zuri being one of them, until about 10 p.m. One of those friends drove me home because I had too much to drink. I went to bed and stayed there all night. I'm sorry to hear that Veronica is dead, but I want to state for the record that I didn't have anything to do with it."

Detective Andrews looked at me stoically, not giving anything away by his expression. I had sounded so sure of myself, but I was freaking out on the inside. I wasn't sure how well they would take my assuredness. I realized I was unconsciously holding my breath.

After what seemed like forever, the detective finally spoke. "Thank you for your explanation, Kary. At this stage we're just gathering information, learning the facts, talking to people. Just to be clear, we aren't accusing you of anything, but we were made aware of the altercation between you and the victim, and it was within hours of her death. That is why we needed to talk to you. I think at this point we have what we came for, but we may need to talk to you again. We'll be in touch."

The interview appeared to be over. I felt relief flood through me. I was hesitant to say anything more, so I simply responded, "Okay."

"Oh, one last question." Detective Andrews played it off like an afterthought, but I knew it probably wasn't. "Do you know the name of the guy Mrs. Calhoun was having an affair with?"

"No, she never told me his name and I never asked for it. I have no idea who he is." I shook my head.

He nodded. "Okay, we'll see ourselves out, then."

Both detectives stood up and started walking out of the room.

I jumped to my feet, suddenly wanting to know more and emboldened by the fact that they appeared to be done questioning me. "Wait! Can you tell us what happened to her?"

"Ms. Flynn," he addressed me formally again, "we aren't at liberty to provide those details to the public yet."

He didn't wait for a response. We watched as both detectives walked out of the room, and a few seconds later, we heard the front door close.

I slumped back in my chair. I hadn't realized I was sitting up so straight, so stiffly. We sat in silence.

After a few minutes, Zuri stood up, walked over to the door and peeked out into the main studio. "Looks like they're gone." She turned back to face me.

"So, I should freak out now, right?" I asked.

"I don't know. I don't think so, though." She sat down in one of the chairs the detectives had been using. "I mean, obviously you didn't kill her. That would be ridiculous."

"But they don't know that. They don't know anything about me, except that Veronica threatened me and now she's dead. You have to admit, it looks pretty bad," I said.

"Okay, I admit it does look bad," Zuri agreed, "but I honestly think it's going to be fine. They have to do their jobs. They have to investigate, but when they finish that investigation, there is absolutely no way they're going to conclude that you were involved. It's a case of terrible timing. You'll be fine, Kary."

"I'm glad you think so," I responded.

"You can think so too," she offered.

The events of the last twenty-four hours started replaying in my mind. I had felt so defeated, so much like the victim when Veronica confronted me. I had wallowed in that defeat for nearly a day. I had played the victim too many times in life, with my old job, with my previous relationships, with other circumstances. There were always reasons to explain why you were being kept down, but that perspective wasn't one I wanted to choose anymore. I could choose to take responsibility and to face the situation head on. I could choose to make sure I would be fine.

I felt a spark of energy as I transitioned from feeling powerless and deflated to feeling strong and committed. "I do think so. I know I'll be okay. I just need to make sure of it."

Zuri looked confused, "I'm not sure I'm following you."

"I understand they have to do their jobs, but I also have to protect myself. I'm going to make sure they don't have the opportunity to come to the false conclusion that I had anything at all to do with Veronica's death," I said.

"How are you going to do that?" she asked.

Ideas hadn't quite formulated yet in my mind, but I knew what the first step would be. "I'm going to see if I can get a little more information about what happened and when. I want to be prepared if they come to talk to me again. I was thrown completely off guard, and without knowing some of the details, I don't feel like I can protect myself."

"But if you just tell the truth, you'll be fine," Zuri offered.

"Will I? You might be right, but you don't know that for sure. I want to be sure," I said firmly.

"Wow, I don't normally see this kind of conviction come from you," she said, clearly surprised.

"Well, I'm starting to realize that I want to take charge of my life, all aspects of it—my business, my relationships, and now this. I'm tired of feeling like I don't have control. I absolutely know that isn't true. It's what I help my clients to see in their own lives. I need to start following my own advice."

Zuri gave me a broad smile. "I'm completely supportive of this take control attitude. You know I've been telling you that for years. This is a unique situation, though. Will you let me help you?"

"Of course. Honestly, I need your help," I said.

"Good. So, what's next?" Zuri asked.

"Do you want to head to Bluegill? We can do a little brainstorming. I know I said I needed to go home and get some rest, but I don't think that's possible now. I'm too wired."

"Sure." She popped up out of the chair. "Let me run up to the apartment to grab my bag and lock up the studio. I'll meet you out front."

"Sounds great," I said.

Twenty minutes later we were sitting at a small table on the patio of Bluegill Grill. The sun felt warm, and I was finding comfort in that. The restaurant was busy, which was expected now that summer season was upon us. The influx of tourists kept most of the businesses in Pineville profitable, based in large part to the revenue they made during the summer season. The winter ski season helped as well, but summer was the main money maker, and everyone knew it.

After ordering appetizers and some non-alcoholic beverages—a soda for me and a water for Zuri—I initiated the topic we came to discuss. "So, my main goal is making sure I have a solid alibi. To do that, I need to figure out where Veronica was killed. The most obvious guess is at her house."

"Her house is the one at the crest of Terrace Court Drive, right?" Zuri asked.

"Yep. That's the one. I've never been there, but I know where it is." I quickly scanned my memory. "Actually, I've never been on that road at all, at least not that I can remember."

"I've been up there a few times for private yoga sessions," Zuri said. "Not at Veronica's house specifically, but at others on the same street. It's a handful of mini-mansions, all the way up the hill. I would assume the higher up, the more expensive. It makes sense Thomas and Veronica would have the one on the top. They love to flash their wealth around." Zuri spoke matter-of-factly and without judgement. The Calhouns made sure their financial success was something everyone in Pineville was aware of.

I started thinking out loud. "So, if that's the case, if she was killed at her house, I think my alibi is pretty solid. I was with you, Dean and Ben all evening and then Ben dropped me off at home around 10 p.m. Assuming the police believe that all of you wouldn't lie for me, that puts me at my house without a car and fairly intoxicated well before midnight. I have no idea what time Veronica was killed, but there are only a few ways I could have gotten to her house." I counted off on my fingers as I spoke. "One, I could have called for a ride, but that would leave a witness and a paper trail. The police could check and confirm that didn't happen. Two, I could have gotten help from someone I know. Again, that would leave a witness or an accomplice. It seems unlikely that two people who don't have criminal records would suddenly commit a murder together. I don't know anyone who would help me do something like that, even if I wanted to do it. Three, I could have ridden my bike to her house. My guess is it's a good five miles, though, and a lot of it is uphill. I'm not sure I could do that sober in the middle of the day, much less drunk in the middle of the night. That just doesn't make any sense."

Zuri jumped in. "There is one other possibility. You could have ridden your bike to town, picked up your Jeep and then driven to her house."

"You're right," I nodded, "and that would have been doable. But I do know my Jeep stayed parked in town all night. If there are cameras somewhere, the police should be able to verify that."

"It seems unlikely you would have had the opportunity to be involved in whatever happened to Veronica," Zuri pointed out.

"That's what I'm thinking, but I want to verify that. The first thing we need to find out is where she was killed. I assume that's the type of information that will eventually be in the news, but until then I'm not sure how to find out. Any ideas?" I asked.

Zuri's brow furrowed and she didn't answer right away. She seemed to be thinking. After a pause, she said a bit cryptically, "I don't have any ideas on that point, but I do have an idea about something else that might be helpful."

"What is it?" I asked, my curiosity piqued.

At that exact moment, our server walked up to the table to drop off the mozzarella sticks, hot wings and potato skins we had ordered to share. My stomach rumbled and I suddenly felt ravenous. I couldn't wait to dig into the food, but I also couldn't wait to find out what Zuri was talking about.

After the server had placed everything on the table and confirmed we had everything we needed, I turned my gaze back to my friend. I realized she was doing her best to avoid my eyes, instead focusing her full attention on the food.

"Zuri," I addressed her and waited, knowing I didn't need to say anything else.

Finally, she looked at me with a pained expression. "I can't tell you, at least not yet."

"Why not?" I was surprised and a little hurt.

"I'm sorry, Kary. I don't want to say anything until I confirm I can actually get this piece of information. Also, it means getting someone else involved and I need to make sure they're okay with that. I promise, I will do whatever I can to help, but you just have to be a little patient. Okay?" she asked expectantly.

I felt a momentary pang of frustration, but I knew what she was asking for was completely reasonable, and I knew Zuri always had my back. "Okay, I promise to be patient."

"Great!" She seemed relieved. "And I promise you won't need to be patient very long."

"Thank you," I said. "I don't know what I'd do without you."

"I don't know either," she agreed.

We spent a few minutes enjoying the food.

Zuri eventually broke the silence. "So, I know those detectives were intense, but that head one, Detective Andrews, he was kind of cute, too. Don't you think?"

"Are you serious? You are unbelievable! I was way too freaked out to notice anything," I admitted.

"Well, he was definitely attractive." She gave me a little wink. "Maybe after this whole thing blows over…"

"Zuri!" I shouted, louder than intended, and a few diners at the neighboring tables glanced in our direction.

"What? I'm just trying to look out for you. Obviously not getting arrested for murder is at the top of my list but getting you a date is right behind it."

"I thought you were pushing the Ben thing," I prodded her.

"I'm not pushing any one person. I just want you to get out there," she said.

At that moment, my phone, which was sitting face down on the table, started vibrating to indicate a call. I still had the ringer off from my earlier coaching sessions. I picked it up, glanced at the caller ID and turned it toward Zuri so she could see the name. *Ben Ferguson.*

"Well, if that's not a sign, I don't know what is," she said.

"Either that or he's somehow listening to our conversation," I said jokingly. I put the phone back face down on the table.

"You're not going to answer it?" she asked.

I sighed heavily, "I just don't have the energy to talk to Ben right now. Actually, I don't have the energy to talk to anyone. I think

I'm going to head out as soon as we finish up here. That exhaustion is setting in again." My whole body felt heavy.

"I get it. It's been a long twenty-four hours," Zuri replied, "Dean will be finishing up his charter soon anyway. It's so nice out. I think I'll go walk down to meet him at the pier."

"When do you think you'll be able to share that thing with me?" I asked, changing the subject back suddenly. I didn't want to push but I wanted to make sure Zuri didn't forget our earlier conversation.

"I'll call you tomorrow either way. I'll definitely know by then," she promised.

"Thank you. I really appreciate it and I really appreciate you," I said, and she smiled.

We spent the next half hour finishing up our appetizers and talking about a class Zuri was taking the following week. She was always expanding her skills as an instructor, learning more types of yoga and various techniques. She had a passion for mental, emotional and physical health. Her business allowed her to share what she learned along those dimensions with others. I admired the drive she had for her own continuous growth and how she took that growth and incorporated it into her business. It was the same thing I was trying to model in mine. I considered Zuri not only my best friend but also someone I could look up to and be inspired by. I was lucky to have her in my life, and I was lucky she had agreed to help me learn more about Veronica's death. I felt strongly that I needed to look into it for my own well-being, but I wasn't naïve. If someone had murdered her, getting involved could be dangerous. There was no telling what I was getting myself into. I felt safer knowing Zuri would be right there with me.

CHAPTER 5

I woke up the next morning feeling refreshed. After leaving Zuri the day before, I went straight home and passed out on the couch in the living room. The lack of sleep the night before, the hangover and the stress of the previous twenty-four hours had all caught up with me. At some point in the middle of the night I woke up, dragged myself up to the loft, threw on some pajamas, curled up under the covers and fell back to sleep. I glanced at the clock on my bedside table. It was nearly seven a.m. No wonder I felt refreshed. I had slept for over fourteen hours! Apparently, I needed the rest.

It was Sunday so I didn't have any work scheduled. When I started my business the year before, I vowed to incorporate balance into my life. During my time as a consultant, I spent the majority of my waking hours on the work side of life. Although I knew starting a business would be hard work, I promised myself at least one day off each week to rest and recharge. On Sundays, I never scheduled coaching sessions, responded to emails or did anything business related. Instead, I spent most Sundays hanging out at home and doing whatever felt most relaxing. Much of the time that looked like reading mystery novels, listening to true crime podcasts, cleaning and organizing the house or weather-permitting, sitting outside on the patio and watching the calm of the lake. It was a day set aside for relaxation and recharging. Based on recent events though, I knew that wouldn't be the case for today.

My thoughts were consumed by Veronica's death. Who would kill her and why? How was she killed? Where did it happen? Was this just the start of something more sinister happening? I suddenly remembered Zuri's promise from the day before. I checked my phone, but there were no messages or missed calls. I knew it was still early, but I could feel my impatience starting to bubble up. Hopefully, I wouldn't have to wait all day to hear from her.

I knew I needed to get my mind off of things. I got started on my morning routine. I had established a routine once I started learning about coaching. It was one of the first changes I made in my life. There are many studies that explain the benefits of morning routines and how they help shape the course of your day. Routines can get you into a positive mindset and can create positive momentum. Prior to establishing a morning routine, I woke up most mornings with a dull sense of anxiety, even a sense of dread when I thought about the day ahead. It didn't matter what the day had in store, which activities or tasks or responsibilities I faced. The feelings were caused by my thoughts about how good enough I was or how capable I was or how successful I was being in my life. All of it was untrue but I had unconsciously created a habit of having these thoughts and starting my days with these heavy, negative feelings. My morning routine gave me something to look forward to at the start of the day, and the routine itself helped me focus on feelings of hopefulness, appreciation and positive expectation.

The routine I established was simple. I made myself a coffee and settled into my favorite armchair in the living room, looking out over Pine Lake. I took time to take in the view and sit in silence for a few minutes. After that, I would close my eyes and meditate for five to ten minutes. Then I would write in my journal, a few pages of whatever thoughts came to my mind. The idea was not to analyze or judge my thinking but to get the thoughts swirling around my mind out onto paper. Much of the time just writing them down took away their hold over me, especially the ones that could be considered negative or anxiety producing. After my brain-dump of thoughts, I always felt better than I had when I started.

On some days, though, I felt the need to dig a little deeper. On those days, I would read through what I wrote and identify thoughts that might not be serving me. I would examine those thoughts in detail, question their validity and decide if I wanted to keep them or not. There was an amazing sense of relief, knowing that my feelings were simply a result of the thoughts or perspectives I was practicing. All thoughts were valid, but all thoughts were a choice. And there was so much to learn about myself in the identification of them. I knew my self-coaching was still in the relative early stages, but my life had changed in significantly positive ways because of it already. It was like finding the key to the universe.

I was just finishing up my morning routine when the phone rang. The caller ID showed it was Zuri. I answered after the first ring and skipped all pleasantries. "Did you get the information?" So much for my post-meditation calm.

"Happy morning to you, too," Zuri responded, not directly answering my question.

"It will be a happy morning if you can help me. Is it a happy morning?" I asked.

"Yes, it is a happy morning, and I can help you," she said.

A wave of excitement filled my chest and I felt jittery. "That's incredible, Zuri! So, what do you know?"

Zuri got down to business. "Well, the headline is, I think I know who Veronica was having an affair with."

For whatever reason, identifying who Veronica's boyfriend was had never occurred to me, but of course it was the perfect angle to start looking into. My excitement mounted, and a number of questions flew out of my mouth all at once: "Are you serious? Who is it? How do you know? Why did you have to make me wait for this information?"

Zuri cut me off. "Slow down Kary. I'll tell you everything. Let me start from the beginning."

"Sorry, I'm just a little excited," I admitted.

"Really? I hadn't noticed," she said, and I could imagine her sarcastic smirk on the other end of the line.

"Okay, I'm calming down now and listening," I said. I looked out over the lake outside and took a deep breath. Most of the time either one of those things would have had a calming effect. Neither one was working now. Oh well. At least I tried.

"So, here's the deal," Zuri explained. "I had to make you wait because I wasn't one hundred percent sure I could get this information, and I didn't want to drag Dean into it if he didn't want me to. You know how he's totally against gossiping and likes to stay out of people's business. It's one of the things I love about him."

"Dean is the one who had this information," I said, more as a statement rather than a question. It all made sense now. Dean was of the mindset that everyone was free to do whatever they wanted in this world and that meant there was no room for judgement or gossip. I loved that about him, too.

"Yep, and to be honest, he didn't offer it up on his own. I had to drag it out of him. He only agreed to tell me because I told him it could help you. Of course, he doesn't completely agree that getting involved in this situation is a good idea, but he knows he can't stop us," Zuri explained further.

"So how did you know he had this information at all?" I asked.

"It was a comment he made to me on Friday night after we left the bar. We were just talking about the Veronica situation, about her husband leaving her. He said that for a woman like Veronica, she would somehow end up on top. Things would work out for her, even if she didn't always have the best interest in mind of the people in her life, even if she might be taking advantage of that boyfriend of hers. It was such an out-of-character comment for him to make. It seemed too familiar, like he knew the guy. I mean, he didn't state that explicitly, but I just got the feeling that he did."

"You know him too well," I said.

"I guess I do, unfortunately for him," Zuri responded with a hint of guilt in her voice. I knew it wasn't easy for her to drag Dean into this. She continued, "Anyway, last night I asked him about it after dinner. He didn't want to tell me but eventually he caved. The guy's name is Greg Marshall. He's a local contractor that Dean knows, and they have some mutual friends in common. I'm not sure if you remember, but over the winter Dean spent that one weekend training ski instructors at that resort in New York."

"Oh right. You slept over here that Saturday night and we binge-watched all the movies in the 'Scream' franchise," I said, remembering our girls' night.

"Yep, exactly," Zuri confirmed, and then continued. "Anyway, while he was there, he randomly ran into Greg. It was totally unexpected to see someone from Pineville there. They said their hellos and chatted a bit. When Dean asked if Greg was there with anyone, he said he was alone, but it seemed like he was lying. Of course, Dean didn't press the issue. It wasn't any of his business. But later that day he caught a glimpse of Greg with a blonde woman as they were leaving the resort. He thinks the woman was Veronica."

"How sure is he that it was her?" I asked.

"He's sure. He tried to put a whole bunch of caveats on it, but I can tell he knows it was her," she said.

"That's fantastic! So, we have to talk to this Greg guy, then. If he was the boyfriend, he'll definitely have some information," I said excitedly.

"Kary, if he's the boyfriend, he could be the person who killed her," Zuri nearly shouted into the phone.

"I know," I admitted, feeling a bit deflated. "What does Dean think?"

"Dean doesn't think he is. He doesn't know him well, but he said he's just a really nice guy, gets along with everyone, and he's known as an honest contractor who does quality work," she shared and then sighed audibly through the phone. "The reality is, though, that you never really know what anyone is capable of."

"True, but that's why we'll be extra careful. Will you come talk to him with me?" I asked.

"Of course, I will. I'm not going to let you go by yourself."

"Thanks. So, do you know where we can find him?" I asked.

"Actually, Dean said that he thinks Greg is working a job outside of town and it's a big one. There should be plenty of other people on the job site so we wouldn't be alone with him. I thought we could stop by tomorrow morning. I have a yoga class to teach at 7 a.m., but am available for a few hours after that," Zuri offered.

"And I don't have clients scheduled until tomorrow afternoon," I shared. "So that's perfect. I can come pick you up."

"Sounds like a plan," she said.

"Good," I replied, feeling hopeful about what we might learn.

"So, can you promise me you'll stay out of trouble until tomorrow? You aren't planning on investigating on your own today, are you? Tell me I don't have to worry," Zuri pleaded playfully, but I knew there was some truth behind her concerns.

"You don't have to worry. I have absolutely no plans to even leave the house today. There has been a lot of drama lately, so I definitely need a bit of a break," I promised.

"Great! I'll see you tomorrow morning, then. Just text me when you get to the studio, and I'll come outside to meet you. Any time after eight-thirty should be fine," she said.

"Will do. See you then," I said.

"Okay bye," Zuri said.

I hung up the phone, feeling satisfied. At least I had a next step planned. I had no idea if Greg would talk to us, but it was worth a try. I thought about the things I would ask him. Do you have any idea how Thomas found out about the affair? Do you have any idea why Veronica would think I was the one who told him? Did you talk to Veronica after she confronted me on Friday night? Do you have any idea who killed her? I knew there was a possibility that Greg was the killer, like Zuri warned. The reality of the situation wasn't lost on me. I was getting involved in something dangerous, but I felt like

I didn't have a choice. Veronica had involved me the moment she stepped into the studio with her false accusations.

The doorbell rang, interrupting my thoughts. I jumped, startled. I wasn't expecting anyone, and it was still relatively early. I had no idea who it could be. I checked the peephole through my front door and felt a sense of relief. It was Ben. This relief was quickly followed by a small wave of nervousness. I knew I would have to address that kiss from Friday night.

I slapped a smile on my face despite my nerves and swung the door open. "Hey Ben. What are you doing here?"

"Hi Kary. Sorry to just stop by like this, but you never got back to me yesterday and I heard about what happened to Veronica. I thought you might want to talk." Ben held up the tray he was holding with two to-go cups in it and added, "And I thought you might want some caffeine therapy. Mocha, right?"

"Tell me there's whipped cream on there," I pleaded playfully.

"There is," he assured me.

"Well in that case, I guess I better invite you in." I smiled and stepped back gesturing for him to come inside.

Ben stepped through the doorway, and I closed the door behind him. I followed him through the short hallway into the main living area. I noticed he was dressed casually in khaki shorts and a fitted white T-shirt. It was a look I didn't often see on him. He tended to dress in button-down shirts and trousers most days while running the antique shop. He told me once that he dealt with mostly wealthy individuals and wanted to exude a level of professionalism in his business. It was nice to see him in more laidback attire. It also made it impossible not to notice that he was in decent shape. The cut of his T-shirt made it obvious that he must work out. That wasn't something he ever talked about.

He walked into the center of the room and came to a dead stop, his eyes taking in the lake through the back windows. "Wow, I forgot how amazing your view was!"

"I know, right? Some days I still can't believe how lucky I was to find this place," I said.

"Here's your mocha." Ben took one of the cups from the carrier and handed it to me.

I accepted it and took a long gulp of sweet sugary caffeine before responding. "It's so good, just what I needed this morning. Thank you."

"You're very welcome," he said.

"Let me take that for you." I gestured to the carrier, and he handed it over, after removing the other cup. I put it on the kitchen counter and then turned back to face him. I suggested, "Do you want to go sit on the back patio?"

"Sure. That sounds great." He nodded in agreement.

A few minutes later we were settled into two chairs on the small patio off the back of the house. It was early but there was some activity on the lake. I noticed a man sitting in a small boat. It looked like he was fishing. I could hear the soft sound of music playing. His boat wasn't close to the house but depending on the wind, sound carried easily across the lake.

Ben's words brought my attention back to the patio and to him. "I'm sorry to just come over here unannounced but I was a little worried about you. You never called me back last night and I heard about what happened to Veronica. I wanted to make sure you were okay."

I felt regret immediately and said so. "I'm sorry I didn't call you back. Honestly, yesterday was a bit of a blur. You know I had way too much to drink on Friday night, so I wasn't feeling well. And I was worried most of the day about how to handle the Veronica situation. Then all of sudden the cops are coming to interview me, and I find out that she's dead!" I felt my blood pressure rise as I recounted the events. Although I knew it to be true, it still sometimes amazed me that my thoughts had such an influence on my body. None of these things were happening at this moment, but just saying them out loud was affecting me physically. I took another sip of my coffee and paused, clearing my mind, interrupting my thoughts and thus calming me down.

"Wait, the police interviewed you?" Ben blurted out. He looked surprised.

"They did, but it totally makes sense," I explained. "Veronica died and somehow they knew about the incident on Friday night."

"But it literally just happened. How would they know about it so quickly?" he asked.

I realized he had a good point; one I hadn't thought of previously. "I'm not sure. They didn't say and I didn't ask. Although, I doubt they would have told me even if I had asked. Zuri was with me. They came to the studio and wanted to know about what happened on Friday night—what was said, why it was said, how I felt about it."

"Do you think they think you did something to Veronica?" Ben voiced the concern I had been trying to downplay, destroying any attempt I had of keeping my stress level under control or avoiding the implications of the situation.

"Ben, I thought you came here to make sure I was okay? As you can see, I am okay. But these questions are freaking me out," I admitted.

His expression softened, his demeanor calmed, and he pushed his glasses up on his nose as he spoke. "I'm sorry. I didn't mean to freak you out. I'm just trying to understand what's going on."

I gave him a smile. I didn't want to make him feel bad. "It's okay. I know you mean well, but the reality is, I don't know what's going on. I don't know if the cops think I did anything to Veronica, but I can't blame them for questioning me. She obviously had a problem with me. She made that abundantly clear a few hours before she was killed. I just hope they realize quickly that I didn't do it and they move on to finding the person who did."

"I'm sure that's what will happen," Ben said encouragingly.

I wasn't sure if he believed what he was saying, but it made me feel better, nonetheless. "Actually, after the police left the studio, Zuri and I walked through all the scenarios of how I could possibly have gotten to Veronica's house that night. After you dropped me off here at home, I didn't have my Jeep. So getting there wouldn't have been easy. I don't think it will take too long for them to realize I didn't have the opportunity to do it."

Ben looked confused. "Veronica wasn't killed at her house. Have you read any of the coverage online?"

I shook my head. "No. I basically passed out early last night and haven't had a chance to look up anything yet today. Where was Veronica killed?"

Ben explained, "It sounds like she was found at Pine's Peak or somewhere near there. At least, that's what is described in the news coverage and what people are talking about around town."

"Really? Pine's Peak? What was she doing there?" I asked. From what I knew about Veronica, the great outdoors didn't seem like a normal place for her to spend her time.

"Who knows?" Ben shrugged.

"I guess that doesn't really change the situation either way for me, though," I said, taking in this new piece of information. "Pine's Peak is still not walkable from here. There's no way I could get there without driving, and you can attest that I didn't drive my Jeep home from the bar."

"Absolutely," he said. "I'll make sure the police know you couldn't have done anything that night." He sat up straighter in his chair.

"Thank you, Ben. I really appreciate it," I said.

"You're welcome," he said, pausing before asking, "Do you think I should reach out to the police directly?"

"No, I would wait. They interviewed me briefly yesterday and like I said, I don't know if they consider me a suspect or not. Who knows? They may not even need to talk to you. I don't want to make things worse than they are," I explained.

"Okay, I understand," he said and then looked me straight in the eyes. "But please let me know if that changes. I'm here to help you in whatever way I can, Kary."

His sincerity was palpable, and I appreciated his friendship and support, but I knew this was the moment I had to address the kiss. I dove in before I lost my nerve. "About Friday night when you dropped me off…"

He cut me off before I could continue, "It's not a big deal. I know you'd had a lot to drink. We don't have to talk about it if you don't want to."

I could feel my cheeks flush. "It's not that I don't want to talk about it but there's obviously a lot going on right now."

"There is a lot going on," he agreed. "Why don't we just chalk it up to one friend thanking another friend for driving them home?"

A sense of relief washed through me. "Yes, let's do that."

"Okay. That's what we'll do," he said.

"Okay," I said.

Our conversation stopped and we sat in an awkward silence for a few minutes, both of us sipping our coffees, unsure what else there was to say.

Ben broke the silence first. "Well, I think my work here is done. You're clearly okay, which was my main point in coming."

"Yes, I'm fine, for now at least. Thanks for checking up on me," I said, truly grateful.

"Anytime," he said and stood up. "I better head out. I have some things to take care of today, but I want you to keep me updated on everything. Let me know if you need me to talk to the police on your behalf. Like I said, I'll do whatever I can."

I stood up as well. "You have no idea how much I appreciate your help, Ben. Really. Thank you."

We hugged briefly and I walked him out with promises to keep him updated if anything new transpired. I knew Ben had my best interests in mind, but I had a sense that he felt protective of me, maybe even over-protective. I decided it was best not to share the plan Zuri and I had to interview Veronica's boyfriend the following day. I would update him afterward, but I didn't want to deal with him trying to talk me out of it.

I heard Ben's car start up and pull away. I walked back to the living room, looking aimlessly around. I felt restless, jittery. The plan to track down Greg seemed like ages away rather than just the following day. I remembered what Ben said about Veronica being found at Pine's Peak. I decided to go online to see what information was available.

I pulled out my laptop and settled onto the couch to see what news articles were available. It dawned on me that I could have checked online earlier. There must be some information publicly available about the crime. There were numerous hits that came up when I searched for "Veronica Calhoun dead Pineville." I scanned the list for the local coverage, thinking they may have access to more inside information than other networks. I found a link for the local network and scrolled down to read the posting from late yesterday.

May 30, 6:30 p.m.

Death of Local Woman Being Investigated

A local woman was found dead early this morning under what police are calling suspicious circumstances. Two individuals discovered the body of Mrs. Veronica Calhoun, a local resident of Pineville, in the early hours of May 30th. She was found at the bottom of Pine's Peak, a popular bluff overlooking Pineville Lake. Initial reports indicated a possible hiking accident. Police announced that after a preliminary investigation, foul play has not been ruled out. No additional details are being released at this time.

It was short but to the point. Just like Ben had explained, Veronica was not found at her home; rather she was found outside at a popular tourist site. Veronica was not a tourist. What in the world was she doing there? And why would she be there in the middle of the night? I scrolled up to the top of the page to read the article that was posted earlier today. It was lengthier than the posting from the previous evening, but based on the headline, it didn't seem likely to reveal much about the crime itself. I scanned through it anyway.

May 31, 1:15 p.m.

Community Mourns Unexpected Loss of Local Philanthropist

Mrs. Calhoun was born Veronica Stahlberg of New York City. She attended NYU for her undergraduate studies and worked as a publicist in the city prior to marrying her husband, Thomas Calhoun. After the marriage, Mrs. Calhoun moved fulltime to their Pineville residence and became involved in numerous local charity organizations. Mrs. Calhoun brought sophistication and class to everything she did.

"Philanthropist" was an interesting label to give to Veronica. She and her husband did contribute money to a number of organizations in the community, so I guess the term wasn't a total stretch, but I had never heard her referred to as a philanthropist while she was alive. I hadn't known what Veronica did for a living before marrying Thomas and moving to Pineville. Being a publicist made perfect sense from what I knew about her, and I'm sure she was good at it. Moving to this town must have been quite a culture shock after living in the city, made worse by Thomas' lack of presence and attention—this was something that had come up in our sessions.

The rest of the article was additional information about all of Veronica's links to the community with quotes from residents about how much she will be missed and how sad they were to hear about her death. The article ended by explaining that the police do not feel the public is at risk. They also reiterated that the investigation is ongoing, and the police are not releasing any additional information at this time.

I wondered how much the police actually knew. How could they possibly know the rest of the public wasn't at risk if the investigation was ongoing? I supposed they had to state something like that so that there wouldn't be widespread fear and panic. It seemed a little preemptive to me, unless they had a good idea of who the killer was. If that was the case, it probably meant it was someone close to Veronica. Who closer to Veronica than her husband? I knew that when a woman is killed, the husband is usually the first suspect. I didn't know much about Thomas. I decided to do a little research on him, and it didn't take long for me to discover something that piqued my interest. It was an article from about fifteen years earlier that had a very similar ring to the one I had just read about Veronica.

Community Mourns Death of Local Woman

Mrs. Janet Calhoun was found yesterday evening unresponsive in her bathtub. She was found by her husband, Thomas Calhoun, around 7 p.m., after arriving home from work. Mrs. Calhoun was rushed to the Pocono Medical Center, where she was declared dead a few hours later. Early reports are suggesting an accidental drowning based on an existing medical condition. The Pineville Community is shocked at the loss of such a vibrant young woman. Information on services will be forthcoming.

Thomas had been married before and his first wife had died. The article made no indication that the death itself was suspicious, but it seemed the likelihood of one man having two wives die is something worth taking a closer look at.

Veronica said that Thomas was leaving her without anything based on learning about the affair, so what would the motive be for murder? Was it a punishment for betrayal? It wouldn't be a stretch to believe that news of an affair could push a husband over the edge. Was it about money? Maybe Thomas discovered that Veronica would be entitled to a certain portion of their finances, and he was unwilling to accept that. There were endless reasons for a husband to want to kill his wife. For a powerful, successful man like Thomas, he may have had more reasons than most. Did he kill Veronica? Did their love turn to hate? Did he do something to his first wife, too?

I felt a chill run up my spine. I became acutely aware of how quiet it was and how alone I was here in the house. I loved my floor-to-ceiling windows, but if I could see out, that meant any-one outside could easily see in. I felt another chill. Was someone watching me now?

I had never felt unsafe in my home before. I was freaking myself out. I knew logically that no one was watching me. It was my mind playing tricks on me. I was sure of that, but just to be on the safe side, I did a quick check of both the front and back doors to make sure they were locked. I settled back down on the couch and turned on the TV for some company. It was time to stop thinking about murders and suspicious deaths, at least for now. I took a good, long look outside, scanning the edges of the lake. It all seemed quiet now, eerily so.

CHAPTER 6

The following morning, I pulled into a parking spot in front of Just Be Yoga. I was ten minutes early. I sent Zuri a text just so she would know I was there. I unbuckled my seatbelt, repositioned myself to get more comfortable, leaned my head back and closed my eyes while I waited for her.

I did not sleep well the night before. I couldn't shake the feeling of being watched, and I spent most of the night tossing and turning. Besides fearing for my own safety, which I knew was ridiculous, my brain kept playing out different scenarios of how Veronica had died. She may have been unjustly angry with me right before her death, but she was still a person, and I still mourned her loss. No one deserved to have his or her life cut short by someone else. I had a small idea that maybe I could do some good for her by looking into her death. Maybe this wasn't all about making sure I wasn't a suspect. Maybe it was about getting Veronica justice as well.

A few minutes later, Zuri hopped in the car, interrupting my thoughts. Sweat glistened on her forehead.

"I will never understand the appeal of hot yoga, especially at 7 a.m. on a Monday morning," I said by way of a greeting.

"I told you, one of these days I'm going to convince you to try it, and I promise you'll be glad you did," she responded.

"You're such a yoga pusher," I joked.

"Well, it is my job." She smiled and shrugged playfully.

This was a conversation we'd had many times before. I knew she was right. Over the last year, I had been learning to push myself out of my comfort zone, but it still wasn't something I enjoyed doing. Did anyone really enjoy it? I guess maybe they did. I think Zuri enjoyed it a lot.

"So, are you ready for this?" I asked.

"Are you?" She answered my question with one of her own.

"Absolutely," I said. "My only concern is whether we'll be able to find this Greg guy, and if we do, if he'll be willing to talk to us."

"I know," Zuri said, "but I think it's worth a try."

"Agreed," I said.

"Do you have an idea of what you're going to ask him?" she asked.

"I have some idea," I said but didn't elaborate. I had thought about this for some time while tossing and turning the night before.

"Good. If we do find him, I'll make the introduction and then turn it over to you," she offered.

"That works," I said, feeling a flutter of anxiety. I was ready to start taking some action, "So, where are we headed?"

"Let me plug it into my map app and I'll be your navigator. I looked it up last night. I think it's about twenty minutes outside of town," Zuri said. She proceeded to type something into her phone.

We both buckled up and I pulled out of the parking spot, heading south at Zuri's direction. We spent the drive itself chitchatting about unrelated things. It was a helpful distraction. There was no use overthinking or over-analyzing the plan. That would only work to stress me out. Zuri knew that about me, and I'm sure that was why she kept to non-murder-related topics during the drive. For that, I was grateful.

Exactly twenty-one minutes later, we pulled up to a worksite with a large white house in mid-repair. There was scaffolding on one side of the building and piles of wood and debris everywhere. About a half-dozen men could be seen performing various activities around the outside of the house. In addition to a number of work vans and trucks, I noticed one vehicle that advertised interior design services. I assumed there were more people inside. Although the house itself was a bit off the beaten path, Zuri was right that there were plenty of people around. With her by my side and in the light of day, I didn't feel at all concerned about talking to Greg at this location. I just hoped he was here.

I turned off the Jeep. "So, do you have any idea if he's here?"

"Dean showed me a few pictures last night, so I know what he looks like. And the last Dean knew, he was driving a big black pickup truck advertising his construction company name on it," Zuri explained, and then paused to look around at the vehicles scattered across the worksite. "I don't think I see it here, though. We should probably just get out and ask someone."

Before we could exit the Jeep, we noticed a tall older man headed toward us. As he approached, he removed his hard hat, and we could see a long white ponytail. It matched the color of his beard and mustache. Despite the construction attire, he gave off a hippy, friendly vibe. The windows were already rolled down, so he walked right up to the passenger side, which was closest to him.

"Hi ladies. Is there something I can help you with?" he asked courteously.

Zuri was closest, so she spoke. "Actually, yes. My name is Zuri, and this is my friend Kary." She gestured over to me.

"Nice to meet you both." He nodded his head and gave a warm smile. "I'm Daryl, the foreman here."

"Nice to meet you, Daryl," Zuri said, and continued. "We're here to talk to Greg Marshall. We were told this is one of his jobs."

"Yes, it is," Daryl said. "Is he expecting you?"

"No, he isn't, but there's something we need to talk to him about. Do you expect him onsite today?" Zuri asked with an air of confidence that I admired.

The older man looked at us curiously and tugged lightly at his beard. I could imagine he was wondering who we were, how much to ask, and how much information to divulge to two strange women who showed up on a worksite without explanation asking to see his boss.

After a moment he made his decision and said, "Greg usually does stop by about mid-morning to check the progress." He looked at his watch. "Looks like it's almost 9 a.m., so he should be here within the next hour or so."

"That's perfect! We'll just sit here and wait for him then," Zuri informed the man, intentionally not asking if it would be okay to do so.

"That should be fine," Daryl said. "But just make sure to stay in your vehicle. We can't have anyone wandering around the site without proper protection."

"That makes sense. We'll stay right here," Zuri said.

"Good," Daryl said with a nod of his head. He paused briefly and then offered, "Do you want me to give Greg a call for you? I can let him know you're waiting for him. Maybe he can try to get over here sooner rather than later?"

I jumped in before Zuri could respond, "No, that's okay. We don't want to get in the way of his normal schedule. We'll just wait to see if we can chat with him when he arrives."

"Suit yourselves. If you need anything, just give a holler to whoever is closest. Ask for me. I'll be somewhere around here all day," he said kindly.

"Thank you so much, Daryl," Zuri responded.

"Yes, thank you," I added.

"No problem at all, ladies." Daryl smiled one last time, and then turned around and headed back toward the house, putting his hardhat back on as he walked away.

I turned to Zuri. "So, it looks like we have some time to kill."

"Do you think you're being insensitive by using that phrase?" Zuri's tone was serious.

"What phrase?" I was confused.

"Time to kill." She tried saying it seriously but couldn't hold back her laughter.

I then realized what I had said, and I knew she was kidding but I felt terrible, "Oh my gosh, I cannot believe I said that out loud. That was terrible." I felt my face getting flushed.

"Kary, it's fine. It's a common phrase and I know you didn't mean anything by it. I'm just trying to bring a little lightness to the situation. This is serious stuff, and it feels heavy. I guess I'm trying to lighten it up more for me than for you," Zuri admitted.

"I totally get it, feeling the heaviness of it all," I shared. "I'm trying not to let it get to me but the whole thing is scary. I totally freaked myself out last night and had a hard time sleeping. I kept thinking someone was watching me."

"Oh my gosh. Do you think someone was really there?" Zuri looked concerned.

"Honestly, no. I'm just all up in my head about this. Who would be watching me? There would be absolutely no reason to. But until the police figure out who killed Veronica, I think I'm going to be a little on edge," I admitted.

"I think we all will," Zuri agreed. She paused for a beat and then added, "Maybe we shouldn't be here at all, inserting ourselves into the investigation. If it's freaking you out, I don't know what good can really come of it. What if by getting involved now, we put ourselves in danger?"

"I know what you're saying makes sense, but I can't stand back and do nothing. Yes, I do want to make sure my name is cleared and that there is no possible way the police could think I was involved. More than that, though, I feel some responsibility for Veronica. She was a client, and she was struggling. I promised to help her, and she was making progress on improving her life. I could tell that things were changing for her in the weeks we worked together. And although she's dead, I want to keep my promise to help her," I said, and then added almost as an afterthought, "And what if choosing to coach with me did somehow lead to her death?" I heard a quiver in my voice and felt a warm sensation rush through my body. I suddenly realized what was driving my actions to look into Veronica's death. I felt guilty.

"Kary, there is absolutely nothing you could have said or done that would lead to someone else murdering your client. You know that, right?" Zuri asked with concern.

I sighed deeply. "Yes, I know that's true intellectually. I know it wasn't my fault and I know my guilt isn't necessary, but I still feel it. I just want to understand what was going on with her. I want to know if I could have done something differently. Maybe I could have helped her in a way that would have prevented this."

"Don't you always advise your clients not to beat themselves up about the past?" she asked.

"Yes, I do tell them that, because there is absolutely nothing to be gained by it." I paused, considering my own situation. "I guess in this case, I'm not beating myself up, at least not yet. I don't know that I did anything wrong to beat myself up about."

"But you think you might have done something wrong. You're trying to find out if you did. You're trying to see if you made some kind of mistake that led to Veronica's death," Zuri pointed out.

"You're right. I am doing that," I conceded, "but for now that's what I'm choosing to do. I am choosing to believe that I might have had some small part in Veronica's death and so I feel guilty. I'm going to try to either prove that my guilt is unwarranted or in the very least see if I can do something, anything to help bring her justice." I could hear the conviction in my voice. The intentions behind why I was getting involved finally became crystal clear to me.

They became crystal clear to Zuri, too. "I understand, Kary, I do. I know I can't change your mind about getting involved, but you have to promise me not to question anyone on your own. And if this does start to get dangerous, promise me we'll stop immediately," she said in a more serious tone than I was used to hearing.

"I promise," I said.

"Good," Zuri said, sitting back in her seat.

We sat in silence for several minutes. Looking out the front windshield, both of us focused on our own thoughts. I felt lighter with the realization that had just come to me. I don't think it had the same effect on Zuri. I sensed a heaviness coming from my best friend.

I decided to try to somewhat lighten the mood, focusing back on the task at hand. I pointed to the clock on the dashboard of the car, which read 9:17 a.m. "How long can you wait?" I asked.

"I have a class at noon, so I we probably should leave here around 11 a.m., just to make sure we're back in time for me to get set up," Zuri said.

"Okay, sounds good. Hopefully we won't have to wait that long, though," I said. I turned on the radio to distract us from getting into another heavy discussion and we settled in to wait to see if Greg would show up.

Almost an hour later, he did.

"Do you think that's him?" I asked, referring to the big black pickup that had just pulled into the far side of the worksite.

Zuri sat up in her seat to get a better look. "It has to be," she said. "See the logo for Marshall Construction Services on the side?

Let's wait until he gets out to make sure but get ready. If it is him, we'll need to hurry to stop him before he goes inside. Obviously, we can't follow him in there."

We watched as a man exited the vehicle. He looked to be in his early forties. He was handsome, with a muscular build, short black hair and evidence of an afternoon shadow on his face, despite it only being midmorning. He had a rugged look, which I guess wasn't all that unusual for a guy who ran a construction business. He looked like someone who would hang out with our group of friends. It was hard to envision Veronica, with her high-end taste and fancy attire, having an affair with this seemingly normal guy. I was sure he was vastly different from Thomas. Maybe that was part of the appeal.

"That's him. Let's go," Zuri ordered, and we both got out of the Jeep. We hurried across the front of the worksite and approached him as he was getting something out of the back of the truck.

He stopped when he noticed us coming, giving us a curious look. As we got close enough to see the details of his face, I noticed he was better looking than I first realized from a distance. He was bigger, too, over six feet tall. More than anything, though, I could see he looked sad and exhausted. His eyes were bloodshot and there were dark circles underneath them. His skin was pale. He looked like a man in mourning, and I felt a hint of regret about bothering him. There wasn't time to second-guess the plan, though. We were here.

Zuri spoke first. "Are you Greg Marshall?"

"Yes, I am, and you are…?" he asked.

"Greg, hi. I'm Zuri Clark, and this is Kary Flynn. I think you know my boyfriend Dean Bradley," she said.

Greg looked confused. "Dean Bradley?"

Zuri gave more details, trying to jog his memory. "Yeah, Dean. He owns the water sport equipment rental shop right on the main street in town. He said you have some mutual friends."

Recollection came over his face. "Oh yeah, I know Dean, obviously not that well but yeah, I know him." He paused and his eyebrow furrowed, his expression shifted back to confusion. "So, what's this about?"

It was my turn to jump in. I took a step forward. "Greg, like Zuri said, my name is Kary. We're really sorry to just show up here but we wanted to talk to you about Veronica…" I let the phrase hang in the air.

He didn't say anything in response, but the expression on his face said it all. It was clear that Dean's suspicion was correct.

I decided to continue. "Greg, I know…" I stopped to glance at Zuri and then turned my focus back to Greg. "We know that you were having an affair with her."

He didn't say anything, but he didn't deny it. I took that as a queue to continue.

"I'm not sure if you know who I am, but I'd been working with Veronica for a while, helping her make some decisions about her life," I explained.

Greg nodded with understanding. "I know about that. I know about you, so you're the life coach."

"Yes, I am. I enjoyed working with Veronica. I thought she was making progress and now she's gone," I said sadly.

"I can't believe she's gone." He said this in almost a whisper, and he dropped his gaze, looking at the ground. After a moment, he raised his eyes back up and there was a spark of energy with his next words. "She was making progress. I saw a change in her lately. She was less secretive, more honest, more focused on the future. She told me she was tired of sneaking around. We'd been together for a year. I never wanted to sneak around. I loved her. I thought she was finally going to leave Thomas."

"I know she was struggling with making that decision, but I don't know if she ultimately decided anything," I shared. "I do know things were complicated. Can you tell us what happened?"

Greg didn't hesitate for a second before rushing to explain. "She did make a decision. It was a few days ago. She finally made up her mind. She chose me. She was going to leave Thomas. It was what I had always hoped for." He paused, and then continued. "But then she told me she wouldn't leave him for two more years. They had a prenup and she wouldn't get anything unless they were married for five years. She told me her future was with me, but if she stayed with Thomas a little longer, the money would help create a life for us." I could sense the frustration and the sadness in his voice.

It wasn't surprising to me that Veronica chose money over love. I knew financial security was important to her from our very first session, based on how she spoke about it. The complication was she had fallen in love with the person she was having an affair with but didn't want to abandon the lifestyle Thomas provided her. We talked at length about the fact that there are no wrong decisions in life and that she could choose whichever path she wanted. It sounded like she was trying to get the best of both worlds by staying with Thomas long enough to walk away with some money. Of course, while we can believe there are no wrong decisions for us, that doesn't mean those decisions will be accepted or approved of by others.

"So, what was your response when she told you?" I prompted.

"I broke up with her. I was hurt and angry. Thomas doesn't love her. He treated her like an object, something he owned and controlled. And the worst part was she let him do it. That was the crazy thing, because in every other area of her life, she was in control, even in our relationship. She seemed vibrant, strong, and opinionated. I never understood it until she told me her decision. It suddenly became clear. It was all about the money. She would endure anything for it, and if that was true, then I didn't know her at all. I didn't know the person I was in love with," he explained, his voice starting to crack.

"We all do that," I offered, trying to help him feel better. "We see what we want to see in the people around us. It's normal to want to see the best in others, or to want those we love to be the best versions of themselves. Thank you for being so open and honest with us."

"Honestly, I'm not sure why I'm telling you all of this. I guess I'd been keeping this a secret for so long, it just feels good to get it out. I don't know anyone else in her life. We have no mutual friends. It's like we lived in parallel worlds that intersected only when she wanted them to. And now that she's gone, I don't have anyone to talk to about it. No one knew about us, so they wouldn't understand." Greg sighed deeply.

Either he was a really good actor, or he was truly mourning the loss of his ex-girlfriend. I got the sense that he did love her but there was a hint of desperation in his words. Although he said he broke up with her, he obviously hadn't wanted to end things. He wanted her to choose him, and when she didn't, did he do something he couldn't take back? He admitted he was hurt and angry by her decision. Hurt and anger could lead to murder. I felt that Greg was telling the truth, but I could be wrong. There could be something darker beneath the hurt exterior he was showing to us now.

"Greg, I'm so sorry for your loss. Veronica was a complicated woman, but it sounds like you really loved her," I said, trying to keep the conversation going. I wanted to see if there was any other useful information he could provide.

"I did," he admitted.

"How long ago was it that you broke up with her? You said it was a few days ago?" I asked.

"It was Tuesday night," he said.

"Tuesday night, okay," I said. I mentally placed that piece of information in the timeline for the week and I decided to transition to the topic I was most interested in. "I'm not sure if you know anything about this, but there was something that happened on Friday night. It was between me and Veronica. I was hoping you could explain it to me."

Greg shook his head, "With you and Veronica? No, I don't know anything about that. What time did it happen?"

"Early evening, about 5 p.m.," I answered.

"No, I don't know about that," he repeated, and then continued without being prompted, "but Veronica called and left me a message late Friday. She sounded really upset and said we needed to talk. She wanted to meet me. I didn't call her back. I shut my phone off so she couldn't get ahold of me. I was tired of jumping at her every request, and I guess I wanted to teach her a lesson. I wanted her to stop taking me for granted. I wanted her to miss me. I wanted her to reconsider leaving her marriage. When I woke up in the morning and turned my phone on, I had a bunch of missed calls and text messages from her."

"Where did she want to meet?" I asked.

"It was our usual meeting place, the lookout off Grandview Road. It's mostly a tourist spot, so anyone who we saw there wouldn't recognize us, and we would usually go at night when people weren't around," he explained, and I could sense he was starting to get emotional again.

Then it hit me. "Is that where she died?" I blurted the question out before thinking it through, realizing I was probably pouring salt in the wound.

Greg nodded sadly, and his eyes welled up with tears. "She was there alone. I'll never forgive myself for not calling her back, for not meeting her."

"You didn't know what would happen. You couldn't know. Try not to blame yourself, okay?" I suggested, but I could tell my heart wasn't in it. Veronica had called Greg to meet him. She died at their usual meeting spot. Maybe I was wrong about believing him. I decided to shift away from her actual death. "Did the police come talk to you?"

Greg's sadness seemed to melt away with the shift in topic, replaced again by the desperation I had sensed earlier. He rushed to explain, "Yes, on Sunday. They came to my house. I was shocked. I don't remember everything they asked but I told them what I knew. I admitted to the affair right away. I told them about the breakup and the calls and texts on Friday night. I'm sure they don't believe that I didn't go meet her, though. I don't know how to prove any differently. I was at home alone all night. I'm afraid they're going to pin this on me."

Zuri had been silently observing the conversation, but at this she interjected. "Greg, if you didn't do it, you have to believe that the police will find the truth. That's why we're here. The police came to see Kary, too. We think there is a small chance they may suspect her. You may both be in the same boat. Maybe if we pull the information we have together, we can help each other out."

Greg looked curious and a bit suspicious. "I think I've given you all the information I have. What can you share with me? Why would they suspect you?"

I jumped back in. "On Friday night, Veronica stormed into the studio and accused me of telling her husband about your affair. Not about you specifically—I didn't know who you were until yesterday— but about the affair in general. She was angry and she threatened to ruin my business. The problem is, I didn't tell anyone about the affair. That's not something I would do. I take my clients' trust seriously. So, because of this confrontation a few hours before she died, the police came to talk to me on Saturday. Do you have any idea at all how Thomas could have found out about the affair? Veronica said he found out and he was leaving her."

Before Greg could respond, we were interrupted by the arrival of a dark sedan. It pulled into the worksite right next to where we were standing. In a matter of seconds, the ignition stopped, both front doors opened, and my stomach dropped. The two detectives who had come to question me were getting out of the car, and they didn't look happy.

CHAPTER 7

The detectives approached our little threesome and my heart started beating faster. It almost felt like it would beat right out of my chest. I hadn't broken any kind of law, but I knew finding Zuri and me here with Greg looked suspicious.

Despite my anxiety, I did look more closely at the men, observing them more than I had when they came to the studio a few days earlier. Detective Andrews wasn't tall, probably close to five foot ten, with a broad chest and strong arms. He had a bald head and nicely groomed facial hair. Detective Williams was a few inches taller, with light brown skin and no facial hair. He also looked to be much younger than his partner.

Detective Andrews spoke first, shifting his gaze back and forth between Zuri and me. "Well, well, well…Ms. Flynn and Ms. Clark, we weren't expecting to find the two of you way out here. I can't imagine this is a coincidence."

I decided honesty was probably best. "No, it's not a coincidence. We came out here to speak with Greg about Veronica and their affair."

He scrunched his face up and pretended to be confused. "The funny thing is, if I remember our previous conversation—and I have notes to jog my memory—you told us you didn't know who Veronica was having an affair with. Yet two days later, here you are." He motioned to our little group.

Zuri chimed in. "Detectives, what Kary told you on Saturday was true. She didn't know who Greg was then. I didn't either. I was just made aware of him through someone I know, and I shared that information with Kary yesterday."

Greg joined in as well. "I can't vouch for what their saying, but I can tell you I've never met either one of them until ten minutes ago when they showed up here."

It was Detective Williams that responded, "So you say."

"It's true," I added, starting to feel panicky. I had been trying to help clear my name by coming here and it was possibly going to do just the opposite. "Zuri found out who Greg was, and she and I decided to track him down. We just wanted to find out a little more information about Veronica. I've been trying to figure out why she thought I told her husband about the affair. I don't know why she thought I was the one who did that."

Before either of the detectives could respond, Greg spoke up again. "I don't know why she thought you were the one who told Thomas about us. I can't answer that question. But the reason I know it wasn't you, is because it was me." He paused and then admitted, "I was the one who told Thomas."

Detective Andrews addressed Greg directly. "Mr. Marshall, when we last spoke you didn't tell us that you were the one who revealed the affair to Thomas Calhoun. In fact, we spoke to Mr. Calhoun, and he told us he's known about the affair for months now."

"What? No, that can't be true!" Greg's voice grew louder with his protest. "After Veronica told me she wouldn't leave Thomas for two more years, I was crushed. I was shocked she would choose money over me. I wanted her to myself. I wanted to share our relationship with the world. I wanted to build a life together. I realized that none of those things would ever happen. She wasn't the woman I thought she was, and I guess I just wanted to hurt her."

"What did you do?" I asked, prompting him to continue.

My question seemed to do the opposite. Greg got quiet, probably assessing what he had just revealed to us. No one else said a word. In the forced silence, the pressure to explain finally got to him. He sighed heavily, and then finally admitted, "I printed out a few pictures I had of Veronica. They were pictures we took while we were together. Private pictures not meant for anyone else. On Wednesday, I put them in an envelope and drove to the city. I pretended to be a delivery guy and left them at the front desk of Thomas' building." Greg's voice wavered and tears formed in his eyes as he added. "I think he killed her after seeing the pictures, not right away but eventually. I know he threatened divorce, but I didn't think he would ever really let her go. It's my fault she's dead."

Detective Andrews took charge and said authoritatively, "Mr. Marshall, we're going to take you downtown to continue this discussion. There is obviously more information you have than what you shared with us during our previous conversation."

"Come with me." Detective Williams took Greg by the upper arm and walked him toward the back of the car they just arrived in.

"Ladies." Detective Andrews turned his focus to both Zuri and me. "I want to stress how important it is for you to stay out of this.

I can assure you we have this covered. There is no reason for you to talk to anyone else who may be involved."

I hated feeling like I was in trouble. I tried to explain, "We know and we're sorry. It's just that after our conversation the other day, I thought maybe you might be looking at me as a suspect."

"You aren't a suspect," he responded, and for a second I felt a sense of relief. He then added abruptly, "You're a person of interest."

My momentary reprieve was gone. I felt my heartbeat start to quicken again and I couldn't find my voice. Zuri spoke up for me. "Now that is ridiculous. Kary is the kindest, warmest person I know. She would never kill someone in a million years."

My breath felt constricted. Was I going to have a panic attack? I focused on trying to clear my mind and breathing slowly, as deeply as I could. It must have been apparent that I was not taking the person-of-interest news well.

Detective Andrews' expression softened, and I could see kindness in his eyes, "Okay, maybe I was a little harsh there. Let me explain. Everyone is a person of interest until they become a suspect or are cleared. Ms. Flynn…"

The momentary shock of his words had passed, and I found my voice again. "Please call me Kary."

"Kary," he said looking me straight in the eyes, "you haven't been cleared at this point, but I will share that in my opinion, you will be cleared in just a matter of time. We're still checking up on your alibi and continuing our investigation of the physical evidence. From what I've been able to gather so far, it is highly unlikely you'll be placed on the suspect list."

"Really?" Both Zuri and I spoke at the exact same time and relief flooded my system once again.

"Really," he assured us.

"But why do you think it wasn't me?" I asked before I had time to think about it, my curiosity getting the best of me.

He allowed himself a chuckle and shook his head. "So now are you going to argue that I should put you on the suspect list?"

"No, of course not. It's just, I guess, I want to understand how you can be so sure I didn't do it. Is it just from my alibi?" I asked.

He sighed and I suspected he was considering how much information to divulge to us. After a moment he finally said, "I can't give away details, but I can tell you there is evidence that whoever committed this crime had large hands, likely a man. And from what I can see, you don't have hands the size that would match what we found." He turned to address Zuri. "And neither do you, for what it's worth, Ms. Clark."

I found myself inadvertently glancing down at my hands. They were relatively small. I caught Zuri looking at her own hands.

Before either one of us could respond, he added with an even more serious tone, "Being able to rule you out as the actual perpetrator is one thing, but that doesn't completely rule you out with having any involvement at all. Although from what we can tell at this point, we believe the perpetrator acted alone. If that changes as we gather more information, you would be added back into the pool of persons of interest. My advice for you, for both of you, is to stay out of this. Don't give us a reason to keep you on our radar."

Zuri and I looked at each other and I knew she felt the same way as I did. I answered for both of us. "Okay, we'll stay out of it."

"I hope that's true. If we have more questions, we'll be in touch." He turned around, walked back to the car and got in the driver's seat.

Zuri and I watched in silence as the car pulled away. Greg was seated in the backseat. He stared straight ahead as they drove away, never glancing in our direction.

"Should we get out of here?" I asked my friend.

"Yep, let's go. We can talk on the way back to town," Zuri replied.

We hopped back into the Jeep, buckled up and I headed back toward town. We drove in silence for a while, both deep in our own thoughts about what we had learned.

Zuri broke the silence first. "So, I guess this means you can stop looking into what happened to Veronica, right? I mean, we don't technically know why she thought you were the one who told Thomas about the affair, but we know now it was Greg who told him."

"Yeah, I'm actually surprised Greg told us as much as he did. I mean, we're basically strangers," I said.

"He seemed like a broken man to me," Zuri offered. "He's either completely devastated by Veronica's death or he's feeling major guilt for being the one who killed her."

"Do you think he killed her? It was despicable the way he revealed the affair to Thomas, but even the way he did it was so passive, dropping off pictures anonymously. I didn't get a violent vibe from him," I said.

"Anyone can be a killer. You know emotions, if left unchecked, can lead anyone to do crazy things," Zuri replied.

I sighed and said, "I guess you're right and that's why there are trained professionals to find out who has broken the law and who hasn't. And we aren't those trained professionals."

"No, we're not," Zuri agreed.

"Just so you know, I was being honest when I told the detective we would stay out of the investigation now. Greg admitted to telling Thomas about the affair, but we may never know why Veronica thought the information came from me. At this point, I guess it doesn't matter."

"It sounds like the police aren't considering you a viable suspect anyway, so I agree there is nothing for you to worry about now and really no reason to stay involved," Zuri said. She sounded relieved.

I was relieved, but I was also curious about one thing we'd learned. I had to bring it up to see what Zuri thought about it. "Did you catch that comment the detectives made that Thomas said he'd known about the affair for a while? Greg said he dropped those pictures off on Wednesday. So, when did Thomas find out? I guess he could be lying, though, about knowing for longer than he did. Finding out about an affair just a few days before your wife is killed looks really bad. I guess…"

Zuri cut me off. "I guess that's something the detectives will need to work out, right?"

She had broken my train of thought and I realized what I was doing. I was allowing my thoughts to suck me back in. She was right, I didn't have to worry about it. "Right," I agreed.

"Right," she repeated. "Now, onto a much more important topic. I think Detective Andrews has a soft spot for you."

"What do you mean?" I asked, confused.

"He didn't have to tell us what he did about the killer likely being a guy and that you were going to be cleared soon," Zuri said.

"I guess that's true," I said.

"He was clearly annoyed that you were there and from a professional standpoint, he had to say that you shouldn't get involved, but I think he might kind of respect what you were doing. I think he's curious about you."

"Now you're completely making things up," I said, shaking my head.

"I know what I saw, and I think there might be some interest there. He might be worth getting to know a little more. He's cute and I didn't see a wedding ring," she said.

"You are relentless about this dating stuff," I whined.

"I know, but I have to be. Someone has to be thinking about your dating life if you aren't. What are best friends for?" She smiled broadly.

I knew she meant well, and she wasn't totally off-base this time. "I will admit he's attractive," I said.

"I knew it! Finally, someone you're interested in." The excitement in her voice was more than the admission warranted.

"I didn't say I was interested. I just said he was attractive," I tried to explain.

"Attraction first, interest next. It's a step in the right direction," she said.

"Don't get too excited. I'm not planning on tracking him down. I'd look like a stalker or in the least he would think I was still trying to get involved in the investigation. For now, I want to stay away from anyone even remotely affiliated with Veronica," I said firmly. I felt a sense of relief that the excitement was over. It was time for me to go back to normal life.

"That makes sense. We'll give it a little time and see how things play out. Who knows, maybe they'll arrest Greg this afternoon or maybe after interrogating him they'll go arrest Thomas. Once they solve this, then I think the coast is clear to track Ethan down."

"Who's Ethan?" I asked, confused again.

"Oh, didn't I mention that I did a little Internet investigating of my own and found out a few facts about Detective Ethan Andrews?"

"No, you didn't mention it, and no, I don't want to know any facts about him," I said.

"Okay, fine, but let me know when you change your mind." Zuri smiled smugly.

I decided to let the subject drop and we drove the rest of the way back to town, back to normal life, in a comfortable silence.

* * *

A few hours later, I was in my office in the studio working with my last client of the day. The afternoon had flown by without incident. There were no client confrontations, news of murders or visits from the police. It was a normal Monday afternoon and it felt good to be focused back on normal things.

I had three sessions back-to-back and they had all gone relatively well. The first session was with a new client named Claire. She was working on her relationship with her husband. They had been married for twelve years and for the last year she found herself feeling bored and uninterested. Although she still loved him deeply, she felt the spark they once had was gone. One powerful concept that I offer to my clients is to consider that relationships are only defined by the way we think about the other person, not by the things they say or do. What that means is that we can work on and completely change our relationship with someone simply by changing our thoughts about them, and the other person doesn't have to change a thing. When we change our thoughts, we show up differently and that changes our experience. Then, because we show up differently, it may change the other person's experience, too. Sometimes that results in changes to their behavior and sometimes it doesn't. What it does do is put us in an incredibly powerful position, not at the mercy of waiting for the other person to do things differently. We focus on ourselves and how we show up, and our experience of the relationship changes. My client Claire was still in the early stages of considering this concept might be true, but she was open to the idea and willing to start to put in the work between our sessions to build this new belief.

My second session was with a client named Kathy, who I had worked with a few months ago on productivity. She had been struggling to get things done, both big tasks and small ones. After just two sessions, she had a few tools and some direction on mindset that seemed to give her what she was looking for. At that time, she wasn't interested in digging deeper to uncover what might be holding her back from creating the results she wanted in her life. I hadn't heard from her until she reached out to me again last week. Apparently, she had fallen back into old habits, which really meant she had fallen back into her old habits of thinking. This time she was more open to uncovering some of the deeper beliefs she had about what getting stuff done or not getting stuff done really meant about her as a person. During the session, she realized she had a belief that her self-worth was dependent on how productive and accomplished she was on a daily basis. It was the breakthrough I had been attempting with her many months ago. She was finally ready to uncover it now, and she scheduled a follow-up session for the following week for me to continue working with her on it.

My last session was with a client named Martha, a petite woman in her late sixties who was working on figuring out the next phase of her life. She had worked as an elementary school teacher for over thirty years before retiring. Just a few months after that her husband died unexpectedly, completely changing the course of what she had planned for her future. She had two grown children and three grandchildren, but without a job to focus on or a husband to share her time with, she had been feeling lost. Her daughter-in-law, who frequented yoga classes, got my information and passed it along to Martha.

She was such a kind and caring woman, and my heart went out to her. Over the past several months I had helped her create a new vision of the next phase of her life and then start to make it a reality. She had done small things at first, like joining a book club and starting a daily walking routine, but now that she had some momentum and some confidence, she was taking on bigger goals. She had always wanted to learn French, and so was taking an online course and she was planning a trip to France with a tour group of seniors in a few months. These were steps she never would have taken when I first met her. She had come far in a short period of time. This was our last session, and although I knew I shouldn't get attached to any clients, I was going to miss seeing her.

"Well, I guess this is it, at least for a while, kiddo. Come give me a hug." Martha stood up and called me over to her side of the office. We embraced briefly and then stepped apart. "I can't thank you enough for what you've done for me," she said.

"It's really what you did for yourself. I just shared some tools and some different ways to look at the world. You're the one who took them and applied them to your life. I'm just happy to see you so happy," I said.

"Me too, kiddo, me too." She said this almost wistfully.

"Well, don't be a stranger. I'm always here if you need me and I'd love to hear updates about how things are going," I said.

"I will miss our sessions, but I'll see you around. Maybe I'll even pop by for a yoga class when I get back into town. I've never tried one before, but why not give it a go, right?" she asked, with a lightness she didn't possess when I first met her.

"Why not?" I agreed and she smiled.

She grabbed her purse and turned toward the door to leave. Instead of opening it, though, she stopped quickly, spun around and said, "Oh wait, I wanted to talk to you about something. I heard about that messy business with Veronica."

I was a little taken aback. We had been having such a lovely good-bye. I was thrown off by the interjection of something so off-topic. I didn't quite know how to respond, so I asked, "What business?"

"Oh, just that she was unhappy with you about something, and she came into the studio to make her point known. I didn't hear the details, but there has been some talk around town, about you possibly being involved in her murder."

"People are talking about that?" I asked, shocked. I had considered the possibility that the police would suspect me, but I hadn't considered other people might seriously think I was a murderer.

"Well, kiddo, people will always talk. You know that. It doesn't mean what they say is true. There are all kinds of rumors going around at this point. I just wanted to say that I know you could never have done something like that. I just want you to know that I'm behind you one hundred percent," Martha said with conviction.

"Thank you," I said, touched by her support but feeling my head start to spin with worries about the rumors going around.

"Of course! Besides, anyone who's lived in this town as long as I have knows that her husband did it," she said.

"Why would you think that?" I asked.

Martha's expression grew serious, "Because Thomas Calhoun got away with murder once before. I worry history may repeat itself."

CHAPTER 8

"He got away with murder?" I blurted out, my voice rising an octave involuntarily.

"I'm sorry, Kary. I didn't mean to be so dramatic," Martha said, after seeing my reaction. "I don't know for certain that he got away with murder, but his first wife Janet died under suspicious circumstances. She drowned in their bathtub. How many adults do you know that drown in their bathtub?"

It was obviously a rhetorical question, so I didn't answer out loud.

She continued, not waiting for a response anyway. "It was ruled an accident. Too many sleeping pills or some nonsense like that. I knew Janet from church, and I knew there were some, let's just say challenges in her marriage. She was getting ready to leave Thomas when she suddenly died. The timing was just too off to be a coincidence. I'm not the only one that believes Thomas had something to do with it."

I was processing the information she had just shared. It was consistent with the thoughts I had when I discovered Thomas' first wife died in the way she did. I explained, "I did read online that Thomas' first wife died, and it seemed strange to me that one man would be widowed twice, both of his wives dying so young. I wasn't able to get too much information on his first wife's death, though."

Martha shook her head and said, "Unfortunately, there isn't much information available. I know Janet's family pushed for an investigation once they learned her death was ruled accidental, but Thomas held a lot of power in this town, even back then. It was a fruitless effort, I'm afraid. And although there are some of us that believe Thomas was involved or even completely responsible, we don't have evidence. We just knew Janet, and we knew that things were not going well in their marriage. An accidental death never made sense."

"Well maybe now that Veronica was killed, the police will go back and have a second look at what happened to Janet," I said hopefully.

Martha agreed. "I suppose that could happen. There is a chance." She paused, and then added with a foreboding tone, "In the meantime though, Kary, stay away from Thomas. He's a danger-ous man."

A chill ran up my spine and I could feel a sense of urgency in her warning. "I will. I don't have plans to go near him."

"Good. Keep it that way," she said. "And I don't mean to scare you, but well, maybe I do mean to scare you, just a little bit. It's best if you stay away from him."

"Okay," I said, feeling unsettled.

"Good. I'm sorry to turn to such a negative topic. I just want you to stay safe and to offer you my support. You've been so good to me," Martha said, with a lighter tone.

"I appreciate your warning and support. I will take both seriously," I promised.

"Smart girl." Martha gave me a wink and left.

I sat at my desk in silence, letting the new information sink in. What Martha had shared was just a long-held rumor. It was something that could be expected when a person passes away unexpectedly, especially someone so young. Their family and friends want to understand why. They want someone to be held responsible. It made sense that the husband would fall under suspicion. I'd like to believe that the police always do the best job they can, and if there were any truth to the rumor, it would have been uncovered years ago. But I knew sometimes the police did make mistakes or just didn't have the proper resources and experience for certain types of investigations. Murders were not commonplace in Pineville, and Janet's death was over fifteen years ago. Forensics had come a long way since then.

I could feel my thoughts racing. I closed my eyes and took a few deep breaths, slowing down my mind. After just a moment, a blanket of calm washed over my body. I slowly opened my eyes.

There was a figure standing in the doorway! I jumped, not expecting to see someone there.

"I'm sorry!" the familiar voice said.

It was Ben. "Ben, oh my gosh, you startled me," I said, putting my hand to my chest to help calm me down.

"I'm sorry," he said again. "I literally just got here."

"It's okay, really. I just didn't expect anyone to be here and I'm a little on edge right now," I admitted.

"Well, then it's a good thing I showed up." He smiled warmly. "I came by to see how you were doing. It sounds like you might need some company. Want to grab a drink or dinner?"

I realized I was happy to see him. I thought it would be helpful to talk through what was going on with someone, bounce ideas off them. I smiled back and accepted his invitation. "It's great that you showed up. I would love to grab dinner."

"Great! Is now okay? Do you have any other work to finish up?" he asked.

"Nope, I'm ready to call it a day. Let me just pack up a few things and then we can go," I said.

"Sounds good. I'll go wait out front. Take your time," he said.

"Okay. I'll just be a few minutes," I said.

Ben left and I leaned back in my chair for another minute or two, gathering my thoughts. Talking this new information through with him would be helpful. He always had such a calm, reasonable perspective on things. I was happy to have a friend like him in my life and I was glad the kiss from Friday night hadn't adversely affected our friendship. I gave a silent thanks for small things and packed up my bag.

As I walked out, I caught Zuri's eye. She was at the front of the studio instructing a class. I mouthed "Bluegill" and she nodded in understanding. I knew she would stop by after the class ended.

I met Ben out front, and we walked amicably to our favorite post-work hangout. Although the day was warm, there were clouds overhead and it looked like it might rain. We found a table inside and settled in. After a few minutes, a server stopped by and we ordered drinks, a lager for Ben and water for me. I usually made a point not to drink alcohol during the week. I liked keeping my head clear and there was way more going on than usual to clutter it up.

"So, how's business?" I asked Ben, referring to his antique store. It sat just a few blocks up from Just Be Yoga on Pine Avenue. I did want to discuss what I had learned from Martha, but I didn't want to jump into that topic right away. There were things going on in people's lives other than my current drama. I wanted to keep sight of that.

"Good, actually," Ben said with enthusiasm. "You know this time of year really picks up for the store with the increase in foot traffic in town. And the online sales have taken off. Henry has learned a lot over the last few months, so I have him running with most of the online responsibilities and we split up the store hours between us. That gives me more freedom to head to estate sales and events where I can pick up merchandise. Honestly, the online sales are really what are keeping the business going. Eventually, I may decide to close up shop here entirely and focus on that. I could find a much cheaper place to store the antiques if I move off Pine Avenue."

"Wow, you'd consider closing the store?" I asked. "I'm a little surprised. I mean, from a financial standpoint, it sounds like it makes sense. But your parents opened that shop before you were born. You've said you consider it a testament to their memory that you took over when they passed away and have kept it running all this time."

Ben looked thoughtful before he responded. "Yes, I guess I have looked at it like a testament in the past, a way to honor them. But lately I'm looking at the future and life is changing; everything is moving online. I doubt my parents would want me to shackle myself to the store if it wasn't going to be the best decision for my life. I think they'd want what was best for me."

"I'm sure they would, Ben, and I'm sure they'd be so proud of how much you've grown the business over the last few years. I know it wasn't in your plans to stay here in Pineville after high school and run the store, but you've definitely made the most of it. It's impressive," I said.

Ben blushed slightly and pushed his glasses up on his nose. It was an involuntary gesture he often made when he was uncomfortable.

"Thanks, Kary. It means a lot that you think that. It was tough at the beginning. I was dealing with the loss of both parents from the car crash and then I was faced with managing the business. They were pretty far in debt, and I had to figure out how to get out of it. My plans of college and an engineering degree fell apart in an instant. I have to admit, I was pretty bitter at the beginning, but I eventually learned to accept the cards I was dealt, and now life is pretty good again," he shared honestly.

"Well, cheers to life being good again," I said as I held up my glass of water and he clinked his beer bottle against it.

The server stopped by for our orders. We both got burgers and fries. After ordering I planned to broach the subject of Veronica's murder, but Ben beat me to it.

"So…" he dragged out the lone syllable, putting me immediately on guard. "I thought I should tell you that the police did come talk to me yesterday afternoon."

I felt my body numb up. This was expected, but the idea of the police checking up on me, even verifying my alibi, still made me uncomfortable. Although I knew I had nothing to hide, it was a strange position to be in. I needed to know more. "What happened? What did they ask?"

"It was probably a ten-minute conversation. They asked about what I did Friday night, if you were with me and if I knew what time I dropped you off at your house. I told them the truth, and that was it. They didn't second guess or push too hard on anything. I got the sense that it was more a matter of closing the loop, just verifying you couldn't have had the opportunity to be involved."

I felt better after hearing his description of the conversation. It really did sound like they were just doing their due diligence to remove me from the person of interest list. I decided to share what I knew. "I saw the detectives today. Detective Andrews basically told me that directly. He said that I was likely going to be cleared soon."

"You saw them today? Did they come question you again?" Ben asked, surprised.

I knew I had to come completely clean. "To be honest, it was more of a chance meeting. Zuri and I were outside of town talking to Veronica's ex-boyfriend."

Ben sounded concerned and a little upset. "Kary, are you serious? Why did you do that? Who was her ex-boyfriend? I don't understand. Why would you get more involved? Aren't you worried the police are considering you a suspect? I would think keeping your distance from anyone associated with Veronica would be the best course of action."

I knew his reaction was coming from concern, but as an adult, I had the right to make my own decisions. I had done what I thought was best at the time. I hoped he'd be able to accept that and be the friend that I needed him to be.

I tried to explain my reasoning. "Ben, I know it probably doesn't make a lot of sense to you, but I felt like I needed to do something, anything to get more information. I felt horrible that Veronica had died, and I was confused about why she thought I told her husband about the affair. I couldn't just sit back and do nothing."

Ben's demeanor shifted slightly, and he seemed more open to understanding my motivations. "I get it, Kary. I do. I'm just worried about you," he said with concern but then asked in the next breath after processing what I had shared, "Wait, how did you know who she was having the affair with, and did you say ex-boyfriend, not boyfriend?"

I smiled, knowing I had piqued his interest, and continued, blurting out the rest of the information I had to share quickly. "Luckily, Zuri was able to figure out who the boyfriend was. His name is Greg Marshall. He runs a construction company, and we decided to drop in on him at one of his worksites. Greg admitted that he's the one who told Thomas about the affair, although he claims he did it anonymously. I called him an ex because apparently, he broke up with Veronica early last week when he found out she wouldn't leave Thomas for two more years because of their prenup. Oh, and it turns out Veronica called Greg the night she died asking to meet up with him. He claims he didn't accept her call or go to meet her, but the police are obviously looking into that. While Zuri and I were there, the detectives showed up and took Greg back to the station for more questioning."

Ben looked stunned. "Wow, that's a lot to take in."

"I know it is. I understand that you're worried about me, and I appreciate it but I'm glad Zuri and I tracked Greg down. We learned a lot, including the fact that he's the one who told Thomas about the affair. I don't know why Veronica thought Thomas found out from me and I may never know, but I'm okay with that now. And based on what the police said to me today and their conversation with you, I'm probably in the clear from ever being considered a real suspect," I said happily.

"That's great, Kary. I'm glad you did what you did then." Ben smiled warmly. "So, it sounds like this whole amateur detective investigation is done."

It was the perfect time to share the new information I had learned from my client. Based on Ben's reaction to my earlier news about going to see Greg, though, I wasn't sure I should talk to him about it. Would he be the calm, rational friend I needed him to be? I decided to give him a chance and broached the subject. "Actually, I would have agreed with that earlier today but something new came up since then. That's part of the reason I wanted to talk to you tonight. I need to share it and figure out what to do about it."

"Okay, what is it?" Ben leaned forward, interested.

I proceeded to tell him what I'd learned from Martha, first about the rumors going around town about me being involved in Veronica's death and second about the suspicious death of Thomas' first wife, Janet. After I finished my story, I asked, "So what do you think? Did you ever hear anything about Thomas' first wife's death?"

Ben looked thoughtful for a moment before answering. "No, I don't remember hearing anything about that. I mean, I've lived here my whole life but if that happened fifteen years ago, I was only eighteen and I know I was completely consumed by my own life at that time. It makes sense that it would have been off my radar, especially hearing that it was ruled an accident. I agree though that it's suspicious by itself and even more suspicious now that his second wife is dead too."

"It sounds like, at least based on what Martha said, Janet was about to leave Thomas right before she died. And we know from what Veronica said, Thomas was leaving her right before she was killed. It seems too bizarre to just be a coincidence. Do you think the police know about this?" I asked.

"I can't imagine that they don't know. You have to believe someone closer to the situation and to the family must have mentioned this to them or it will come up when they look into Thomas' background," Ben said.

"I hope so," I said.

Ben's face lit up and he said, "Actually, this makes me think about a case I heard about not too long ago. It happened a few towns over. I'm not sure which one, though. There was a minister whose first wife died in a car accident. He was in the accident too, but he survived. It was late at night. They were on their way to the hospital because his wife was feeling sick. He was driving and he said a deer ran out in front of the car. He swerved to avoid the deer and hit a tree. His wife died immediately. The community rallied around him and everyone at his church was supportive. Of course, his wife's death was ruled an accident and life went on. But then, just a year later, he married a woman from the church. She was younger and had been married previously as well. Her husband died unexpectedly from what looked like a heart attack a few months earlier. Well, sure enough, people started talking. Two people, who work together, end up married after both of their spouses die within a year of each other? Family and friends brought their suspicions to the police and after a few months of investigating, they charged the minister with his wife's murder. They eventually uncovered evidence that proved she was dead prior to the car accident. He set the whole thing up. I think he's in jail for life now."

I was intrigued. I watched and read a lot of true crime but wasn't familiar with this particular case. I asked, "What about the new wife? Was she charged with anything? Did she kill her husband?"

"As far as I know, she was never charged with anything," Ben said, shaking his head. "I don't think they were ever able to prove that the heart attack wasn't natural. Who knows, maybe that part was a coincidence. Maybe it was just fate that her husband died, clearing the way for her to marry the minister. But then that marriage led to questions and suspicions and ultimately a conviction for his previous wife's murder."

"Fate," I pondered out loud. "Maybe that's the same thing happening in this case. Or maybe Thomas did kill them both. I just hope the police can bring Veronica's killer to justice, whoever it is. And if someone killed Janet, hopefully they're brought to justice, too."

Ben nodded in agreement and then said, "So, you started out telling me you wanted to share some new information and then figure out what to do about it. I assume you're referring to Thomas' first wife Janet and the rumor that he may have killed her. I don't understand why you need to do anything about it."

"I know I don't need to do anything about it, but I want to do something. It's hard to explain. I just feel connected to Veronica and somehow responsible for what happened. I want to make sure she gets the justice she deserves. Earlier today I had basically decided to drop the whole thing but after hearing about Thomas' first wife, I just want to find out a little bit more. I know it doesn't make sense." I hadn't even acknowledged that it didn't make sense to myself until sharing it with Ben. I did want to continue investigating—and I would, regardless of what anyone else thought about it.

"Kary, I agree that it doesn't make sense and it could be dangerous. You realize that, right?" Ben asked.

"I do," I said, "but all I'm thinking about doing is contacting a few people, asking a few questions, nothing too outrageous or risky. I might find out something I can share with the police."

He sighed audibly with a hint of frustration. "I can tell I'm not going to talk you out of this."

And I could tell by his response that Ben probably wasn't going to help me come up with a plan for who to contact or what questions to ask. It was helpful, though, to at least share the new information I'd learned. Saying it out loud was helping me formulate some possible next steps in my own mind.

At that moment, I caught sight of Zuri entering the bar, followed by Dean. I waved my hand to get their attention and they walked toward our table. Zuri had the usual bounce in her step, but something seemed to be wrong with Dean. His normal smile was replaced by a small scowl, and he was leaning slightly forward as he walked.

Zuri offered an explanation as soon as they got close enough to the table to speak, "Hi guys. Dean threw his back out." She plopped down in the chair next to mine and watched as her boyfriend shuffled over to the other side of the table and lowered himself slowly into a seated position next to Ben. He looked incredibly uncomfortable, but he gave Ben a fist bump and me a smile in greeting.

"Oh my gosh! I'm so sorry. What happened?" I asked.

Dean readjusted his position seemingly preparing to answer. He didn't look any more comfortable than how he was originally sitting. Before he could answer my question, Zuri jumped in to answer for him, "He was showing off again."

Although he could have taken that negatively or as a reason to get defensive, Dean did just the opposite. It was one of the things I appreciated about him, his laidback attitude and his general acceptance of others, especially those he cared about. I'm sure he knew anything Zuri said was just caused by her concern for him.

Dean nodded in agreement. "She's right. I was showing off. I had a charter to take these college kids waterskiing this afternoon and they were cool. They didn't have much experience but were totally up to try anything. So, I had fun pushing them a bit. I'd demo a few moves first and then let them give it a try. Honestly, it was a blast."

"Sounds awesome! So, how'd you take it too far?" Ben asked.

"I tried to do this type of flip I haven't done for like a decade, and I guess I twisted in the wrong way. I felt this pinch in my lower back immediately, but it seemed okay for a while. Then over the next hour it got worse and worse. Now it's pretty awful," he admitted with a wince.

"Are you going to see a doctor?" I asked. "Maybe there's something they can do for you."

Dean waved his hand in dismissal. "Nah, I'm just going to see how it feels in a few days. This has happened before and there's usually nothing they can do. Besides, I have something that does a decent job of pain management."

My confusion must have been apparent on my face. I didn't ask a thing, but Zuri cleared it up for me anyway.

"He's talking about pot," she explained, and Dean smiled sheepishly with a shrug.

I knew Dean smoked occasionally but it wasn't something we usually discussed. I didn't think Zuri did, but honestly it was none of my business. I knew they didn't bring it up because they knew I wasn't a pot smoker. I had tried it one time back in college and I ended up feeling pretty sick for several hours afterward. I vowed never to try it again.

"No pharmaceuticals?" Ben asked.

"Not for me. Not if I can help it. I'd rather stick to the natural stuff," Dean said.

"I get it, man," Ben said. "I had a slipped disk in my neck a few years ago. It was the worst pain of my life. The doctor prescribed some meds, but I didn't end up taking them. I was a little concerned I would get addicted, so I just dealt with the pain."

"Well, if anything like that happens again, I can help you out," Dean offered with a sly smile.

"I'll remember that," Ben said.

I decided to change the subject. "Are you guys staying? We ordered food a little while ago."

"We can't." Zuri shook her head and gestured across the table to her boyfriend. "I've got to get this guy home to rest, but we wanted to stop by to say hi." She turned to look more directly at me. "And I also wanted to see how you were feeling after our outing this morning."

I knew she was being evasive because she didn't know if I wanted Ben to know what we had been up to. "It's okay," I assured her, "I just told Ben all about it. I'm assuming you told Dean what happened."

Zuri nodded. "Great! So, we're all up to speed. I don't like having secrets between us."

"Me either," I agreed. I knew I would share the information I learned from Martha with Zuri at some point, but she had other things to worry about right now. I would get her up to speed later. Besides, at the moment there really wasn't much to tell. It was just some old gossip. I would talk to her about it once I gathered more information.

"Alright, well enjoy your dinner. We'll talk tomorrow, Kary." Zuri gave me a quick hug and stood up. She waited patiently while Dean struggled to push himself back into a standing position.

Once he was upright, he gave us a smile and a quick wave. "Bye guys."

Ben and I said our good-byes and watched them head toward the door. A minute later our server stopped by with our burgers, and I suddenly realized how hungry I was. I also realized how tired I was. I felt both physically and emotionally drained.

Ben must have sensed something. "What's wrong?" he asked as soon as the server left.

"I'm just hungry and tired and I guess I have a lot on my mind," I said.

"Totally understandable. Let's eat and then you can get home. I'm sure it's been a long day," he said.

"It has been a long day," I agreed. Little did I know, I had some much longer days ahead of me.

CHAPTER 9

I woke up early the following morning feeling refreshed, energized and focused. After I had my coffee and did my morning routine, I looked ahead at my calendar for the day. I didn't generally see clients on Tuesdays. I reserved those days to work on my business as a whole.

There were two things I had on my plate for today. One was writing blog posts. Once a week I published a post related to a lesson from life coaching that I had learned firsthand or from working with my clients. I would then link that post to my business Facebook page. It was a way for me to put myself out into the world, giving potential clients an opportunity to discover me, while at the same time hopefully learning something from what I shared. I had been doing it for a few months with minimal success. The blog posts didn't seem to be capturing much attention.

The second thing I was working on was creating an area of focus for my business. Up to this point, I had been doing general coaching on any topic or problem. Every session was different, based on the client need. I was trying to decide on a niche, an area of focus, and then create a program around that. The niche would help narrow down my marketing and ideally result in attracting more clients. I had a lot of decisions to make concerning my niche, my program and my marketing, and I was wallowing in confusion about all of them. I coached numerous clients on decision-making, and I knew the best way to move forward was to just pick something, just decide. I kept telling myself there is no wrong decision, it's all just a learning process, but I was continuing to choose to keep myself stuck.

Therefore, it was an easy decision to procrastinate today. I had been using any excuse that came up lately not to work on my business as planned on Tuesdays. Looking further into Veronica's death was the best excuse I'd had in a long time. I had a backlog of blog posts that I'd written previously, so I chose one and published it. The whole thing took me ten minutes. I then turned my focus to some amateur sleuthing ideas I had come up with the previous evening.

First on my to-do list was contacting Veronica's best friend. From our sessions, I remembered her name was Fiona. It was not a common name, so it stuck with me. Veronica mentioned her friend on multiple occasions, and it sounded like they were close. If anyone knew what was going on in Veronica's life with respect to her husband, the affair and possible divorce, it would be Fiona.

The amazing thing about technology today is how easily you can find people. I logged onto Facebook and found Veronica's page. It wasn't private, so I was able to see all the people she was connected to. Sure enough, there was a Fiona Graham listed. I scrolled through a few posts and saw the two women together often. This had to be the woman I was looking for. I clicked on Fiona's name and sent her a private message. I explained who I was and how I was connected to Veronica. I expressed my condolences for her loss and asked if she would be willing to talk to me about her friend. I included my cell number and asked that she contact me back.

After sending the message to Fiona, I thought about how it might be received. I had no idea what she knew about the situation or Veronica's misconception of my part in it. I had no idea if she'd be willing to talk to me at all, and even if she was willing, how long it would take for her to get back to me.

I turned to the second item on my to-do list, getting more information about Thomas' first wife's death. This one would require a little more work. I hoped someone on her side of the family might be open to talking to me about it. Of course, I was a total stranger and had no business asking them about it. I wasn't in law enforcement and there likely wasn't anything I could do myself to help them if they did still feel Thomas was involved, but perhaps the desire to talk to someone who was open to listening, especially after all these years, would be something they would consider.

I did a little research online and found some old articles about Janet's life. I eventually found her obituary. I learned her parents predeceased her, but she did have a brother who was named Phillip Cranston. Her brother had been alive fifteen years ago when she died. I decided to see if Facebook could help me find Phillip. Sure enough, after some searching, I found a Phillip Cranston who lived in Whispering Hills, a town several miles away from Pineville. His page was private so I couldn't see any of his details, but I decided to reach out, taking a chance that he was Janet's brother. I sent him a message with a short explanation of who I was, why I was interested in talking to him and my cell number.

After sending the message, I sat back in my chair to think. Now what? I had woken up with such a sense of focus, ready to take action to investigate Veronica's death. The reality was, reaching out to Fiona and someone related to Janet were the only two actions I had come up with. I had accomplished those in no time at all and now it was a waiting game. I racked my brain to see if I could come up with any other ideas. Was there anyone else I could reach out to? Was there any other avenue of investigation to explore? The answers to both of those questions were "no." I couldn't think of anything else to do, and I felt a sense of powerlessness. I glanced down at my laptop and realized I didn't have an excuse not to work on my business for the rest of the day.

Just as I was about to refocus on niches and marketing and program creation, my cell phone rang to save me. It was a number I didn't recognize. I answered it after two rings. "Hello, this is Kary Flynn."

"Ms. Flynn? This is Phil Cranston. I just got your Facebook message. I figured it was easier to call than to message you back." The voice was deep, with a hint of hesitance in it.

"Mr. Cranston, thank you so much for calling! You can call me Kary." I tried to keep my voice from giving away my excitement. I couldn't believe he contacted me back so quickly, and I didn't want to scare him off.

"Kary, then. You can call me Phil," he said.

"Okay, great. Phil, I'm sure my message was unexpected and a little vague." I tried to explain. "As I mentioned in it, I have a connection to Veronica Calhoun who was recently killed. I wasn't sure if you knew who..."

He cut me off. "I know all about Veronica and her death. I've been watching the news, and as you can imagine it was of particular interest to me based on my history with Thomas."

"I bet. I've never met the man myself, but I did know Veronica. After what happened, I started hearing some stories about Thomas and your sister's death. If you'd be willing to speak to me about your experience, I'd be so grateful," I said.

"What's in this for you, Kary?" he asked bluntly.

I should have expected the question, but I hadn't. It was a tough question to answer even for myself. I answered as truthfully as I could, "To be honest, I'm not sure. I didn't know Veronica well, but I feel terrible that she was killed. At first, the police came to speak with me because Veronica and I had a disagreement the day before she was killed, and I was on their radar as a person of interest. I know I had nothing to do with it, so I started asking some questions, just trying to clear my name. I recently found out the police don't suspect me, but now that I've started looking into things, I want to learn more. I knew there was strain in Thomas and Veronica's relationship, and then I found out about Thomas and your sister, Janet. Two wives, both dying so young. It just seems too coincidental. So, what's in this for me? Nothing really. I just want to try to get to the truth."

There was a long pause on the other end of the line. Finally, Phil said, "It's been a long time since anyone has shown interest in my sister's death." There was another pause, and I involuntarily held my breath, waiting for him to continue, not sure of the right response. Before I could say anything, he said, "I'll meet with you."

"Thank you," I blurted out, unable to contain my excitement. "When would you like to meet?"

"Are you available now?" he asked.

"Yes, I am. Where would you like to meet? I can come to you. Maybe we could meet at a coffee shop or a restaurant somewhere near where you are?" I suggested.

"I'm at work. It's a realty office in Whispering Hills. There's a coffee shop a few doors down, called Café Chill. I could meet you there as soon as you can get here. My first appointment isn't until noon today, so I have a little time," Phil explained.

"That sounds perfect. Give me a minute to check the directions from where I am now," I said.

"Okay," he said.

I put the call on speaker phone, opened my map app and typed in the name of the coffee shop. "Looks like I can be there in about forty-five minutes," I said, and then asked, "Since I'm not completely familiar with the area, can we say an hour from now?"

"An hour sounds fine. I'll see you then, Kary," he said.

"See you then," I said, and disconnected the call.

I was excited that Phil decided to meet with me so quickly. That wasn't a guarantee when I reached out to him. I knew I had to get moving if I didn't want to be late. I glanced down at my laptop and felt a moment of guilt that I was choosing to abandon my work for the morning. I took a minute to see if I could redirect my thoughts. I decided I wasn't completely abandoning my business by going to speak to Phil. I assumed the rumors were still flying around town that I had some involvement in Veronica's death. Surely, anything I did to investigate, anything I learned, could help to clear my name in the public eye, and that in turn, would help my business. This thought pushed my guilt to the side. I grabbed my bag and headed out the door.

Just short of an hour later, I walked into Café Chill. It was small, with a handful of two-person tables positioned in front of a low counter. I scanned the room and saw a man who appeared to be in his early fifties looking my way. He was attractive and clean-cut with salt-and-pepper hair. His button-down shirt, slacks and black loafers didn't seem to fit the vibe of the place, which had a more bohemian feel to it. This was reinforced by the reggae music that was playing over the speakers. I wasn't surprised when he waved me over.

"Are you Phil?" I asked, approaching the table.

He nodded and said, "You're Kary, then."

"Yep," I confirmed.

"Please sit down," he said and motioned to the chair across from him. "As I said on the phone, it isn't usual for anyone to ask about my sister these days, so I'm curious to hear what you'd like to know."

"And thank you for responding at all. I know it was an unusual request," I said. Before taking a seat, I noticed he didn't have a drink in front of him. "Before we get started, can I grab you a coffee?" I offered.

"Sure, that would be great. I just got here and wanted to make sure to get us a table. I'll take a regular coffee, black, nothing in it," Phil said.

"Coming right up," I said.

I took a few steps to the counter and ordered two coffees, black. Based on the reason for our meeting, it didn't seem appropriate to order a fancy espresso drink for myself. A few minutes later I was back at the table, sitting across from the older man. I couldn't read his expression. He seemed wary of me, which was understandable. I was a stranger about to ask some personal questions about his family. I would be wary, too. I cleared my throat, a bit unsure of how to begin.

Before I could say anything, Phil spoke first. "Just to make sure I'm clear on the situation, you knew Veronica Calhoun and you suspect her husband Thomas is the person who murdered her. And so, you want to hear about what happened to my sister because there's a possibility Thomas murdered her, too. Is that right?"

"Well, I wouldn't say I suspect Thomas of murdering Veronica, but the husband is always a suspect. So, I think it's possible he did it," I clarified, not wanting to start my own rumor. "But yes, I learned about your sister's death and that there are some people who believe Thomas was responsible. I do think it's suspicious that he's been widowed twice now. Maybe there are similarities between what happened in their relationships with him, some kind of pattern. I know the deaths were very different, though. There's no doubt that Veronica was murdered. In Janet's case, I understand that's the over-arching question—was it an accident or was it murder?"

Phil nodded his head in agreement and explained. "That's the part we've struggled with all these years. There is no way to prove that Janet didn't take those sleeping pills herself. There's absolutely no evidence. The police refuse to reopen the investigation and so as long as it remains listed as accidental, nothing can be done. Just so you know, once I heard about Veronica's death, I did call the police and make sure the investigating officers knew about Janet. I assumed they would tie the two deaths together eventually, but I hoped my call would get the ball rolling more quickly. So far no one has called me back, though."

I could sense anger rising to the surface as Phil explained the situation with the police. That was understandable. I would be angry if I were him too. However, I needed to learn more about Thomas and Janet's relationship and why Phil thought Thomas was respon-sible. I tried to steer the conversation in a more personal direction. "That's terrible. I'm so sorry this happened to your sister and to you. It's awful to lose someone and I'm sure these circumstances make the loss even worse."

"Thank you. It is terrible. It's been a nightmare," he admitted. I sensed his anger subside a bit, replaced by sadness.

"I spoke to someone who knew your sister and I understand there were some problems in the marriage. Can you tell me about their relationship? Were you aware of their problems?" I asked.

Phil sighed heavily before sharing. "That relationship was doomed from the very beginning. I tried to talk Janet out of marrying him, but she wouldn't listen to me. I could tell right away that the guy wasn't genuine. He said all the right things, but I could tell it was an act. Guys can read guys, and I knew he was one of those assholes who like to have the perfect wife at home while they go out and do whatever they want. My sister was smart and capable. She could have done so much in her life. I wanted better for her than to be the stay-at-home trophy wife of a guy who didn't really love her."

"Did Thomas prove you right, then, after they were married?" I asked.

"Not right away, but after the first year, I could tell something wasn't right. Janet seemed sad, not her usual self. She was spending more time without Thomas. He was always working, and he never came to family functions after the wedding. I kept trying to get Janet to tell me what was going on, but she refused at first. Eventually she broke down and told me she found out he was cheating on her. Even back then he had a penthouse in the city, along with the house in Pineville. He was sleeping with someone from his office when he stayed in the penthouse. When my sister found out, it had been going on for about six months. She was devastated. No one deserves to go through that." He shook his head. "But you know what was even worse? Thomas made her feel like it was her fault. She wasn't being a good enough wife. She wasn't meeting his needs. She wasn't attentive enough. I could have killed the guy when she finally told me what was going on."

"What did you do?" I asked, on the edge of my seat to hear what happened.

"I showed up at Janet's house, we packed a bag, and she came to stay with me. I wasn't going to let her stay in a situation like that," he said with pride.

"I don't blame you. It sounds like you were really looking out for her," I said.

"She was my sister. Isn't that what a big brother is supposed to do?" he said, not expecting an answer.

I knew we were getting to the worst part. I prompted Phil to continue. "So, if she came to stay with you, how did she end up back with Thomas?"

"He wouldn't let her go. He kept calling and stopping by and apologizing and sending gifts. Eventually she agreed to go back, to give the marriage another shot," he explained. "I was not supportive. I couldn't believe she was being so weak. I didn't understand why she would go back to such an unhealthy situation. And I told her that. I told her I couldn't support her decision and that I wouldn't be there again if something happened. I was so angry. Looking back now, I realize I handled the situation all wrong."

"Why do you think that?" I asked.

"Because after that, Janet wouldn't tell me anything. She pulled away. We didn't see each other very often, and when we did, it was surface-level conversation only, nothing too deep. I made it so she didn't feel comfortable opening up to me. I didn't realize it at the time. I was so mad at her for going back to him. And then just three months later, she was dead." Phil stopped speaking abruptly and I could tell he was trying to hold his emotions back.

"I'm sorry to dredge up these memories for you," I apologized, feeling guilty. I wanted to learn more about the situation, but I hated asking this man to relive what was probably one of the worst times of his life.

"You haven't really. They're with me all the time," Phil said. "I've been trying to get Janet justice since the day she died. I know it's too little too late, but it's all I can do. I wasn't there for her when she needed me."

"It's sounds like you tried to be. You did the best you could and you're doing what you can now," I assured him. "I'm sure Janet would be grateful."

He nodded but didn't respond, his expression full of regret and sadness.

I nudged the conversation forward again. "Just so I make sure I know the full story; do you know if Thomas was ever abusive or violent with Janet?"

"I know he said terrible things to her. I would classify that as verbal abuse, and his behavior was manipulative. He made her feel so bad about herself. She withered away right in front of all of us after marrying him," Phil explained.

"Anything physical?" I asked to confirm, not that mental and verbal manipulation weren't abuse, but it seemed to me that jumping from no physical violence to killing someone was probably unusual.

"No, I looked into that after she died and I was never able to find any evidence of physical abuse," Phil admitted and then quickly added, "although, that doesn't mean it didn't happen. It just means no one knew about it."

"And it doesn't mean he wasn't involved in her death," I said. I could sense he was getting defensive. I needed to keep him on my side. "I just want to make sure I know the whole story."

Phil nodded. I got the sense he was still with me. That was good, because my next set of questions would take us into an even more a sensitive area.

"Do you know if Janet took sleeping pills? Did she have a prescription?" I asked.

Phil nodded as he replied, "She did. She started to have trouble sleeping after our parents died. That was a few years before she met Thomas. That's the thing about it, she had taken that medication for such a long time. It's impossible that she accidentally took too much and fell asleep in the bathtub."

I swallowed hard before asking my next question. I wanted to be sensitive, but I had to broach a fairly obvious explanation, one that Phil had not brought up. I decided the straightforward approach was best. "Is there any chance she did it on purpose?"

"Suicide? No! Never!" he answered adamantly, and then tried to defend his reasoning. "She wouldn't have it in her to do that. She had way too much to live for and there was no note, no sign that it was even a possibility. I heard later that she told people she was leaving Thomas. She was getting things ready. Why would she kill herself? That doesn't make any sense."

I could tell this was an explanation he wouldn't feel comfortable exploring further, so I decided to agree with him. "You're right. It doesn't make sense." I was starting to feel a little deflated. While Thomas did sound like a jerk and the timing of Janet's death was concerning, if she really was planning to leave him, it didn't sound like there was any evidence to support the idea that Thomas killed her. I understood why her brother and those close to her might have suspicions, but I was starting to understand why the police may not agree with them. "Is there anything else you can tell me that might be helpful?"

"The only thing I can think of is Thomas had a personal assistant back then. Her name was Cheryl Barclay. She did everything for Thomas, and even spent time at the house with Janet. They were friendly. I tried to talk to Cheryl afterward, and she was respectful but not very open. I got the sense she was holding something back, that she knew something. She was completely dedicated to Thomas, though, had worked for him for years. I figured she was scared of losing her job. I kept tabs on her over the years and eventually she moved on to a different job. I gave it a few months and then reached out. I was hoping since she no longer worked for Thomas, she'd be more open to speaking with me. She never called me back, though. I tried a few more times and then stopped. That was probably at least five years ago. Maybe now she'd be more willing to talk. Maybe she'd be more willing to talk to someone other than me," Phil explained.

"It's definitely worth a try," I said, my spirits rising a bit with this new avenue to explore. "Do you have a way to contact her?"

"I have a cell phone number, but I don't know if it's good anymore," Phil said and pulled out his phone. He looked through the contacts and then read it out loud while I entered it into my own cell.

"Thanks," I said.

"Sure. So, what do you think?" he asked me expectantly.

I knew he was looking for assurance that I believed his theory about Thomas killing Janet. From what he shared, though; I couldn't do that. After a brief pause to gather my thoughts, I said, "From what you've shared with me today, there isn't concrete proof that Thomas had something to do with Janet's death, but that doesn't mean he wasn't involved. With Veronica's murder, I think that does warrant looking back at what happened to your sister a little more closely. I obviously can't promise you anything. I'm not in law enforcement, but I am going to continue to ask questions. If I come across anything at all that could benefit your sister's case, I'll let you know."

"I understand. I know there isn't much there, despite my best efforts over the years, but thank you for meeting with me and listening to me and keeping my sister in mind. I would appreciate hearing about anything new you learn. I feel terrible that another woman is dead, but I also feel hopeful again after so many years. It's hard to explain." He dropped his head, trying to keep his emotions under control.

"I'm sorry for what you've been through and for what you're going through. I'm sure it's not something that's easy to talk about. Thank you for sharing what you know with me," I said with gratitude.

He lifted his head and said, "You're welcome." He smiled but there was deep sadness behind his eyes.

"I guess I'm going to head out," I said. I stood up, put my bag over my shoulder and grabbed my still half-full to-go cup. "Thank you again, Phil. I'll be in touch if I learn anything at all."

"Thank you, Kary. I really do appreciate it." He stayed seated as he spoke.

I gave him a final smile and walked out of the coffee shop. I ran through the things I learned as I walked back to my Jeep. For the most part, what I learned was how dysfunctional Thomas and Janet's relationship was. There were a few similarities to the little I knew about Thomas and Veronica's relationship. I had no idea if any of it was relevant to Veronica's death, but I filed it away in my mind for future reference.

After getting into my Jeep, I decided to try to contact Thomas' former assistant. I tried the number Phil had given to me. It went straight to voicemail, one of those standard pre-recorded messages, so I had no idea if it was still Cheryl's number. After the beep, I asked to speak with Cheryl and left my name and cell number. I decided there was a better chance of her calling me back if she didn't know what I was calling about. I hung up after leaving the message. Now that was a waiting game too. I turned on the Jeep and headed back toward home.

I was about halfway there when I had a thought. If I took a slight detour, I could stop by Pine's Peak, where Veronica's body was found. I felt a twinge of anxiety. Was it a good idea to stop by the scene of the crime on my own? I checked the time. It was 11 a.m. on a Tuesday in June. The sun was shining. It was the perfect day for spending time outside. Pine's Peak was a popular spot for tourists to admire the lookout point and it was located along a well-known hiking trail. I highly doubted the place would be completely empty. There would likely be at least a few people around. I decided to make the detour.

Just minutes later, I pulled off the road into a small parking lot. It was just big enough for three or four cars. My Jeep was the only vehicle there at the moment. That didn't mean no one else would be at the lookout since you could reach it from the trail and other turn-offs further up and down the road. I turned off the ignition, grabbed my phone and hopped out. I knew the police had done their jobs and had combed the area for clues, so I didn't expect to find anything. I just wanted to take a look at it for myself, to see where Veronica had died. It was an impulse I couldn't explain.

I walked down the short path surrounded by trees. It went straight back about a hundred feet. The path then rounded to the left and I could see this is where it joined the longer hiking trail. After another hundred feet or so, there was an offshoot to the right with a sign about the lookout point. I followed the sign and found myself standing on the edge of a rocky cliff. There was a low railing constructed to prevent people from walking out too far. I looked out over the valley, and you could see the lake far below. The view was breathtaking. No wonder people liked to visit this spot. I had been here when I was in high school but hadn't been back since. It looked about the same as I remembered it.

I glanced around and realized there was no one else here. That was surprising and I felt a chill run up my spine. I wouldn't stay long. From where I was standing at the railing, I could see that there was a drop, but the brush and rocks on the other side of it were obstructing my view. Apparently, whoever killed Veronica must have pushed her over the railing, which was about waist high. The person had to be strong. I understood, with my smaller stature, why the police didn't think I was a likely suspect.

I was just debating whether there was anywhere I could go to get a better view of the drop-off itself when I heard a rustling sound behind me. I hadn't realized how quiet it was until the sound broke through the silence. I jumped involuntarily and spun around to see where it was coming from.

Standing just a few feet behind me was a man. My breath caught in my throat and time seemed to stand still. I recognized him immediately from the pictures I'd seen. It was Thomas Calhoun.

CHAPTER 10

I unintentionally made eye contact with him. His expression was blank, no recognition that he knew me but no warmth in the greeting of a stranger. Being alone in the woods with a possible killer was not the ideal time to strike up a conversation, much less make accusations. It was probably better to play it off like I didn't know who he was.

"Oh sorry, I didn't realize anyone else was here. You startled me." I didn't have to fake the nervous laugh that followed. He said nothing, so I asked, "It's a beautiful day out here, isn't it?" I moved a few feet over where I could pretend to still be looking at the view but where I could see his movements from the corner of my eye.

He paused for an uncomfortable amount of time before answering, "Yes, it's very beautiful today." He started walking in my direction and came up to the railing to my right, turning his gaze from me to the view once he was beside me.

He looked older in person than in the pictures I had seen, and although I knew he was nearing sixty, I could see he was strong and tall. With his salt-and-pepper hair and chiseled features, he was traditionally attractive, but knowing what I knew about him, I knew that was only physical. He was an ugly person on the inside. There was no denying I was scared of him. I could feel my heart pounding in my chest. Could he hear it? Did he know who I was? Did he kill his wife? The questions swirled around my head while I tried to work out the best thing to do.

We both looked out side-by-side. I wished someone else would come along the trail and join us. I wanted to turn and run away, but I didn't want to seem like a crazy person. A few minutes passed. It was long enough that it wouldn't look suspicious if I left. I was about to do just that when his voice broke the silence.

"I know who you are," he said flatly, without emotion. He spoke so quietly, for a second I thought I imagined it.

I turned my head, and he was still looking out over the valley, expressionless. Had I imagined his words? I was shocked into silence. I just stood there, frozen.

"Apparently you knew my late wife," he said coldly. He turned to face me and said, "Apparently you put all kinds of ideas into her head."

I turned toward him now as well. He was about five feet away from me. He was too far to reach out and touch me, but he could always lunge. And he could have some kind of weapon. I braced myself and got ready to run. I pulled together all the courage I could muster and replied, "Yes, I knew Veronica. You must be Thomas."

"Ms. Flynn, I find it very curious that a woman who spent weeks manipulating my wife, encouraged her to ruin her marriage and then had a very public fight with her hours before she was killed would be hanging out at the scene of the crime just a few days later." His tone remained flat, but his expression darkened.

I had expected some amount of anger from this man, but I was thrown by the accusation. I involuntarily stuttered, "I, I'm, I'm sorry, but what are you implying?"

"I didn't take you for stupid, Ms. Flynn. You know exactly what I'm implying," he said. His voice remained steady and calm. It was almost more terrifying than if he had been angry and lashing out. I envisioned a tiger stalking its prey, waiting for the perfect time to strike. I wouldn't give him that chance.

I said nothing. I walked quickly toward the tree line. My senses were in overdrive, everything seemed to be happening in slow motion. I could sense that he wasn't following me. After a few steps, I turned around and saw that he hadn't moved but he was watching me. I turned back around and picked up my pace. When I rounded the corner and was out of sight, I broke into a run. In a few minutes I was back in my Jeep with the doors locked.

I was slightly out of breath, partly from the run but mostly from the fear. I kept a view of the entrance to the trail. Thomas didn't walk out. I noticed a red BMW parked behind me, which must belong to him. I started up the Jeep and pulled out onto the road. My heart was still pounding, and I felt my body start to shake. I was literally shaking with fear. Not in a million years had I expected to run into Thomas at the lookout. I guess going there by myself hadn't been my best idea.

After a few minutes of driving, I could feel my body start to calm down. The shaking had subsided, and I could tell my heart rate had slowed. I was starting to think more clearly again. I decided it wasn't so silly not to expect Thomas to be at the lookout, but there had to be a reason he was there. Was he coming to the spot his wife died to pay his respects or mourn her death? Or was he coming back to the scene of the crime to make sure he hadn't left anything behind?

All at once a totally different set of questions came to my mind and they sent shivers down my spine. Was Thomas following me? Am I what brought him to the lookout? Why would he be following me at all? Was he trying to pin Veronica's murder on me? That's exactly what his comments had implied. Martha had warned me to stay away from Thomas, that he was a dangerous man. I may not have a choice in the matter. I was on his radar. I didn't know what my next move should be. I decided to focus on getting home. I longed for the comfort of my own space. I needed to take some time to calm down. Then I would figure out what to do.

An hour later I had finally relaxed. When I got home, I ran inside, locked myself in and burst into tears. I had a flood of emotions that needed to be released. It was mostly relief I think, from not being hurt out there on the ridge. Suddenly the reality of the situation and what I was getting myself into became very, very real. I took a hot shower and let the steam and water wash the emotions away. I felt about a thousand times better once I was showered and dressed again.

Although I had been terrified out there on the ridge with Thomas and I knew staying involved was potentially dangerous, seeing him, seeing how imposing he was, understanding what Veronica may have been going through with a husband like that, only strengthened my conviction to keep digging. I would just be more careful moving forward. No more going off into secluded areas on my own. Honestly, that's a general rule I follow in my life, even when nothing related to murder is going on. I had let my curiosity overrule my sensibility. I would not let that happen again.

I had just made myself a turkey-and-cheese sandwich and was outside on the patio eating it when my cell phone rang. I looked at the caller ID. "Hi mom," I said, trying to sound upbeat and normal when I answered, putting the call on speaker so I could talk and eat at the same time.

"What's wrong?" she asked abruptly.

"Nothing. I'm just sitting here eating a sandwich," I said.

"Nope, it's not that. I can hear you mumbling but there's something else. Tell me what's wrong," she said.

It was impossible to get anything past my mom. She had a sixth sense when it came to my sister and me. Secrets were not a thing in our household growing up, which was great in some respects but completely frustrating in others. Now as an adult, I usually appreciated the fact that no topic was off limits, and we generally did talk about everything. Sometimes I just wished I could bring things up in my own time. Somehow though my mom always knew when something was going on.

I decided I could at least put her off for a few hours, "You're right, there is something going on, but I'd rather not get into it over the phone. I'll tell you about it tonight."

"So, you are coming tonight? That's why I was calling. Family dinner." She sung the last two words.

"Mom, do I ever not come to our weekly family dinners? I don't know why you insist on calling me every Tuesday afternoon to double-check," I said, pretending to be frustrated. This topic would be a great way to distract her.

"Kary, you know how happy I am that you moved back here last year, and I just want to make sure you keep these dinners on your schedule. I know how life can be. We all get so busy, but we need to make time for each other," she explained.

I had heard this before and I did love hanging out with my family. They were a big reason I had moved back here to begin with. Of course I wanted to see them. And I had to admit that I really didn't mind my mom checking in every Tuesday to make sure I'd be at our weekly dinner. I just liked to give her a hard time about it. "I'll be there tonight and every Tuesday night, as long as you are cooking. I promise."

"And do you promise to tell me what's going on over dinner then?" she asked.

"Yes, I promise. I'll tell you, dad and Paige everything. Actually, I could use your advice," I said.

"Okay then. I'll hold you to that promise. We'll see you around six-thirty, sweetie," she said.

"Bye mom," I said and hung up.

I was looking forward to dinner with my family tonight. After living far away for so long, I appreciated spending time with them. And although I would have loved to keep this whole situation from them, I knew it would be far better to get them up-to-speed. My family was open-minded and resourceful. They may have some ideas for what I should do. I also knew they would have no concerns about me doing my own investigation. In fact, they would probably think I was doing Veronica and myself a disservice if I didn't get involved. Flynns took action. Flynns made things happen. It was our family motto. In general, it was a very positive way to approach life. However, it was one of the things that made me feel so inadequate when I quit my previous job without a plan. I knew my family was relieved once I made some decisions and appeared to have direction in my life again. I guess I was relieved, too.

I finished up my sandwich, put my plate in the sink and checked the time on my cell phone. It was 1:13 p.m. I had several hours until I needed to head to my parents' house for dinner. The afternoon stretched ahead of me, and I felt a sense of overwhelm. I still hadn't worked out what to do next about the Veronica, and now Thomas, situation. I also knew there was no way I would be able to focus on working on my business. I was too distracted by the events of the morning.

I decided a walk might help. Sometimes getting out of my house into the fresh air, allowing my mind to wander, getting my heart rate up a bit, was all I needed to settle into work mode. I put on my sneakers and got ready to head out. I had a forty-minute loop that I liked to walk around the neighborhood. That was usually enough time to get my brain ready to focus on a few solid hours of work. I could still salvage some of this day.

I always made sure to bring my cell phone with me on my walks in case something happened and I needed to call for help. Today unlike other days, I had a cloud of concern hanging over my head because of my encounter with Thomas. I wasn't sure if my fear of him following me was an overreaction, but I didn't want to take any chances. So, I decided to bring a small can of pepper spray with me as well. When I first moved to Boston, I was living downtown, and a friend had given it to me for protection. I used to carry it at all times in the city, although I never ran into any trouble. Once I moved back, I had set it aside, not feeling the need for that level of protection in Pineville, at least not until now. I wondered if it still worked. It was a few years old at this point. I put it in my pocket before heading out and made a mental note to order a new can when I got back. I'd feel better having a brand-new can.

Luckily my walk went without incident, and I felt calmer and clearer-headed after nearly completing my usual loop. I was in the final stretch. I rounded the corner and gained a view of my house. There was a car parked on the street right in front of it. It was a dark color, and it didn't look familiar. I put my hand in my pocket to ensure that the pepper spray was still there. It was. I slowed my pace, unsure of how to proceed. If I wanted to get to my front door, I would have to walk either right in front of or behind the car. Or I could loop around behind my neighbor's house instead, avoiding the car altogether. I was still contemplating my next move when the driver's side door opened, and Detective Andrews stepped out. Relief flooded through me. It wasn't Thomas coming to confront me or a stranger that I needed to fear. My relief was replaced almost immediately by a sense of alarm though. This was the detective in charge of investigating Veronica's murder. What was he doing here?

I gathered up my courage and approached him, noticing his partner wasn't with him. My voice displayed a confidence I didn't feel inside. "Detective Andrews, is there something I can help you with?"

"Ms. Flynn, I'm so glad I caught you. I noticed your Jeep in the driveway and rang the doorbell but there wasn't any answer. I was just about to leave. Good timing," he smiled as he addressed me.

"I guess you could call it that. Please, call me Kary," I said, repeating my earlier request. I hated being called Ms. Flynn. It made me feel old.

"Kary, that's right," he acknowledged but he didn't say anything else.

"I was just taking a walk," I said, stating the obvious and filling in the silence. His lack of an explanation for being here was making me uncomfortable.

"Nice day for it," he said, nodding as he continued. "In fact, I heard you were taking a walk earlier today too." For a second, I was caught off-guard. I didn't understand what he was talking about. I'm sure my expression gave my confusion away because he added, "Pine's Peak."

Realization hit me and I blurted out without even thinking, "Thomas called you."

"That he did," Detective Andrews said.

I needed time to pull my thoughts together. I said, "Detective, do you want to come in for a few minutes? I could really use a glass of water after my walk, and you obviously want to talk to me about what happened."

"I would like to talk to you. We can do that wherever you'd like," he said, making a motion for me to walk in front of him so he could follow me toward the house. As I passed him, he added, "and you can call me Ethan."

"I can?" I asked, a little taken aback. Knowing his first name was incongruent with him being the big scary detective that I pictured him as in my mind.

"There are no rules about what you can and can't call me. I think we've met enough times at this point to be on a first-name basis," he explained. "I'm okay with it if you are."

"Yes, of course I'm okay with it. Ethan it is then. It just kind of threw me." I was tripping over my words now.

"Because I have a name and so therefore, I'm a real person?" he asked with a slightly teasing tone and a slight smile.

I realized he was enjoying this. I also noticed what Zuri had mentioned before. He really was attractive. I smiled back and felt a warm rush of something that certainly wasn't alarm or fear. "I'm glad you're finding my discomfort so amusing."

"Can you blame me? I've got to have some fun on this job." He shrugged.

I shook my head and said, "Follow me."

When I got to the front door, I unlocked it, and we went inside. He followed me through the hallway into the main living area, removing his sunglasses.

"Wow, this is an amazing view!" he said, admiring the lake through the floor-to-ceiling windows.

"It's my favorite part about this place. I love it! It's even more beautiful first thing in the morning," I said without thinking. After the words came out, embarrassment hit me hard and I felt my face flush. I didn't want to give him the wrong impression or have him think I was flirting with him. Or did I? Did I want to flirt with him? Did I want him to flirt with me? Did I want him to be here first thing in the morning? My mind was all over the place.

He graciously let my unintentional innuendo go and simply replied, "I'm sure it is."

I took the opportunity to change the subject. "So, can I get you anything to drink?"

"No, I'm fine," he said.

"Okay. Let me just grab myself some water and we can go sit on the back patio. You can head out there if you'd like. I'll just be a minute," I said.

Ethan went out to the patio while I poured myself a glass of water. I took two huge gulps and then filled it up again. I took a big breath in and let it out slowly, allowing the release of my breath to release some of the tension I felt in my body. I knew I hadn't done anything wrong. There was nothing to be afraid of. I would tell the truth.

I walked out to the patio, settled into the chair next to him and initiated the conversation instead of waiting for him to start. "So, what did Thomas tell you?"

Ethan smiled, possibly amused by my approach and then explained with a matter-of-fact tone, "Thomas called to let me know he had stopped by Pine's Peak to see where his wife spent the last few minutes of her life, to mourn her death. When he arrived, he came across you, the woman who he believes killed her, clearly coming back to admire the scene of the crime."

I got defensive immediately and nearly jumped out of my chair. "Are you serious? You can't believe him? That isn't at all what I was doing there…"

He cut me off. "I don't believe him, and I know exactly what you were doing there. You're still investigating after we discussed you should stay out of it."

I sighed heavily and gave him the truth. I admitted, "Yes, I am." I paused for a beat. I didn't think I owed him more information than that, but I felt comfortable with him and decided to share more. "Look, I know it may seem like a dumb idea to you, but I need to look into this. I just want to ask a few questions, learn more about her life. I feel some sense of responsibility and connection to Veronica. I can't explain it."

"You're right. I do think it's a dumb idea, and I wish you would let the police handle things. But I can't stop you from doing what you're doing, as long as you're not impeding the investigation," he said with only a hint of resignation.

"You can't?" I asked.

"No, I can't. You can obviously talk to whoever you'd like and go wherever you want. I can't stop you, but I came here to ask you to please be more careful. Will you do that?"

This wasn't what I was expecting at all, and I rushed to agree to his request. "Yes, of course I'll be more careful. After this morning and running into Thomas, I was telling myself the exact same thing. I promise, I won't let anything like that happen again."

Ethan looked at me quizzically. "I'm trying to decide if I believe you."

"Well, I can't force you to believe me just like you can't force me not to talk to people and ask questions. But I assure you, I have every intent of being more careful from this point on," I said.

"I hope so. Thomas certainly does seem to believe you're somehow responsible for his wife's death. And although I'm new to this town, I gather he isn't someone you want to make an enemy of. I would be extra cautious when it comes to him," he advised.

"How can he possibly think I killed Veronica? Did you tell him that you cleared me?" I asked.

"I don't think it would matter what I say. He's pretty adamant. He thinks it was you, or Greg or you and Greg together," Ethan explained.

"What? That doesn't make any sense. Besides, I just met Greg for the first time yesterday," I said in my defense.

"I know you said that yesterday," he acknowledged. "Greg backed up that story when we interviewed him. He said he'd never met either you or Zuri until you stopped by the work site."

The way he phrased his response didn't seem right. He wasn't agreeing that Greg and I just met but rather stating that our stories matched. Maybe he wasn't as convinced of my innocence as he led me to believe. I wondered if this whole nice-guy thing was just an act. I realized I still needed to keep my guard up with the detective. I also realized what Thomas might be up to—trying to cast suspicion away from himself. Let me cast some suspicion back on him. I said, "Speaking of Thomas, I wanted to make sure you knew about his first wife, Janet, about how she died."

Ethan nodded and said, "I know all about the first wife. Believe me, we're looking into it. We're giving this investigation all the time and resources it needs. So, as I've said before, there really is no need for you to get more involved than you already are. But if I can't dissuade you from doing that, I just request that you do it carefully. Bring a friend. Don't go off by yourself to obscure places. And lock your doors. Okay?"

"Yes, okay. I will be more careful," I promised again. I wasn't sure how to read his tone. Did he still suspect me? Was he concerned about me? Was I annoying him? All the above?

"Good. Okay, I better get going," he stated and stood up.

"Okay," I said and stood up as well. "I'll walk you out."

He followed me back through the house and I opened the front door so he could leave.

Before walking out, he turned to face me one more time. "And Kary, if anything happens again, just call me directly, okay?" he handed me a card.

I accepted it and glanced down to read it briefly.

"That has my cell phone number on it. Call anytime, day or night, if you need to. I'd rather hear it from you than hear it from somebody else if something comes up," he said.

"I'll keep that in mind," I told him. And I would. It might come in handy to have a direct line to the detective.

"And I have to caution you again to keep your distance from Thomas. Stay away from him," he stated seriously, "and I've told him the same thing about you."

"I have no intentions of going anywhere near that man. He totally creeps me out. I will keep my distance," I said.

"Good. Thank you for your time, Kary." He smiled warmly and turned to head toward his car.

"You're welcome, Ethan," I responded and closed the door.

I leaned against the wall. There seemed to be a million thoughts racing through my mind. I didn't quite know what to make of the encounter. In one respect, I knew he was doing his job by warning me to stay away from the investigation. But in another respect, it almost seemed like he was egging me on. He certainly wasn't under any illusions that I was going to stop.

And even beyond the whole investigation, there was the underlying attraction, the chemistry I felt between us. I didn't know if it was real or imagined, but I did know things had gotten more complicated than they had been just twenty-four hours earlier.

CHAPTER 11

A few hours later, I pulled my Jeep up to my parents' bungalow, which sat back in a small clearing surrounded by trees. They had moved in about three months ago and it was the perfect home for them. They followed a light minimalist lifestyle, so didn't need much space for their possessions and the land allowed plenty of room for their black lab, Molly, to roam free. It was an idyllic scene to drive up to and I appreciated the simplicity of their living arrangement. The reality was my parents had become fairly wealthy over the last decade and could certainly afford much more than a modest bungalow on a small piece of land. They set an example when it came to what was important in life, and for them it wasn't money. It was connecting with loved ones and spending their time doing things they enjoyed and that brought them happiness.

The thing my parents enjoyed most was owning and running Mountain Peak Inn, one of the most successful bed and breakfasts in Pineville. Over ten years ago, they used the inheritance money my mom received when my grandmother died to buy land on the outskirts of town and fix up a large farmhouse that was positioned on it. My mom had a lifelong dream to run a bed and breakfast and my dad was on board for the challenge. They were in their mid-50s when they embarked on the adventure together. They both quit their previous jobs—my dad had been an accountant and my mom had been an elementary school teacher—and jumped into the unknown. They worked hard for the first few years, getting the house and property in shape to provide the level of accommodation they desired for their future guests. It was inspiring for my sister, Paige, and me to watch. While most of our friends' parents were talking about and longing for retirement, riding out jobs that they had been in for years, our parents were taking a leap of faith and pursuing a dream.

Eventually that dream paid off. The first few years were a financial struggle but over time their vision came to life and now the B&B was one of the most sought-after places for visitors to stay. They specialized in romantic getaways and never had trouble keeping the twelve rooms in the building fully booked most of the year. Just two years ago they expanded their offering to include wedding services, and it took the Mountain Peak Inn to another level. The beauty of the location, the character of the building, and the kindness and knowledge of the staff quickly resulted in the Inn becoming not only a favorite spot for getaways but one of the most popular wedding venues in the Poconos.

It was such a success that my parents were able to move off the property itself and hire enough full-time staff to cover everything. This bungalow was their personal getaway, although my mom still spent most of her time at the B&B itself or helping to run the weddings they had there. My mom was always coming up with new ideas to expand the offerings and there was an energy and excitement in her that only seemed to grow over the years. On the other hand, my dad was starting to take a step back with this move. I knew he was spending more time fishing and reading and enjoying a revolving set of hobbies. He wasn't officially retired, but I could tell he was slowing down. I understood that the B&B was really my mom's dream and he had helped her achieve it. Now it was time for him to take some time for himself. They seemed to have settled into a comfortable rhythm lately and I was happy for them.

I noticed my sister's Toyota was already there. I usually was the one to get here first for our Tuesday night family dinners, but I realized that with the school year winding down, she probably had more time on her hands. She had followed our mom's footsteps and was a teacher, although she taught high school rather than elementary school.

When I stepped out of my Jeep, my parents' black lab came up to me and I reached down to pet her in greeting. "Hi Molly girl."

She leaned into me for a few seconds and then darted off toward the front door. She was still young and energetic. Our family always had dogs over the years, and I planned to adopt my own someday, once I felt more comfortable with my coaching business. Of course, depending on how the rumor mill went concerning my situation with Veronica, feeling comfortable with my business may have taken some steps back. I shuddered, pushing the thought away. I was planning to tell my family about what was going on, but I didn't have to allow my thoughts to devolve into negative speculation. My focus had to be on learning more about Veronica and who might have hurt her. The truth would make the rumors go away, or at least I hoped it would. I closed the Jeep door, walked to the small front porch and let myself inside.

"There she is," my mom called out across the room from the kitchen. The bungalow was open concept, with the living, dining and kitchen areas all combined.

"Hi mom!" I called back, letting Molly into the house as well.

"Kary, come over here for a minute," my dad said from the couch where he was sitting next to my sister, Paige. "I want to show you something I've been working on."

"He's discovered Mystery Box," Paige explained with a hint of amusement, shaking her head and pointing to the table that was covered with a variety of items. Her dirty blonde hair was piled on top of her head in a messy bun, one of her favorite looks.

"I don't know what that is," I said.

"Ken, let her get in the house and settled before you bombard her with your newest hobby," my mom called out.

I gave my dad and sister each a quick hug and said, "I'll be right back. Let me go say hi to mom. I definitely need to hear about this Mystery Box thing. It sounds intriguing."

My sister and I gave each other a knowing look. Our dad spent much of his free time, stumbling on new things, delving into them like he was obsessed and then after a short period of time, moving onto something else. He had always been this way and we liked to make fun of him for it. We called him a "serial hobbyist," which he agreed was a fair classification. Despite making fun of him, I admired how he was able to learn deeply about something, usually master whatever skills it required and seemingly enjoy every minute of it. He had a curiosity that drove him. I liked to think that I had some of that drive in me as well.

"Hi mom," I greeted her and gave her a quick hug. "What's for dinner?

"Homemade lasagna," she said, beaming. Her smile and energy made her look years younger than her true age of 61. It also helped that she watched her diet, worked out three times a week and never missed a hair appointment to "keep away the grays," as she liked to call it.

"My favorite," I said.

"I know," she said with a slight wink.

"Wait, is there a reason you're making my favorite dinner?" I questioned. I was suddenly suspicious.

"Well, I thought you might need a little pick-me-up because of everything going on," she said.

"I didn't think you knew what was going on. We just talked a few hours ago and it seemed like you didn't have a clue," I said with exasperation. It was impossible to keep secrets from my family.

"I told her what I knew," my sister called out from the couch.

"Told her what?" I asked. "I haven't talked to you either."

"Kary, how could you possibly think we wouldn't find out? The murder is all over town. It's practically the only thing people are talking about. We were bound to find out eventually," Paige said.

My mom jumped in to explain further. "We had all heard about Veronica's murder but had no idea you knew the woman. Paige called this afternoon after we spoke to let us know about the rumors going around at the school. Paige…" she prompted Paige to add to the story.

"Kids in high school can be dramatic, so I wasn't sure what to believe at first. Oh, and I didn't hear your name directly, but I've been hearing about some kind of therapist that may have been involved with the murder. Today someone used the term 'life coach,' and that's when I realized they were most likely talking about you." As a high school English teacher, she always had the inside scoop when it came to town gossip. Teenagers heard a surprising amount of information from their parents.

I looked back-and-forth between the two of them and asked, "Why didn't either of you call me?"

"I did call you, honey, and you didn't want to talk," my mom said.

"I knew we would be seeing you tonight and we wouldn't let you leave until you told us everything," my sister said with a mischievous smile. "We have you trapped here."

"Kary, why wouldn't you call us as soon as this happened?" my dad asked.

I collapsed into a chair at the dining room table and repositioned it in a way that gave me a view of all three of them. I sighed before responding, "I don't know. I guess I just didn't want to bother you with it. I wanted to try to handle it on my own."

"Don't be ridiculous. Family is family. We're here to help," my mom said, coming over to give me a big hug.

"She's right. We're here to help and we can't do that if you don't share things with us," my dad said in a serious tone.

Paige agreed.

"I know. I guess I'm just used to handling things on my own. I lived far away for a long time. I know I've been back for a year, but I'm still not used to having all this support around," I admitted.

"Well, we forgive you honey," my mom said, effectively ending the topic of me not reaching out for help. This was not the first time it had come up since I'd moved back. My mom then suggested, "the lasagna will be done in about twenty minutes. Why don't you find out what your father is all excited about and once dinner is ready, you can tell us everything while we eat."

I liked the sound of that plan, and I did want their support. I'm not sure how much any of them could help me, but their support would mean a lot.

"Okay, sounds good," I agreed. I got up and went over to sit on the couch with my dad and sister. "So, tell me about this Mystery in a Box thing."

My dad's eyes lit up, drawing attention to his bushy white eyebrows, as he shared the details. "You get to solve a mystery from the comfort of your own home. They send you a new box every month, which has a bunch of clues inside. It's your job to narrow down the list of suspects based on those clues to ultimately decide who you think committed the crime. I've done two months so far and guessed right both times. It's so fun! One of these months, you girls should come over and we can work on one together. It usually only takes a few hours to solve."

His energy, while usually infectious when talking about one of his hobbies, wasn't enough to eliminate the dull sense of anxiety I felt. In fact, the topic of eliminating suspects and solving crimes was hitting pretty close to home. I found my mind wandering back to my own situation while my dad spoke. The next twenty minutes didn't fly by.

During dinner I gave a full rundown of the situation, starting from Veronica's confrontation in the studio on Friday up to Detective Andrew's visit to my house this afternoon. There were a few questions throughout my account, but for the most part my family just listened.

"So, what do you all think?" I asked when I finished my story.

"Well, I understand why you're pursuing this on your own," my mom responded.

"I thought you would," I said.

"Yes, it makes perfect sense. You have an obligation to Veronica as a former client and you want to clear your name and the name of your business from being associated with anything as nasty as murder. It's what a good person and a good businesswoman would do," she nodded approvingly.

"Thank you. That's exactly the way I'm thinking about it," I said.

"I think it's awesome that you're doing your own investigation," Paige said. "Although the police say you're not on their suspect list anymore, I'm not sure I'd believe them, not until you're officially cleared. And even then, you'll still have to deal with the rumors. Speaking of rumors…" Paige left the last phrase hanging in the air.

"Oh no, you heard something more than just that rumor about the therapist who killed their patient. What else have you heard?" I asked and felt my stomach churn. Nerves about what Paige might have to tell me were already affecting me physically and I hadn't even heard what she had to say yet.

"Nothing else about you," she assured me with a shake of her head. "Like I said when you got here, there is a lot of talk at the high school about the murder itself. Most of it sounds completely ridiculous, but late this afternoon, I heard something you might find interesting, especially after hearing your story."

"Tell me," I begged. I was on the edge of my seat.

"The name Greg Marshall has been floating around," she said.

"So, the word is out that he was Veronica's boyfriend," I replied.

"It appears so, and it makes sense if the police have questioned him. There were witnesses when they came to the job site yesterday and who knows who saw them when they brought him downtown.

It was probably only a matter of time before more people started to suspect he might be involved or that he was in the very least tied to Veronica in some way. Why else would the detectives be questioning him? And for a single guy to be tied to Veronica, an affair is an obvious conclusion." Paige's green eyes looked thoughtful as she spoke, like she was trying to work out a connection in her mind at the same time as she was talking.

"So, what was being said about Greg specifically?" I asked, feeling impatient.

"Just that if he was dating Veronica, it couldn't have been very serious. Apparently, he's been dating a number of other women as well," she said.

"Recently?" I asked, surprised.

"I don't know," Paige said, shaking her head, "but from what I was able to gather, from what I overheard, the guy gets around and has been known at times to date high school girls."

"That's disgusting," my mom blurted out. "How does a parent let something like that happen?"

I quickly jumped in, not wanting the conversation to veer off in a different direction. "Just to be clear, you've heard Greg Marshall's name in connection with Veronica, he might be involved in her murder, he was also dating other women and he's been known to date high school girls." I counted off the four points on my fingers as I summarized them.

"Exactly," Paige confirmed.

I sat back in my chair, feeling confused and a little shocked. When I met Greg, I had to admit I kind of liked him. He seemed like a good person caught up in a bad situation. Had I completely read him wrong? Of course, rumors were rumors, so there could be little truth to any of this, besides his affair with Veronica.

"What are you thinking about Kary?" my mom asked.

"Just what my next move should be. I'm going to have to talk to Greg again," I concluded with a shrug. Both my sister and mom nodded in agreement.

My dad had been sitting there silently during most of the conversation. He cleared his throat to get our attention. He looked directly at me from his side of the table and said, "You know I support you in all things, Kary."

"Of course. I know you do," I confirmed.

His tone was serious, "All I ask is that you be careful moving forward, more careful than you have been, more careful than you think you need to be."

"I will dad," I promised with sincerity.

"She'll be careful Ken," my mom offered on my behalf.

My dad turned his focus to my mom, "Donna please don't discount this. It's not a game. These are real people and there was a real murder."

"I know it's not a game, dad," I said, wanting to ease the tension that had just sprung up between my parents, "and I will be careful. I will."

"That's all I ask," he said.

Silence followed. It was broken after a few moments by my mom. "Time for dessert." She stood up and started clearing the plates.

The conversation had effectively ended. That was fine with me. There was nothing left to say. I was glad I shared what was going on with my family and their moral support was nice; however, there was nothing they could do to change the situation. And hearing the rumors about Greg just made me feel sad. Based on our sessions, I knew Veronica loved him deeply. What if it turned out his love was all a lie?

During dessert we changed the subject to the wedding that was held the previous weekend at Mountain Peak Inn. My mom described lost rings, drunken groomsmen, spilled wine and a missing DJ. It seemed that whatever could go wrong, did go wrong. While at the time it was a stressful situation for my mom and everyone else working the wedding, it offered a fun story to tell, and we all found ourselves laughing. The mood had lightened considerably.

We were just finishing up our brownies with vanilla ice cream when my phone rang. I checked the caller ID. It was a number I didn't recognize.

"Sorry," I said to my family, "but I need to answer this." I accepted the call and got up from the table to limit the disruption. "Hello, this is Kary."

"Kary, this is Fiona Graham. You sent me a message earlier today," a soft, feminine voice greeted me on the other end of the line.

"Yes, Fiona. Thank you so much for calling me," I said. I motioned to my family that I was heading outside to the front porch to get a little privacy.

"To be honest, I was thinking about reaching out to you anyway," she said.

"You were? Why?" I asked, surprised. I closed the door behind me and walked out onto the porch. Molly had followed me out.

"Well, there's something that I think you should know…" she said, allowing her voice to trail off.

"What is it?" I asked, feeling my stomach churn yet again.

"I don't feel comfortable talking about it over the phone. Would you be willing to meet with me?" Fiona asked. I noticed a level of urgency in her voice.

"Of course," I said, feeling a chill run up my spine.

"What about tomorrow afternoon? I know you work in that yoga studio in town. I could come by around three?" she posed it as a question.

I mentally checked my schedule for the following day. I had two sessions in the morning and one in the early afternoon. I said, "Three works for me."

"Good. I'll see you then," Fiona said.

"Okay," I said.

She abruptly ended the call.

I was left standing on the porch, watching the dusk settle around the bungalow, feeling spooked. What in the world would Fiona have to tell me? A had imaged there was a chance that she would be angry with me, depending on what Veronica had told her. I had been ready for that reaction. However, I didn't sense any anger in her tone. I sensed fear. I quickly scanned the porch and the yard around it, making sure I was alone. I was, besides Molly who was standing at my feet now after exploring the yard for a few minutes. I breathed a sigh of relief. I was sure there was nothing to be afraid of here. I vowed not to let my imagination run wild. And I would just have to wait until tomorrow when I would learn what Fiona had to tell me.

I went back inside the house with Molly to join my family.

"So, who was that?" Paige asked when I sat back down at the table.

"It was actually Fiona Graham," I said.

"Veronica's best friend?" Paige asked knowingly.

"Wow, you really do know what's going on," I said.

"I told you. There is gossip and stories are flying around the school nonstop. Apparently, Fiona and Veronica did everything together. Both of their husbands work and stay in the city during the week, so they had a lot of free time on their hands," she shared.

"Why was Fiona calling you?" my mom asked.

"Oh, I left that part out," I said, realizing I hadn't shared how I had contacted her earlier in the day. I had only told them about Janet's brother, because I had actually met with him. "I contacted her on Facebook this morning. I wanted to see if she'd talk to me about Veronica, about their friendship, about Veronica's marriage and about the affair. I wanted to see if she had any idea who might have killed her friend. I wasn't sure she'd contact me back, but I guess she's open to talking. We're going to meet tomorrow afternoon."

I decided it was unnecessary to share the specifics of the call and the uneasiness I felt after speaking with her. There was no need to concern my family. I had no idea what Fiona had to tell me. It was possible I was misreading her tone and there would be nothing to be concerned about.

"And you'll be meeting her in a public place?" my dad asked.

"Yes," I said with a nod, "she's coming to the studio. They'll be plenty of people around."

"Good," he said.

"You will keep us updated, honey, on what you learn, right?" my mom asked.

"I will," I agreed.

"And I'll let you know if I hear anything else at the school," my sister promised.

"That would be great. Thanks Paige," I said.

Our conversation transitioned to less serious topics for the rest of the evening. A short while later, I was driving the fifteen minutes back home and feeling a sense of calm. It was good to have shared what was going on with my family. My sister gave me some information about Greg to follow-up on, and I was meeting with Fiona the next day. It felt like I was making some headway, however small, and that felt better than doing nothing.

I had been lost in my thoughts for a few minutes when I became aware of a car behind me. It wasn't following closely, but I realized it had been behind me for quite some time. I took a series of back roads to get from my parents' house to mine. It wasn't a well-known route, and this car had been following me at every turn. It was dark by now, so I couldn't see the make or model. It was after nine and the roads were all but deserted in this area. I hadn't seen a single other car during the drive so far. Was it just a coincidence that this car was following the same route? Was I being paranoid?

I decided to do a little test. The roads I had been taking were moving me in the direction of town. While following me, this car was going in the direction of town as well. At the next intersection, I took a sharp right turn onto a road that I knew would take me back in the direction of my parents' house, back the way I had come.

A checked my rearview mirror and a few seconds later the car made the same right turn. My heart started pounding in my chest. I was definitely being followed.

CHAPTER 12

For just a moment, I allowed myself to panic. My heart was pounding in my chest, and I could feel my hands shaking on the steering wheel. I took a deep breath and put my focus on the road. The last thing I needed to do was accidentally crash. I had to pull myself together and make some quick decisions.

I decided to head back toward town, toward people. I knew I could make it back to my parents' place quickly since I was closer to it now, but I didn't want to put them in any danger. This was my problem, and I would deal with it. At the next opportunity, I took a few turns until I was heading back toward Pineville. The car trailed behind me at a distance, but it continued to mimic each and every turn. There was no doubt in my mind that it was following me.

Once I was headed back toward town, I needed to decide exactly where to go. I didn't want to allow the car to trail me back to my house. That wouldn't do me any good. Instead, I could allow it to trail me somewhere more heavily populated. Should I call 911? Was this an emergency? Should I call someone to meet me? Maybe I should call Ethan. He did tell me to call if I needed anything, and I did have his card. I glanced down at my bag. It was resting on the passenger seat. I knew it would take time to rummage through it to find the card, though. Why didn't I just put his number directly into my phone? My phone was out where I always kept it, in a car holder for easy access. Who else could I call? Zuri? I didn't want to put her in danger either, and what could the two of us do against whoever was trailing me?

The answer suddenly came to me: Ben. I knew he would help me. I found his name in my contact list and called.

After four rings he answered. "Hey Kary. What's up?"

"Ben! I'm so glad you answered," I nearly shouted out. I was relieved to hear his voice, "I'm sorry to bother you but I need some help."

He must have sensed my urgency because he immediately asked, "What's wrong? Where are you?"

"I'm outside of town, coming back home from my parents' house and I think someone is following me," I explained, trying to stay calm.

"Are you sure? How can you tell?" he asked.

"I'm pretty sure," I said. "I took a few turns heading in the opposite direction from town and they took the same ones."

"What about the car or the driver? Can you see anything? Make? Model? Is there more than one person inside?" He probed for more information.

"The car is pretty far behind me. I really can't see anything, just the lights. Would it be okay if I came to your house?" I asked. Ben lived above the antique shop on the main street in town. Although it was after 9 p.m., with the warm weather, I knew there would be people around.

"I'm not home right now. I just finished a business dinner and I'm driving back to town too," Ben said, and my heart fell momentarily, but he quickly continued, "I'm not that far away, though. Let's stay on the phone. You can keep me updated on where the car is and then we can meet once we both get to town. Does that sound like a plan?"

"Yes, it does," I said gratefully. "Thank you, Ben. Thank you so much."

"Well, don't thank me yet. Let's wait until we're together. Where exactly are you now?" he asked.

"I'm on Knight Road," I said.

"So, you're driving south," he said, "and I'm coming from the opposite direction. I'm probably about ten minutes away from your house."

"I'm about the same," I said.

"We can either meet at your house or each drive a little further to meet at mine. I think we should meet at your house. It isn't as populated, but we can both get there more quickly."

"Okay, that sounds good," I agreed. I hadn't wanted to head there originally, but if Ben was going to meet me, I thought it would probably be just as safe as meeting somewhere else. At least I wouldn't be alone.

"Good," he said. Now that a plan had been created, he turned his focus to me and asked, "How are you doing, Kary? Are you okay?"

"I'm okay," I blurted out, and it was clear from my tone that I was really not okay.

That must have been obvious to Ben. He directed me in a calm and reassuring tone, "Just try to focus on driving. You'll be home in no time, and I'll be there with you."

"I will. I'm focusing," I said.

"Good," he said.

I took my next left turn. After a few seconds, I glanced in the rearview mirror, expecting to see the car follow. Instead, I caught a glimpse of it making a right turn and heading in the opposite direction. I felt relief flood through my system, and I shouted out without thinking, "Oh my gosh, Ben!"

"Kary what's happening?" He sounded alarmed.

"Sorry, no, it's a good thing," I said. "I think the car just stopped following me."

"Are you sure?" he asked.

"Yes. I'm looking back now, and it's definitely gone," I explained, continuing to glance in my rearview mirror off and on to double-check that I no longer saw any cars following me.

"Okay, good. Let's stay on the line, though; I still want to meet you at your house. Kary, keep an eye out and let me know if it starts following you again. Just talk to me while you're driving."

I did exactly as he said and less than ten minutes later, I pulled onto my road. Ben was still a few minutes away, so I did two loops around the block until he confirmed he had pulled into my driveway and that no one else was there. I pulled the Jeep up right next to his car and hopped out, meeting him at his driver's-side door. He pulled me into a warm embrace.

"You're safe now. I'm here," Ben whispered, stroking my hair.

I let my nerves cool down with the warmth of his hug and the kindness of his words. After a few minutes, I pulled away and looked at him. "Is it okay to thank you now?"

"Yes, now you can thank me," he nodded with a smile and we both laughed lightly.

"Will you come inside?" I asked.

"Of course," he said and followed me in.

After getting Ben a beer and myself a bottle of sparkling water, we sat down on either end of the coach so we could talk.

"Kary, I have to admit, I'm worried about you. What's going on now? Who do you think would be following you?" Ben asked with concern on his face.

I sighed heavily, knowing that I probably should share everything that had happened with him. He deserved the truth, especially after rushing so quickly to my rescue. But I knew he wasn't supportive of me continuing to investigate and I wasn't in the mood to hear a lecture. On second thought, though, maybe a lecture was exactly what I needed to hear. Did I want Ben to talk some sense into me?

I decided to just give him the highlights, and explained, "You knew I was going to keep looking into things, and so that's what I've been doing. I got in touch and met with Thomas' first wife's brother. He told me more about her suspicious death. Then I stopped by the site where they found Veronica and ran into Thomas there. He was not happy to see me."

"Is that who you think was following you?" Ben asked.

"Well, I don't know for sure if someone was following me," I said with some hesitancy. Now that I was home safely, I was second-guessing myself about what had happened. Was I being paranoid? I couldn't be sure, so I put a disclaimer on it, "but if some-one was following me, Thomas or someone associated with him is my best bet."

Ben looked confused, "Why would he follow you or have you followed?"

"Apparently, he found out Veronica had been meeting with me and he blames the situation their marriage was in entirely on my coaching. Detective Andrews stopped by this afternoon and let me know that Thomas called him. It sounds like he's trying to turn sus-picion onto me," I explained.

"Suspicion about the murder? That's completely ridiculous!" Ben's face grew a shade darker with frustration. "The cops don't believe him, do they?"

"No, not as far as I can tell or at least from what Ethan told me. But I'm not sure if I can trust him."

"Ethan?" he asked.

"Oh, I mean Detective Andrews. He told me to call him Ethan," I said.

"Oh." Ben looked puzzled and said, "That's a little weird, don't you think? Being on a first-name basis with the detective investigat-ing a crime for which you're at least remotely under suspicion?"

"I think he may be trying to get me to let my guard down, but you know I'm not hiding anything. He says that he doesn't believe Thomas, but I can't be sure. That's why I'm going to keep looking into things. I need to figure this out."

"Do you really think that's a good idea? Come on, Kary. You realize you could be putting yourself in real danger here, right?" He looked at me with a worried expression.

"That's the thing, Ben. I have this feeling that I'm in danger anyway, even if I do nothing," I admitted. I had been feeling unsettled and spooked for days now.

"What do you mean?" he asked.

"I'm not sure how to describe it," I said, deciding there would be no benefit to trying to get him to understand something I didn't understand myself, so I dismissed it. "Maybe it's just my nerves."

"Well, you know where I stand. After tonight, I really think you should back off. Let the cops do their job. Stay away from Thomas," Ben said.

"I'm not planning to go anywhere near him. I just hope he won't come anywhere near me," I said.

"So, what's next then? I assume you're not going to take my advice to back off," he said. I shrugged, not verbally agreeing or disagreeing with what he said. My response was clear though, so he continued. "If I can't talk you out of pursuing this, can you at least tell me what you have planned? Maybe I can help you. I don't think you should be meeting with people alone."

"Actually, I'm meeting with Fiona, Veronica's best friend, tomorrow. And don't worry, we're meeting at the studio. Besides, she isn't someone I feel like I have to be afraid of. I highly doubt she killed her best friend. We're just going to talk about Veronica."

I decided to leave out the part where Fiona had freaked me out by saying she had something important to tell me. I didn't want to make Ben more concerned than he already was.

"Do you want me to be there?" Ben asked.

"No, I'll be fine," I said quickly. I had a feeling that what Fiona had to tell me was probably for my ears only. I didn't want to spook her by bringing someone else with me. "And honestly, like I said before, I can't be sure I was being followed tonight. Now that we're here talking about it, I feel silly about the whole thing. I may have overreacted."

"I don't think you overreacted. With everything going on, it's better to be safe than sorry, and you know you can call me anytime to help you, right? I'll always be here for you, Kary," Ben said with a serious tone.

His words hung in the air. There was a deeper meaning behind them, and things suddenly felt awkward. I knew we had agreed to just stay friends, but I wasn't sure that would be enough for him. I was so grateful for his friendship and for him rushing over to help me, but I didn't want to lead him on.

"Thanks, Ben. You're a really good friend," I said, putting a slight emphasis on the word "friend."

If he was hurt by my response, he didn't show it. "Do you want me to stay here tonight? I could sleep on the couch," he offered.

"No, that's okay. Now that I'm home, I feel much better and like I said, I really may have been overreacting. I'm sure I'll be totally fine here tonight. But thank you for the offer. I really do appreciate it," I said.

"Of course," Ben said and stood up. "I guess I'll head out then but call me if you need me. And please be cautious when you meet with Fiona tomorrow, okay?"

"I will," I promised, and stood up as well.

I walked him to the door, and we said our good-byes. I heard his car start up and drive away. Then I was alone. Although I had assured Ben that I was fine, the sudden silence and emptiness of the house felt eerie. I turned on the TV for background noise and curled up on the couch with a blanket. Thoughts of the day replayed in my mind, and I felt exhaustion wash over me. I closed my eyes and fell asleep.

On the surface, the following day looked like a normal Wednesday. I went through the motions and kept to my schedule, but there was an underlying sense of anxiety beneath it all. I kept watching the clock, wishing for it to be 3 p.m., when I would finally get a chance to hear what Fiona had to tell me.

I did see three clients as planned, two in the morning and one in the early afternoon. The first client was a regular, and in fact, my only male client. I was helping him work on building a business. I didn't have any knowledge about his particular line of work, which happened to be high-end landscaping, but I did have knowledge about how the brain works. That is where I could provide him value. As a small business owner myself, I knew success was dependent on a person's ability to set goals, go after them and learn from the failures that would inevitably occur along the way. Success was a mind game, and it was one that I was still in the early stages of playing myself. This made it easy for me to coach this client because I was going through the same things myself, just a few steps ahead of him. He had been making really good progress over the last few weeks of us working together, and although I had to admit my head wasn't 100% in it, I thought the session with him went fairly well.

I couldn't claim the same for the other two sessions, though. They were both new clients and I could tell I was distracted and having a hard time staying present. Neither had previous coaching experience and so probably didn't have anything else to compare it to, but I knew I hadn't given it my all and that was what mattered most. They both seemed satisfied with how things went but neither scheduled a follow-up session.

While assessing what had happened, I made a decision. Moving forward, no matter what was going on with the investigation or my life, for that matter, I would not allow it to affect the work with my clients. It wasn't fair to them. After making that promise, I also decided to be kind to myself. It would not be helpful to continue to beat myself up for not doing my best in today's sessions. That would only end up resulting in me not showing up in the way I wanted to in future sessions. What was done was done. I hadn't given it my all. I acknowledged that but would self-adjust and move on. Learning from failures but continuing to show up was what success was all about.

After I finished my self-assessment of the day's sessions, which was really just me coaching myself, I had about twenty minutes before Fiona was expected to arrive. I was antsy and couldn't sit still. I ventured out of my office to see what was going on in the studio. There wasn't a class in session, but I hoped that Zuri would be around. Luckily, she was. I found her in the equipment room, and it looked like she was taking inventory.

"Hey there," I said as I approached.

"Hi Kary. I'm so sorry I didn't call you yesterday. In-between classes, I was basically babysitting Dean. You would not believe what a baby a thirty-five-year-old guy can be," Zuri said with playful exasperation. I knew she loved taking care of him.

"I can only imagine," I said with a roll of my eyes.

She smiled and asked, "So what did I miss? Did anything happen yesterday?"

I took a few minutes to give her the highlights, including my meeting with Phil Cranston to discuss his sister, my unexpected run in with Thomas, Detective Andrew's visit to my house, the car following me, Ben's help and my upcoming meeting with Fiona.

When I was done explaining everything, she had an overwhelmed expression on her face. She paused for a second and then threw a bunch of question at me, one after another. "All of that happened yesterday? Are you okay? Do you think someone was really following you? Are you scared of this Thomas guy?"

"Do you want me to answer anything, or do you want to just keep asking me questions?" I said with a smile.

"Sorry, that was just a lot to take in all at once. Yes, please go ahead and answer," she said, putting her hands up in fake surrender.

"Overall, I'm fine. I think there's a chance someone was following me but I'm not sure why. I'm a little scared of Thomas, but I doubt he would actually do anything. The police are all over this right now. It just wouldn't make any sense," I explained.

"You seem so calm about it all," Zuri noted.

"I seem calm but I'm freaking out inside," I admitted.

"Good. I'd be more worried if you weren't freaking out. So, this meeting with Fiona is happening soon?" she asked.

I pulled my cell phone out of my back pocket and checked the time. "Actually, she should be here any minute."

"Do you want me to talk to her with you? I have time right now," she offered, and then explained, "I just want to be home by 6 p.m. so I can get Dean all settled and get to bed early myself. I have that class I told you about in Naperville tomorrow. It starts early, so I have to leave here by five in the morning. I want to get a good night's sleep."

"No, I'm fine meeting with Fiona on my own. In fact, I think she'll open up more if it's just me. And I totally forgot about your class. I know you're really looking forward to it. Have a great time. I want to hear all about it."

"Thanks! And you be safe, okay? Please call me if anything happens. Even if I'm out of town, Dean is around and despite his back issues, I'm sure he'd be more than willing to help you if you need it," Zuri said.

"I will," I promised and then gestured to the door. "I'm going to go up front to wait for Fiona. I want to make sure to be ready when she gets here."

"Okay. Good luck, Kary," Zuri said.

"Thanks!" I responded. I left her to her to finish the inventory and headed toward the front of the studio.

About ten minutes after 3 p.m., the studio door finally opened, and a woman came in. She was short and pretty, with fair skin, blonde hair and blue eyes. She was dressed in yoga gear, and I could have mistaken her for a patron, except for the look of concern she had on her face and her disheveled demeanor. She had dark circles under her eyes, and they were bloodshot. She didn't look like a person who was about to partake in a class. She looked like someone who was worried.

Her eyes settled on me. "Kary?"

"That's me. I assume you're Fiona," I said.

"Yes," she confirmed, and approached me glancing around the open and empty room. "Is there anyone else here? I was hoping we could talk privately."

I motioned toward the back of the studio and explained, "There's a class starting at 4 p.m., so people might start arriving in twenty or thirty minutes. I thought we could head over to the coffee shop right down the street."

"I'd prefer we just talk here. I don't think this will take too long and the last thing I need is more caffeine." She laughed but it sounded forced. She was clearly nervous about something.

I hadn't planned to meet in the office, which could qualify as private, but based on her size and demeanor, I had a sense I would be safe. Besides, Zuri was here as well, and people would be coming soon. I said, "Sure, follow me. We can meet in my office."

I showed her to the small room, and we sat down. I made sure to leave the door open just in case. It made me feel better not to be closed into such a small space. She seemed harmless but she was a stranger, and this was not a coaching session. I decided to err on the side of caution.

"Thank you so much for meeting with me. I really appreciate it," I said, hoping to kick-start the conversation.

"Like I said on the phone, I did want to talk to you anyway so when I got your message, I figured it was a sign," Fiona said, her voice soft just like it sounded when we spoke the night before.

That was all she said, and an uncomfortable silence settled between us. I was dying to know what she had to tell me, but she didn't seem to be forthcoming. I realized I would have to be the one to move the conversation forward. "So, the reason I contacted you is to learn more about Veronica. I don't know how much you know about my coaching with her and the misunderstanding we had before her death."

"I know all about it. Veronica and I told each other everything. She was my best friend," she said, tears forming in her eyes. "I can't believe she's gone."

"I can only imagine what you're going through. I'm so sorry for your loss," I said, and offered her a tissue from the box I kept on my desk. It wasn't unusual for clients to get emotional during our sessions.

Fiona accepted my offering and wiped the tears from her cheeks. She took a deep breath and sat up straighter, looking more determined, and spoke. "I apologize for breaking down like that. It really isn't like me. I'm a strong person and I know I can deal with what's going on."

"I'm sure you can," I said supportively.

She didn't acknowledge my comment and instead said firmly, "I came here to talk to you because I think there's a chance you might be in danger."

I felt my breath catch and my body suddenly felt numb. This was not where I had expected this conversation to head, and I was confused. "What do you mean?"

"I'm sorry," she apologized again. "I have to go back to the beginning to explain. I'm getting ahead of myself."

"Okay," I said and gave her a nod to continue.

"What you have to know about Veronica is that she came from a wealthy family from Chicago. Her dad ran some kind of investment fund, and her mom was a socialite. She grew up living with more money than anyone could ever need. It was all she knew until she was fourteen. It turned out her dad had been embezzling money from the fund for years and he was finally caught. He went to jail and she and her mom ended up living in a tiny two-bedroom apartment on the outskirts of town. They lost everything—their money, their house, their social status, their friends."

"That's terrible," I commented, not knowing this part of Veronica's past.

"It was terrible but that wasn't the worst part," she explained. "Her mom couldn't handle it. She started drinking all the time and she took all her anger out on Veronica. She said horrible things. For a while, Veronica tried to maintain a relationship with her dad, but he refused to communicate with her or let her see him in jail. He was humiliated and didn't want to face either his wife or daughter. It's like in an instant, she became an orphan, yet both her parents were still alive. They just weren't there for her. The financial loss ruined them."

Fiona paused and I felt like I was on the edge of my seat. I didn't say a word. I didn't know what words to say.

She continued. "The day she turned 18, she left home, moved to New York City and never looked back. She vowed to rebuild what she had lost. Becoming wealthy was the single most important driver in her life for years. She believed it was the answer to everything. When she finally met Thomas and married him, she thought she had achieved everything she had worked so hard and so long for."

"And she was miserable," I said, knowing where this was headed.

"She was," Fiona confirmed. "Of course, at first, she enjoyed living the life of a wealthy wife and I think she even fooled herself into believing that she loved Thomas. That didn't last long, though. Their entire relationship was under his terms. He decided when he'd be in the city and when he'd be in Pineville. He dictated when she could come with him to the city and when she had to stay here. He controlled the money, giving her an allowance but monitoring her spending like a hawk. It became clear that she was playing the role of the young, beautiful wife, while he was continuing his life much like he did before they were together."

"I gathered some of this in our sessions, but I had no idea the relationship was this dysfunctional," I admitted.

Fiona shook her head with disgust and said,"What's even worse is she found out he was having affairs. When she confronted him, instead of apologizing, he said it was his right and that she should be grateful for the life he was affording her. Although she knew going into the relationship that it wasn't true love, she had felt affection for him and believed it was reciprocated. Thomas isn't someone who's capable of affection and love, though. He's the kind of man who wants what he wants and then when he gets it, he gets off on controlling it, exerting his power over it. She had been the object of his affection and once he had her, the relationship changed completely."

"No wonder she had an affair," I said. "She was probably dying for affection. And when I spoke to her, it sounded like she really did love Greg."

"I know she did. He was absolutely the love of her life, and it wasn't just because she was trying to escape the Thomas situation. They were perfect for each other. I was the only person who spent any time with them, and I could see it myself. They were meant to be together," Fiona said wistfully.

"That's the sense I got when I spoke to her about their relationship. I know she was struggling though with the financial aspects of leaving Thomas," I explained.

She nodded her head and agreed. "It all goes back to the money. Veronica was so afraid of being poor again, of having nothing, that she wouldn't leave Thomas yet. She believed that the money was worth more than her happiness, and if she could just hold off a little longer, maybe she could have both. Unfortunately, when she told Greg about waiting to leave, he didn't feel the same way about it."

"Fiona, so are you saying I should be afraid of Thomas? Is that what you came to tell me?" I asked, still feeling confused about her earlier suggestion that I might be in danger. I couldn't connect the dots between that and what she was telling me.

She shook her head. "That's the part I'm about to get to, and no, it's not Thomas. He's a horrible human being and an awful husband but he's not physically violent. I don't believe he would kill Veronica. He got off too much on controlling her and making her life miserable. It was like a game to him. He had too much to lose by committing murder."

"So why do you think I might be in danger?" I asked, no longer able to hide my impatience.

"I'm sorry, Kary. I didn't mean to drag this out." She paused and looked me straight in the eye. "There's a guy named Steve Moretti. I think he killed Veronica. He's the one you should be afraid of."

CHAPTER 13

Silence hung in the air between us. Fiona continued staring at me, her eyes wide, and I realized she was waiting for some kind of response. My mind was racing with questions, but I held myself back from spilling them all out incoherently. Instead, I opted to ask simply, "Steve Moretti?"

"Steve Moretti," she repeated his name back to me.

"That name doesn't sound familiar to me," I said, realizing I may have to ask some of those questions directly. "Who is he, why do you think he killed Veronica and why should I be afraid of him?"

Fiona took a deep breath before starting to explain. "First of all, I didn't know anything about Steve until just before Veronica's death. The whole situation is bizarre. I really thought she was over-reacting when she told me, but then she died and I think he's the one who killed her and if only I had believed her, made her go to the police…" She started to choke on her words and tears streamed down her cheeks. She used the tissue to wipe them off, sniffling lightly.

I spoke kindly but firmly. "Fiona, again I'm so sorry about Veronica and I know this is hard, but you're scaring me. You're telling me I should be afraid of the person who you think killed Veronica. Please tell me what's going on!"

She swallowed hard and closed her eyes for a second. When she opened them, she looked calmer and more focused. She finally started to explain again. "Steve Moretti is a bartender who was hired for a black-tie event Thomas and Veronica had at their home a few months ago. I guess Steve showed up much earlier than he was supposed to and saw Veronica and Greg together in the pool house. Thomas wasn't home for the weekend yet, and it was hours before anyone was supposed to come for party preparations. They didn't even know they had been seen, but a few days later Veronica got a text from an unknown number with a photo of the two of them together. The message demanded $3,000 or else the photo would be sent to Thomas."

"Oh my gosh, he tried to blackmail her?" I asked.

Fiona nodded and clarified, "He did blackmail her. She paid him. She had too much to lose if Thomas found out about the affair, so she responded to the text, set up a meeting and handed over the money. She recognized Steve immediately from the party. He didn't even try to hide his identity. She begged him to delete the photo and any others he had taken. He just laughed at her, thanked her for the money and said he was going to hang onto the photo for a while. He suggested that she should be a little more careful hiding her indiscretions."

"That's awful," I blurted out. I knew there were unkind people in the world, those who would jump at the chance to take advantage of others for their own personal gain, but for some reason it always surprised me to hear specific stories. In my life, I tried to focus on the good in people, believing at their core that most people meant well and cared about others. I knew that wasn't always the case. I said, "I'm assuming it didn't stop with that one meeting and that single payment then?"

Fiona shook her head and continued. "I guess at first she thought it was over. A few weeks went by, and nothing happened. But then he showed up at a farmer's market she and I like to go to on Friday mornings. When she told me about all of this recently, I remembered the day he was there. I knew something seemed off, but at the time she tried to hide it. He walked right up to us with a big smile, said they were old friends, and what a surprise to run into each other. It was a quick conversation and she seemed uncomfortable. I asked her about it after he walked away, and she told me he was a creep who had tried to date her before Thomas. I knew she wasn't telling me the whole story, but I let it go. Now I wish I had pressed her for more information at the time."

"So, was that when the blackmail started up again?" I asked.

"Apparently, yes. It was all a sick game to him. He would show up somewhere unexpectedly, pretending to run into her. Usually a few hours after the conversation, she'd receive a text with a dollar amount and a day and time to hand over the money. It was always small amounts, a few thousand dollars each time. She would usually have two days to pull the money together and meet him for the handoff."

"Where would they meet?" I asked.

"I don't know. Veronica never told me that," Fiona said regretfully. "She never told me any of this until last week when Greg broke up with her and Thomas found out about the affair. Last Thursday she told me everything. She suspected you were the one who told Thomas. I didn't know if it had been you or not, but I just tried to be supportive of her. She was heartbroken to lose Greg and devastated to lose her chance for all that money, but she was relieved to be done with Steve. With Thomas learning about the affair, there was no reason to pay the blackmail anymore. She felt like a huge weight had been lifted off her shoulders."

"So why do you think this Steve guy killed her and why would he be after me at all?" I asked, unsure if Fiona was doing a bad job of explaining things or if I was having trouble following. Either way, I was still at a loss for how all of this added up to Veronica's murder and how it had anything to do with me.

"I guess in the midst of all this, she was supposed to meet Steve to give him some cash on Thursday. She didn't go. She didn't see the point," Fiona explained, and then her expression turned dark. "She didn't expect Steve to react the way he did, though. When she got home on Thursday night, he was waiting for her outside her house. He demanded his money, and she told him to go to hell. She had no reason to pay anymore. She finally felt like she had control back. He was a leach, an opportunist, a snake but she wasn't ever afraid of him, not until that moment. Once he learned that she wouldn't be his personal ATM anymore, something in him shifted. She said there was a look in his eyes, a coldness that she'd never witnessed in anyone before. He told her that if she wouldn't give him money, she would have to pay in a different way. It was clear what he was threatening. She feared for her safety, even her life. She didn't know what to do. No one else was around. She told me she was terrified, and I don't blame her, but what she did next wasn't good. She decided to deflect, to protect herself. She told him if he wanted to blame someone for the situation changing, he should blame you. You were the one who told Thomas. You were the one who put all of this into motion. You were the one he should make pay."

"Oh my god," I gasped, and my hand flew up to cover my mouth involuntarily.

"I know. It's terrible. She did a terrible thing. She realized it as soon as the words came out of her mouth, but they appeased him. He asked a few questions about you and left. That's when she called me. I came over and she finally told me about everything—Greg, Thomas, Steve, the affair, the blackmail and you. I'm not sure that she truly thought you were the one who told Thomas, but during that conversation, I realized she was trying to make herself believe it. If it was true, then maybe what she did wasn't so bad after all. Maybe you had it coming. Maybe she wasn't a horrible person..." Fiona trailed off.

I knew she was waiting for a response, but I was at a complete loss for words. How could Veronica do something like that to me, someone who had only been trying to help her? How could she?

Fiona finally broke the silence. "I know it wasn't right. I know you probably didn't tell Thomas, and even if you did, that wasn't the way to handle it. I can't change what happened, what she did, but I can apologize. Veronica wasn't a bad person. She was just scared. She was afraid of what was going to happen if Thomas divorced her. She was afraid of losing the love of her life. She was afraid of this Steve guy and what he was capable of. Now she's gone, and I just want to make sure you don't get hurt as a result of all of this. I know Veronica wouldn't want that."

I needed to take some time to process everything that Fiona had told me. I wasn't sure how to feel. I wasn't sure what to think. I chose to focus on getting the rest of the facts and then getting her out of my office. I asked, "So why do you believe that Steve is the one who killed her? Because of that threat?"

"Of course. Who else would it be? It can't be a coincidence that this happens on Thursday, and she's killed the next night," Fiona said.

"The timing does seem suspicious," I agreed. "I assume you told all of this to the police?"

Her face flashed a crimson color, and she shrunk slightly in her chair. Her response was short. "No."

I couldn't hide the frustration in my voice. "No? Why not? If you think this guy killed your friend and might be after me, why in the world wouldn't you tell them?"

"I was scared. I didn't want to get involved. They came to talk to me a few days ago and they were asking all these questions about Thomas and their relationship and Greg and their relationship. But they never asked about Steve. I figured they would find out about him eventually, especially if he's the one who did it. I didn't want to be the one to tell them about him, but then I realized he might be after you. I couldn't live with myself if something happened to you, and I never did anything to stop it. That's why I was so glad you reached out to me," she said.

"Fiona, I appreciate you thinking of me and coming to tell me this, but you need to tell the police, too. You have knowledge about a blackmail scheme and a threat to Veronica's life. You have knowledge about a suspect they may know nothing about yet. You need to tell them, for Veronica's sake, and I guess for mine as well," I said firmly.

"I know you're right and I'm going to tell them. I just wanted to tell you first. I have no idea if this Steve guy is after you, but I think you should be extra careful just in case. And I'm sorry I didn't tell the police right away. I know now that I should have," she admitted and looked at me expectantly.

"Thank you for telling me and for being concerned about my safety. I really do appreciate it," I said, "and I'll accept your apology about not going to the police right away, as long as you go there now."

She looked relieved and said, "That's my next stop."

"Good. Thank you, Fiona," I said, mustering up what I hoped looked like a warm smile. I certainly wasn't feeling warm inside.

"You're welcome, Kary. And I just hope I'm wrong about Steve coming after you. All I can go by is what Veronica told me and the way she described him was pretty scary. Please be careful," she warned me again.

"I will," I said.

Fiona stood up and said, "I guess I better go."

"Actually, before you leave, I do have one more question for you," I said as an idea started forming in my mind. Fiona sat back down and looked at me expectantly. I asked, "Do you know where Steve could be now? You said he was a bartender. Does he have a job?"

"Um, I think so," she drew the words out and seemed to be searching her memory as she spoke. "Veronica did mention that he worked at a local restaurant. It stuck with me because I remember thinking it was kind of fancy. It didn't seem like the type of place such a slimeball would work. Which one was it?" she asked herself out loud.

I sat without saying a word, letting her focus on the name.

After a long pause, she nearly shouted out, "The Carriage House! That's it! She said he worked at the Carriage House."

"The Carriage House. Interesting. Thank you, Fiona," I said gratefully. I knew the place well and her fancy descriptor was right.

It was considered upscale and located on the outskirts of town. I had never been there myself. I knew some of the guests at my parents' B&B frequented it during their stays. Considering this Steve guy, though, I supposed working at an upscale restaurant didn't necessarily mean you were a good person or that you weren't a criminal.

Fiona stood up again and said, "I'm not even going to ask why you wanted to know where to find him."

"That's probably best," I agreed.

"Good-bye, Kary," she said.

"Bye," I responded.

She left and I was alone once again. Learning about Steve Moretti was both promising and complicating. He clearly had a motive to hurt Veronica, and he was yet another suspect to add to the mix. And there was the added concern that he might now have turned his focus to me. Was he the one who was following me? I shuddered. Freaking myself out wouldn't help at all.

Instead, I would do something productive. I had an idea. It probably wasn't a good idea, but based on the way Fiona described Steve, it might give me a sense of whether I had anything to worry about. I gave the Carriage House a call and checked to see if he was working this week. The woman on the other end told me he was working the next few nights. I thanked her and hung up. I was a little surprised that she didn't ask who I was and why I wanted to know his schedule, but I'd take the good luck while I could.

I went to find Zuri. She was getting set up in the front of the studio. There were students trickling in. I checked the clock. There was still plenty of time before the class started but this would only take a minute anyway.

She caught my eye as I approached, and asked, "So did you learn anything from the best friend?"

"Actually, I did. I know you can't go tonight, but is there any chance you'd be up for getting a drink at The Carriage House tomorrow night?" I asked.

She looked at me curiously. "The Carriage House? Why?"

"It's kind of a long story, but the short version is that there's a bartender who works there named Steve Moretti. Fiona thinks he killed Veronica," I explained.

"So why in the world are we going to see him?" Zuri asked with an exasperated expression.

"We won't stay long, just for one drink. I want to see if he recognizes me or acts strangely toward me," I said.

"Why would he recognize you or act strangely? I don't get it," she said.

"That's part of the long story. I promise I'll tell you everything tomorrow, before we go," I said.

Zuri shook her head and said, "This sounds like a terrible idea."

"It might be, but it's something I have to do, and I'd really prefer if you went with me. Besides what's he going to do? He'll be working. I'm sure it will be totally safe." I said this not just for Zuri's benefit but for mine. I was trying to convince myself that it would be.

One of the women called out to Zuri to ask her a question about the class. She walked over to the student to speak to her and then came back to the front of the room where I was still standing.

"Do you want to think about it? You can text or call me tonight to let me know if you're in," I suggested.

"No, I'm in. I don't fully understand what's going on and you have to bring me up-to-speed tomorrow like you promised. I can see there is no talking you out of going, though, and I'd feel better if I went with you," she said.

"I knew you would," I said, relieved. I knew she wasn't happy about what I was doing, but she would always support me in my choices and always be there for me. I was grateful. "I'll pick you up around seven tomorrow night then."

"Okay, seven it is," she said with a smile.

I turned to gather my things from the office and head home. I wondered what I would do to distract myself all evening, counting down the hours until I could drop in on Steve Moretti the following night.

* * *

Later that evening, I found myself sitting in my Jeep in the parking lot outside of the Carriage House. I guess the truth was I didn't just happen to find myself there. I let my curiosity and impatience supersede all thoughts of caution and safety. I decided to head to the restaurant on my own instead of waiting for Zuri to come with me the following night. While it was easy to make the call about driving over, going inside was a different story. I had been sitting in the parking lot for over an hour now, debating whether I should go inside on my own. It was a Wednesday night, but the parking lot was full, so there would be plenty of people inside. Assuming Steve was working, all I had to do was go in, sit at the bar, order a drink and see if he acted like he knew me. No big deal. At least that's what one side of my brain was telling me. The other side was telling me I was being an idiot. I finally decided to follow the "no big deal" theory and got out of my Jeep.

I walked into the restaurant and let the hostess know I was just going to have a seat at the bar. She pointed to a room to the left side of the entranceway. As the name implied, the restaurant was an old Carriage House that had been converted years ago into a restaurant. I noticed the room off to the right side of the entrance was decorated with dark rugs and old pictures in golden frames. A small chandelier hung from the ceiling. There were six tables in the room with diners at each of them. I could see another room behind it that looked similarly decorated. There was a cozy but sophisticated vibe about the atmosphere.

I entered the bar area, which was a long rectangular room. A lone bartender appeared to be waiting on a handful of people who were seated at high-backed stools. The bartender glanced over as I walked into the room and greeted me with a smile. He was short and stocky, with a dark complexion and black hair. I noticed his nametag read "Steve." I could only assume this was my guy. I took a seat on the stool closest to the entrance, a few spots away from the rest of the patrons.

Steve approached me. "Hi. What can I get for you?" His tone was friendly and upbeat. He didn't give any indication that he knew who I was.

"I'll just have a vodka soda," I said. I wanted to keep a clear head, so wine was out of the question. I could get hard liquor and just sip it.

"Sure! Do you want to start a tab?" he asked as he started to make my drink.

"No, that's okay. I'll just have one for now," I said.

"Alright," he replied. He made my drink like a pro, rung up the tab and placed both my receipt and my drink in front of me on the bar. "Enjoy!"

He walked to the other end of the bar and handled a few more drink orders. Then he grabbed some plates that diners were done with and walked out of the bar area through a door on the far side of the room. I assumed he was taking them back to the kitchen. He reappeared a few minutes later and took another drink order.

I sipped my drink while I observed what he was doing. He didn't appear to recognize me at all. He certainly wasn't paying extra attention to me or doing anything out of the ordinary. He was just doing his job. I'm not sure what I expected to happen. Had I hoped he would recognize me? Had I hoped he would say something or even threaten me? What in the world was I doing here?

I swirled the ice around my drink while thoughts swirled around my mind. Coming out here at all suddenly felt silly. And although he didn't appear to know who I was, confronting him about the Veronica situation seemed like a bad idea. If any of what Fiona said was true, then it wouldn't be smart for me to question him on my own. I didn't expect him to do anything to me here in the restaurant, but I didn't want to incite something unnecessarily. I decided to go. My drink was still half-full, but I grabbed my bag and pulled out some cash to pay the bill.

I hadn't noticed that Steve had approached my side of the bar again and was standing in front of me. He asked, "Leaving so soon? Was something wrong with your drink?"

I was caught off-guard and fumbled around for a response, deciding on a little white lie, "Oh no, nothing's wrong. My drink is fine. I just found out the person I was supposed to meet isn't coming, so I'm going to head out."

"Too bad. I was looking forward to having a conversation, Kary." He said this in a menacing tone and stared me straight in the eyes.

Chills ran through my body as I processed his words and took in his cold, dark stare. I felt the switch in him, from warm and friendly to something quite the opposite. I pushed my fears aside and spoke with more confidence than I felt. "You looked a little too busy for a conversation, Steve. But if you have time, I'm more than happy to stay."

"Please stay. Let's talk," he offered with false joviality.

I decided to get right to the point. "I heard you had some dealings with Veronica Calhoun before she died."

"Dealings. I like that," he said with a chuckle. "Sure, I knew the woman. I worked some of her parties."

"Is it true you were blackmailing her?" I asked.

"Blackmail is quite an allegation," he said, without answering my question.

I tried a different approach. "How do you know who I am?"

"You know, I'm under a lot of pressure these days. I've been thinking I need to see someone, talk to someone. Maybe a life coach," he said with mocked seriousness.

I didn't respond.

After a pause, he added coldly, "Kary Flynn, Certified Life Coach. Certified to get all up in people's business where she really shouldn't be."

My heart started beating faster. No wonder Veronica was scared of him. Before I could answer, I felt the presence of someone to my left.

"Kary." It sounded like Ben.

"Ben?" I asked as I turned to look over. Ben was standing right beside me. Confusion clouded my mind.

Suddenly there was a commotion behind him. Ethan and his partner walked through the entrance and up to the bar. Ethan did a double take when he saw me sitting there, but he quickly turned his focus back to Steve.

He flashed his badge. "Steve Moretti, I'm Detective Andrews and this is Detective Williams. You're going to have to come answer some questions for us."

CHAPTER 14

Steve started to argue with the detectives about going with them in the middle of his shift. An older man with a pronounced scar across his cheek appeared from the back and joined the heated conversation. I could only assume he was the restaurant manager or owner. It was impossible not to overhear what they were saying. It was such a small room. After a few minutes, they came to an agreement that one of the servers would take over handling the bar patrons and Steve would go with the detectives as they requested. He came out from around the bar and gave me a cold, hard stare as he passed.

I swiveled my bar stool 180 degrees and watched him walk out the door. The whole thing happened so fast. I felt like I was watching a movie. I was brought back to the present when I realized that Detective Williams had walked out with Steve, but Ethan was standing in front of me.

"Kary, I'd like to talk to you out front," he said. It was not a request and that annoyed me.

Before I could respond or make a move to get up, Ben responded for me. "She doesn't have to talk to you. You can't force her to." Ben took a slight step forward, toward Ethan.

I put my hand up to Ben's chest to direct him to step back. I could tell his anger was starting to get the better of him, and I didn't want him to do something he'd regret. I needed to diffuse the situation quickly. I assured him, "It's okay Ben. I don't mind talking to him. In fact, I want to talk to him."

Ben's shoulders lost some of their rigidity, but he didn't step back. He turned his gaze from Ethan to me and said, "I'm coming with you." That wasn't a request, either.

I could feel my own anger start to rise. Suddenly everyone seemed to think they could order me around. I understood they each had their reasons, but I wasn't a child. "Fine," I said to him curtly. By his expression, I knew he could tell I wasn't happy.

Ethan nodded and stepped aside. I gathered my bag and walked out of the bar with Ben and Ethan right behind me. I saw the sedan parked right in front of the entrance. Steve was sitting in the back seat. His gaze was fixed on us, and he looked pissed. Detective Williams was in the driver's seat, also staring at us, waiting for Ethan.

I suddenly felt an overwhelming sense of anger, frustration and annoyance all at once. I turned to Ben first. "What in the world are you doing here? Are you following me?"

I turned to Ethan without allowing Ben to answer. "And before you say anything, yes, I was coming here to check out Steve on my own. You may not think that was a smart idea but the last time I looked, this is still a free country so if I want to grab a drink at a bar by myself, I believe I'm free to do so."

Both Ben and Ethan looked taken aback by my outburst. I wasn't one to lose my temper easily or often, but I had had more than enough lectures lately and I had a sense that was what was coming. Even more importantly, though, I knew coming to check out Steve on my own was not a good idea. I was mad at myself, and it felt better to take my anger out on someone else.

Ben put up his hands in a gesture of defeat. "Look, I'm just trying to be a good friend here. Zuri called me. She's been trying to get ahold of you for the last hour and you haven't responded to any of her calls or texts. She's stuck in the middle of helping Dean. His back is still really bothering him. Anyway, she asked me to drive by your house, and when you weren't there, she asked me to see if you were here. I have no idea what's going on, though. I just drove out here, saw your Jeep and headed inside to see what's up. Who's this Steve guy?"

I rooted around in my bag until I found my phone and pulled it out. Sure enough, there were five missed calls and numerous texts from Zuri and Ben. I realized I had forgotten to turn the ringer back on after my client sessions earlier in the day. No wonder Zuri was worried about me. It wasn't like me not to respond.

Ethan spoke before I could apologize to Ben. "Of course, you're allowed to go wherever you want to, Kary. I know why you're here. Fiona told us everything. Although, I don't agree with you coming here on your own, there is nothing I can do to stop you. I wanted to talk to you to see what Mr. Moretti had to say to you tonight. Anything at all he said might be helpful to the investigation, and I'd like to know what was said before we question him."

A flash of warmth from embarrassment flooded through my system. There were no lectures coming. My displaced anger had nowhere to go but right back to me. Coming here had been a mistake, and yelling at two people, who were apparently not trying to control my actions, made me the bad guy. I really was acting like a child. Why would I expect to be treated any differently than how I was showing up?

I took a deep breath. I looked back-and-forth between the two of them. It was my turn to apologize. "I'm sorry. I really am. Coming here wasn't a great idea to begin with, and to make it worse, I didn't tell anyone where I was going or make myself reachable. That was a mistake."

They both looked at me expectantly but didn't say anything. I took that as a signal to continue.

I turned to Ben directly. "Ben, thank you for coming to check on me."

"You're welcome," he said, and then explained, "I sent Zuri a text to let her know you were here before I went inside, but you should call her. She's really worried about you. She'll want to know what happened." He paused and then added, "And she'll probably want to yell at you herself."

"I deserve it," I admitted, and turned my focus toward Ethan. I said, "As for your question, Steve didn't tell me much, just enough for me to confirm that he knows who I am. He basically told me to mind my own business. He didn't admit to anything about Veronica, except that he used to work some of her parties. He did creep me out, though. I can see why Veronica might have been afraid of him."

Ethan nodded, and then asked, "So he didn't say anything else?"

"No, nothing. We had just started talking when Ben showed up," I said, glancing over at my friend.

"Did he say anything to you, or did you overhear any of the conversation?" Ethan directed his questions at Ben this time.

Ben shook his head. "No, I walked up to Kary right before you guys came in."

"And neither of you met Mr. Moretti before tonight?" Ethan asked.

"No," Ben and I said in unison.

"Okay, thank you both," Ethan said. He then asked Ben, "Can I expect you'll make sure she gets home safely tonight?"

"That's what I plan to do," Ben said, and the men nodded at each other.

Once again they were treating me like a child. My frustration was palpable now and I didn't disguise it. "I may have had a momentary lapse in judgment by coming here on my own tonight, but I'm not completely incapable of taking care of myself. I can get home just fine without anyone helping me."

Before either of them could respond, I got into my Jeep and drove away.

* * *

I woke up early after a fitful night of sleep. The events of the previous few days were playing on a loop inside my mind. I was second-guessing my decisions about every move I had made, and I was mad at myself for alienating my friends through it all. I called Zuri on my way home from the restaurant, and although she was relieved that I was okay, she was really mad at me for going there alone and for making her worry. I completely understood and apologized profusely. She told me she accepted my apology, but I still felt terrible. And Ben, he was just trying to help. I yelled at him essentially for caring. And Ethan, he was understanding of my ongoing interjection into his investigation, but I knew I was trying his patience. I suspected at least some of that understanding was because of his interest in me. I was interested in getting to know him more when this was all over. Would he still want to get to know me if I continued to push the limits?

After allowing myself a good thirty minutes of ruminating on all of these thoughts, I forced myself to get out of bed. There was no benefit to wallowing in self-pity or worrying about what might happen in the future. I needed to keep moving forward, and that meant figuring out my next move.

It was Thursday. That meant it was another "work on my business day." Unlike earlier in the week, I didn't have illusions that I would get any normal work done. I was too distracted by the case. It felt too important to put on the back burner for even a day. A plan started to form in my mind. I had a few clients to see in the evening, but until then my day was open, and I knew exactly what I would do. I showered and dressed and then started in on my plan. I felt a surge of energy.

First, I called Greg Marshall. All I could find was the main number to his business, but I left a message and crossed my fingers that he would call me back. I needed to talk to him about Steve and about the rumors that he was cheating on Veronica. Could you call it cheating if the other person was still married? I guess technically cheating is what it was. The whole situation was so complicated. I had never gotten caught up in any kind of love triangle myself. The lies, the deceit—it all sounded so exhausting.

Next, I called the number Phil had given me for Cheryl Barclay, Thomas' old assistant. I got the same generic message again and I left the same generic voicemail. I still didn't know if I was leaving messages for the right person. I would try a few more times before giving up on this number. I would have to figure out if there was a way to find a more current number if this one turned out to be a bust.

Then, I pulled out my laptop and started some online research on Steve Moretti. I found very little information. He didn't appear to have accounts on any of the usual social media platforms. A general Google search provided a list of links that I methodically made my way through. I came up with nothing. Not a single link appeared to refer to the Steve Moretti here in Pineville. After more than an hour of fruitless effort, I gave up. The guy was a ghost. I didn't know if that was intentional or not. I hadn't run across anyone who lived so below the radar before. That made me even more concerned about him. If he didn't have a presence online, what was he trying to hide? I wondered if there was a different way for me to find out information about him. Maybe I could track down some of his coworkers.

I stopped myself mid-thought. What was I doing? I already knew the guy was bad news. I could tell that from the little Fiona had shared with me and our minimal interaction the night before. What would I hope to gain by learning any more about him or seeking out any of his coworkers? I'd probably only piss him off more, and if I wasn't on his radar after my little trip to the restaurant, I would guarantee myself a spot on it. I didn't know if Steve had anything to do with Veronica's murder, but I decided to let the cops deal with him. The other leads I had seemed reasonable to pursue—even Thomas to some extent. He wasn't a good person, but he didn't seem physically violent. Up to this point, the only people he may have hurt were his wives. I wasn't sure he would put his freedom in jeopardy by doing something to me. I didn't think the same held true for Steve. I made a decision to stay away from him entirely, at least for the time being.

Despite the decision about Steve, I knew I still had to be extra careful. Someone associated with Veronica had killed her and I was going to continue to ask questions. I went to the table by the front door to make sure my pepper spray was still safely inside my bag. It was.

My cell phone rang from the other side of the room. I rushed over, hoping it was Greg or Cheryl returning my call. The caller ID read *Ben Ferguson*. My spirits fell a bit. I didn't mind talking to Ben, but I couldn't wait to talk to Greg or Cheryl. I answered anyway and tried to force cheerfulness in my voice. "Hi Ben."

"Kary, hi. Uh, I just wanted to call to check in. Um, see how you're doing today." Ben's words were stilted. I could sense the awkwardness spilling over from the night before. I hadn't exactly left him at the restaurant on good terms and we weren't close enough to have had arguments in the past. This was new territory for our friendship.

And although I felt badly about how I had spoken to him the night before, I wasn't sure I should bring it up immediately. "I'm okay. Just getting some work done here at the house," I lied. There was no need to admit what I was really doing, and I didn't want to make things worse between us. I knew he wouldn't approve.

"That sounds good." Ben paused awkwardly. "Sounds productive."

"I guess so," I said, letting my response hang in the air between us.

After a short pause, Ben blurted out, "Look, Kary. I wanted to apologize for last night. I know it was a little weird for me to just show up out of the blue there. Like I explained, Zuri was worried, and she talked me into tracking you down. I don't want you to feel like I'm overstepping at all."

I was relieved he brought it up first. I said, "It's okay Ben. Really. I understand why you did what you did. And I understand why Zuri was upset with me. I should have told her what I was planning to do, or in the very least made sure my ringer was on. I did call her last night on my way home and apologized."

"Are the two of you okay?" he asked.

"We are. We're always okay," I said.

"Good. And we're okay too, then?" Ben prompted hopefully.

"We are," I said, my heart warming a bit. I was blessed to have friends who cared about me. I made a silent promise to myself not to take that for granted.

"That's a relief," Ben said.

"For me too," I admitted. "Again, I'm really sorry about how I acted. Thank you for coming to check on me and for caring about me."

"What are friends for?" Ben said, and then changed the subject. "So, do you have any plans tonight? I thought we might grab dinner. There have obviously been some developments since we last hung out. I'd love to hear about them. Maybe I can offer another perspective on things."

"Unfortunately, I can't. I have two client sessions tonight and I want to get over to the studio at least an hour before to prepare. I've been a little off my coaching game this week. But we should do our normal Friday night thing at Bluegill. I'm not sure if Dean will be feeling up to it, but I know Zuri will definitely be in."

"Okay, sounds like a plan," Ben said.

"Great. See you tomorrow night then," I said.

"Bye Kary," he said.

"Bye Ben," I said, ending the call with a sense of relief. I felt like I had settled things with both Zuri and Ben. We were all hopefully in a good place again. The last thing I needed to worry about in the midst of all of this was ruining my relationships. And having people who cared about me was a good thing, something I hadn't been relying on enough. I made a decision right then and there. I would be smarter moving forward. That included asking for help and accepting it when it was offered.

* * *

Later that day, I was sitting at a two-person table in Stews & Brews, sipping a piping hot mocha while I waited for Greg to meet me. He eventually had returned my call and agreed to talk in person.

After waiting for nearly thirty minutes past our scheduled meeting time, Greg finally walked in, looking exhausted and harried. He spotted me right away, came over to my table and plopped down in the seat across from me.

"I'm sorry I'm late. There was an issue at one of the work sites I had to take care of and…" He paused and gestured toward himself. "You can probably tell I'm not really operating at my best right now."

"It's fine," I assured him. "I'm just enjoying a coffee. Do you want one?"

"Nah, it's okay." He shook his head and added, "I probably had too much coffee today as it is. There's only so much help caffeine can give you." He glanced intentionally at his watch. "I do have to get going soon though, so…"

I could sense his urgency. I'd have to get to the point quickly, "Of course. First of all, thanks again for meeting with me. I know you didn't have to."

"I have to admit, it's nice to talk to someone who knew Veronica and actually seemed to like her. I don't have many people I can talk to as it is, and with this whole murder thing hanging over my head, I don't feel comfortable sharing much in general. I can tell that you're trying to help, though," Greg said.

"I am trying to help. I want to find the person who hurt her, and I don't believe that person was you," I stated as firmly as I could. I honestly didn't believe Greg was the killer, but I knew there was a chance I was wrong about that. I needed him to trust me, though, so he'd answer my questions.

"I wish the police felt the same way. I know I'm still under suspicion. Thomas has so much money and influence in this town. I can't fight against that. I think he's going to make sure I go down for this and I can't do anything about it." Greg's head fell in defeat.

I knew I needed to get moving with my questions before Greg let his emotions take over. I decided it was best to wait to ask him about other relationships, especially with minors, the rumor my sister had mentioned. I would start first with something less sensitive, so I asked, "Do you know a guy named Steve Moretti?"

Greg lifted his head slightly and seemed to have a renewed interest in the conversation. "Steve Moretti? No, I don't think so. Why?"

"The police haven't asked you about him or mentioned him to you?" I asked.

"No, nothing about him at all," he said.

"That might be because they just found out about him yesterday," I shared.

"So, who is he?" Greg's eyes grew bigger as his interest peaked. "Are you saying he might be the one who killed Veronica?"

"I don't know. What I do know is that Steve was blackmailing her. He had pictures of the two of you together and was forcing Veronica to pay him small sums of money so he wouldn't send them to Thomas," I explained.

Greg's face contorted angrily, and he blurted out, "That bastard!"

We both looked uncomfortably around as the handful of other diners glanced at us, Greg's outburst drawing attention. After a few seconds, the room lost interest in us.

Greg leaned toward me and spoke in a much softer tone. "Why didn't she tell me? I could have done something. I could have protected her."

"I don't know. I'm not sure anyone will be able to answer that question now. I'm sorry Greg," I responded.

"She had secrets that she didn't share with me." He said it like a statement, but I knew he was coming to terms with the truth himself. It appeared that although he loved her deeply, Veronica had kept things from him—more things than he realized, important things.

This seemed like the perfect way to segue to a different topic. "Speaking of secrets or rumors or whatever you want to call them, I wanted to ask you something else."

He looked at me but didn't say anything. I took that as a signal to continue. "I heard something about you. I'm not saying that it's true or that I believe it, but it is something that has come up, so I wanted to ask you about it directly." I paused and then asked as lightly as I could, "Have you ever been involved with a high school girl, someone underage?"

I expected him to get angry or lash out. I did not expect the response he gave. Greg laughed. It was a deep belly laugh, and after a few beats I found myself chuckling in response. I was confused but also curious. Who in the world would find a question like that funny? I waited until his laughter died down.

He wiped a tear away from his eye. "I'm sorry. That was probably inappropriate, but I just can't believe the ridiculousness of this entire situation. I lost the love of my life. I've been accused of murder. And now I'm a pedophile."

"I didn't say that you were," I cut in.

"I know you didn't say it, but that's what you implied," he said. "What's next? What other criminal activity can be pinned on me?"

"I'm sorry, Greg. My understanding is that this rumor is going around the high school, so I had to ask you about it," I explained.

"I get it. It's fine. I know exactly where that rumor started. It's not the first time I've heard it. It's just been a few years. I thought all of that was behind me," he said.

"You know where the rumor came from?" I asked, surprised.

"I do. It came from the daughter of a woman I used to date. Her name was Beth, and she had some issues. I dated her mother, Kate, for a few months a couple of years ago. When Kate and I were together, I would sometimes drop Beth off at school in the mornings. One day, Kate got a call from the school counselor asking her to come in. Apparently, Beth was telling everyone that I was her boyfriend. She was just trying to get attention, fit in with the popular crowd. She thought having an older boyfriend would make her seem more interesting, more mature. I guess it worked for a while, until one of the parents of her friends found out and reported it—reported me—to the school. Kate explained the situation to the counselor, but the school had to file a report and the authorities came to talk to both of us. Eventually I was cleared. Beth admitted it was a lie, but the damage was done. I couldn't bring myself to stay in the relationship with Kate after that, so I broke up with her. For the next few months, I would hear the rumor come up, but it eventually seemed to go away. It's been a few years now. I had hoped it was something the town had forgotten about. Unfortunately, I guess it hasn't."

"I'm sorry Greg. I'm sorry that happened to you and I'm sorry this is happening now," I said. I felt bad for him, but the guy did seem to have bad luck when it came to relationships. Or was he just really good at playing the victim?

He sighed deeply. "I can't wait for this whole thing to be over. I hear what you're saying about this Steve guy, but I'm telling you, it was Thomas. I just know he did this and he's trying to pin it on me."

"You could be right," I said, but I was on the fence about Thomas. The existence of Steve created a new angle on the situation. And I had to admit, after this conversation with Greg, I wasn't sure how I felt about his innocence anymore. He was saying all the right things, but I didn't know how much I believed him anymore. How could someone be so unlucky in love?

Greg checked his watch again. "I better get going. Was that all you wanted to ask me about?"

"Yeah, that was it. Thanks again for coming to meet me," I responded.

"Sure." Greg stood up from the table and continued talking. "Like I said before, I think if we can share information, it would be best for both of us. And I don't mind doing that with someone who I know wants to find the real person responsible for hurting Veronica. Please call me if anything new comes up."

"I will," I promised.

He gave me a nod and left.

I sat there going over the conversation we just had in my head. I had learned very little. The only new item was Greg's explanation of the high school girl-dating rumor. I supposed I could follow-up with Paige to see if she could validate what he said. Would the school keep records like that? Or I could try to track down the mom and daughter. Would they be willing to talk to a stranger about that type of situation? Maybe I would be better off sharing the information with Ethan, although it didn't seem all that relevant to what was going on now. And if there had been a complaint filed, I would think the police would already have come across that report. Maybe there was nothing to be done with this new information at all.

I finished my mocha and waved to Misty, who was working at the register, as I walked out. I had two hours before my client sessions were scheduled to begin. I needed to clear my head and get focused on my work. I had promised myself that I wouldn't allow this situation to affect my ability to help my clients. That was a promise I intended to keep.

* * *

By 8:30 p.m., I was feeling great about doing just that, keeping my promise. After meeting with Greg, I went to my office and did some calming exercises and some thought work to get myself into a coaching headspace. That allowed me to be completely focused during my sessions. I thought they went well and both clients left seemingly satisfied. I reminded myself of how grateful I was to be doing work that I loved and that was making a positive impact on other people's lives. I was proud of myself.

I pulled into my driveway and hopped out of the Jeep. I was deep in thoughts of appreciation, gratitude and satisfaction as I walked toward my front door. I was distracted and not paying attention to my surroundings. Suddenly, I caught sight of a dark figure emerging from the side of the house quickly moving in my direction. I didn't have time to get my key in the door before he was upon me.

CHAPTER 15

I jumped back from the doorway, which created some space between me and the figure. It was all happening so quickly. My eyes finally came into focus on the person's face. It was Thomas. Fear flooded my system. I didn't have time to run. He was less than an arm's length away.

"Ms. Flynn. I have been made aware that you are asking questions about my first wife. Things you have no business asking about." His tone was cold, but as he spoke, he stopped advancing toward me.

I allowed myself a breath and then cleared my throat, trying to get my bearings, unsure how to respond. I slowly moved my hand into my bag, searching for my pepper spray.

"Well?" he pressed, his expression dark.

I wasn't sure if Thomas was planning to hurt me. If that was his intent, he could have done that already. Based on what I had learned about him, he was probably trying to intimidate me. That realization gave me courage to respond, "I have been asking questions. I'm trying to find out what happened to Veronica."

"And how do questions related to my first wife's unfortunate accident have anything to do with what happened to Veronica?" He spoke with anger this time. I could see veins bulging in the side of his neck.

Keep calm. I had to remain calm. I continued moving my hand surreptitiously around the bottom of my bag, still searching for the pepper spray.

I answered with false bravado. "Well, Mr. Calhoun, I find it hard to believe that you've had two wives who have both died extremely young. What are the odds of that happening? Being widowed twice? Who drowns in their bathtub? Who gets killed in this town? You must be one unlucky husband. I feel sorry for your next wife."

"Look, Ms. Flynn," he said, his words reeking with disdain, "you can play your little game, trying to cast suspicion on me, but we both know the truth will come out. I know you killed her, and I've told the police all about it. It's only a matter of time before they arrest you. But until then, if you know what's good for you, you'll stay out of my business. I don't want to hear about you asking questions about Janet."

My hand finally clasped the pepper spray. I could pull it out at any time. I felt a rush of exhilaration, knowing I could defend myself. I wouldn't let him intimidate me. Instead of backing down, I pushed back. "And I know your game, Thomas. You keep trying to pin Veronica's murder on me. Do you know how illogical that sounds? What about her boyfriend? What about her blackmailer? You'd be better off trying to pin it on one of them. Trying to pin it on me only makes you look more suspicious."

His expression froze and something shifted in his demeanor. He looked at me curiously. Tension sizzled in the air between us. After a long pause, he asked, "Her blackmailer?"

"You didn't know?" I asked, somewhat surprised.

His eyes grew even darker than before. "Tell me." It was an order.

I focused on the facts. The words tumbled out quickly, "His name is Steve Moretti. He knew about the affair. Veronica was paying him off not to tell you."

He nodded slowly, taking in the information. I could sense anger, even rage, simmering below the surface.

There was another pause. Silence fell between us. I felt my breath catch, unsure of what he would do next.

"Stay out of things that don't involve you, Ms. Flynn, or there will be consequences," he said coldly. Then he turned and walked away, down my driveway and then farther down the street until I lost sight of him. He must have parked somewhere else, so I wouldn't know he was waiting for me.

I let go of the pepper spray and grabbed my keys. I managed to unlock the door and get inside, my hands shaking terribly the whole time. All of the adrenaline that had rushed through my system when he approached was now subsiding. I felt shocked and relieved and still scared. I needed to call someone. I grabbed my cell phone and dialed the one person I knew could help me.

"Kary, is something wrong?" Ethan spoke, answering on the first ring.

I didn't waste time on greetings. My words rushed out. "Thomas Calhoun just showed up at my house and threatened me."

"Is he still there?" he asked.

"No, I think he's gone," I said.

"Make sure the door is locked. I'll be there in ten minutes," he said.

"Thank you, Ethan," I said and hung up the phone.

I went into the bathroom and looked at myself in the mirror. I was white as a ghost. I splashed water on my face and took some deep breaths. Right here, right now, I'm okay. I repeated this phrase over and over, allowing the truth of it to calm me down. It was a phrase that I used when I felt like circumstances were out of control. And although things did seem a little crazy right now, I knew it was my thoughts about them that caused my experience. My body was still reacting from the confrontation, but I was telling myself that the experience had passed. I really was okay right now in this moment. It would just take a few minutes for my body and my senses to catch up with that understanding. Deep breaths and calming thoughts, these are what I focused on. Ten minutes later when there was a knock on my door, I was in a much better headspace.

"It's me, Ethan," he spoke from the other side of the door. His words were muffled but I could tell it was him.

I opened the door. "Thank you for coming," I said gratefully. Please come on in."

He walked in. I closed and locked the door behind him. I felt butterflies in my stomach. Maybe it was the idea of having him rush to my rescue. Maybe it was being in such a close space alone with him. Was I that cliché? I had been working to take care of myself for such a long time. I didn't want to need a man to save me. I didn't even want to want a man to save me. But I couldn't deny how grateful I was that he was here.

When we got into the living area, he turned to face me and said gently, "First of all, are you okay? Did he do anything to you?"

"I'm fine. He didn't touch me. He just scared me," I assured him.

"Well, just the fact that he showed up here is completely out of line," Ethan said. "Let's sit down and you can tell me exactly what happened."

"Okay," I agreed.

Ethan took a seat in the chair, and I took my usual spot on the couch. I told him everything I could remember; from the moment I stepped out of my Jeep up to Ethan's arrival on my doorstep a few minutes ago. I ended my story with, "That's basically it. It happened so quickly and honestly there wasn't much said at all now that I'm thinking back on it."

"But he did threaten you?" Ethan asked.

"Yes, he did," I confirmed, "but I don't know how seriously to take his threat. Do you think he might do something to physically hurt me? Do you think he killed Veronica?"

"You know I can't share details about the investigation with you, but Thomas is still a person of interest," he assured me.

"What about Steve? What happened when you questioned him? Is he a person of interest?" I asked.

"We're still looking into Mr. Moretti," Ethan offered.

"And Greg? Are you looking into him too?" I asked.

"We're still looking into Mr. Marshall as well," he said.

It had been nearly a week and it didn't sound like the police were any closer to solving this thing. I allowed my frustration to surface, as I said accusingly, "So you really haven't cleared anyone or made any progress at all, then."

"Well, we did officially clear you," Ethan said with a smile.

His words did nothing to help my mood. I scoffed, "Thomas still seems to think I'm the one who did it, which is completely ridiculous."

"He's just projecting, trying to turn the heat onto everyone else. He's tried to pin it on both you and Greg. At one point he even implied there was jealousy between Veronica and Fiona, so maybe she did it," he explained.

"The guy is a rich asshole," I blurted out.

"That he is," Ethan agreed, "but being a rich asshole doesn't make him a murderer."

"I know," I said. "I'm sorry. This whole experience has just been a little overwhelming."

"Hey, it's okay. It's understandable. This situation would be a lot for anyone in your shoes to handle. I think you're doing a pretty good job," Ethan assured me with another smile.

I felt a warm rush through my body. I couldn't place the exact feeling, but it was a good one. "Thank you," I said warmly.

Ethan's smiled turned serious as he continued, "Let me clarify something, though. Being a rich asshole doesn't make Thomas a murderer, but it also doesn't mean he isn't a murderer or that he couldn't be dangerous in a different way. I'm going to have a talk with him myself. You might not intimidate him, but I'm a different story."

"Okay," I said.

"And I'd like you to file an official complaint to get it on the record. It won't be enough for any kind of restraining order, but it will be a start. Is that okay with you?" Ethan asked.

"I guess so. This is just so out of the norm for me. I never have problems with people or have to file complaints or even talk to the police. My life has taken this sharp turn in the last five days. I don't even recognize it anymore." I couldn't hide my sense of being overwhelmed as I spoke.

"Hey, it's okay. Most people don't have to deal with complaints or police or murder investigations. It isn't normal, so don't feel bad about not feeling like you have a handle on everything," he offered kindly.

"It's normal for you," I said.

"Well, it's my job. And from what I hear, it isn't normal for Pineville. That's one reason I moved here. I was tired of dealing with death," he shared.

I was surprised by the transition to something so personal, but I was also intrigued. I decided to take the opening he had offered and asked, "Where was all that death you wanted to get away from?"

"I was a detective in Philly for ten years, in the robbery and homicide division. It was important to me to make the biggest impact I could. I helped bring a lot of criminals to justice, but what I saw on a daily basis took a toll," he explained.

"I can only imagine. And I guess, if I'm honest, it's the kind of thing I don't really want to imagine. I'm not sure I'd be able to sleep at night. I can understand why someone might want to make a change, transition to something less intrusive to the psyche," I said.

"Less intrusive to the psyche? That's an interesting way of putting it," he said with a curious look.

"I'm really interested in the way the human brain works. Everything in life generally comes back to it," I explained. Usually, I could go on all day about my interest in the brain, psychology, and coaching, but I suddenly felt shy. I turned the conversation back to him, "So why Pineville? I mean this is a pretty far cry from the city."

"It's completely the opposite, and it's exactly what I was looking for," he explained, and then continued. "I have a sister who comes here for summer vacations with her family. I came up once with them, a few years ago. I remember feeling so calm and comfortable that week. For whatever reason, this place felt like home to me immediately. I could envision myself living here. So, when I decided to move somewhere that was the opposite of Philly, this is the first place that popped into my head. Luckily, they were looking for a new detective. My first month here was exactly what I expected—drugs, burglaries, domestic disputes—standard stuff."

"And then Veronica was killed," I added.

"And then Veronica was killed," he echoed.

"So, does this make you want to leave Pineville now that it isn't exactly what you were hoping for?" I asked, concerned that he might leave before I would ever really get to know him.

His eyes met mine and I could feel my breath catch. There felt like a pulse of energy flowing in the air between us. After a pause, he answered, "I think there might be some things here worth sticking around for."

My heart started beating faster and I could feel my face flush. I was able to squeak out a response. "I think there might be."

There was a long pause between us.

Ethan finally broke the silence. "What about you? Have you lived here your whole life?"

With his words, some of the charge between us dissipated. I was able to pull myself together to answer his questions. "I grew up here and moved away for a number of years. I was a consultant up in Boston. I did the whole corporate rat race, worked crazy hours, traveled all over the place, but I got tired of it all a few years ago.

Kind of like you. I was looking for a change, a slower pace. Once I decided to start my business, I realized it was something I could do anywhere. My family is all here still, and so is Zuri, who's been my best friend forever. They convinced me to move back here last year. I'm glad I did."

"Sounds like you have good friends and family. That's important in life," he commented.

"I agree. So, is your family at all close by? Does your sister still come here in the summer?" I asked.

"They all live in Bethlehem, about an hour south of here. That's where I grew up," he shared.

"Oh, I know Bethlehem. I've been there plenty of times," I said.

"Yeah, it's a great town. So, I'm a little closer to them now than I was when I lived in Philly. And yes, my sister is still planning to come up here for vacation. She and her husband and kids rent a lake house for a week every July. It will be nice to spend time with them while they're here," he said.

"Assuming there are no murders to solve to distract you," I said, only half joking.

"Assuming there are no murders to solve," he chuckled and shook his head. "Speaking of murders, I better get going. I have a long day ahead of me."

"Oh, okay," I couldn't hide the disappointment from my voice, so I rushed to add, "Thank you again for coming over so quickly."

"You're welcome," he said as he stood up.

I stood up as well.

"If anything happens again, let me know," he said.

"I will," I promised, and I knew that I would. I felt safe and protected with Ethan.

We started walking toward the front door. He led and I followed.

He spoke as he walked, "I know it goes without saying, but try to be extra careful. Keep your doors locked and make sure you're aware of your surroundings when you go out." Almost as an afterthought, he stopped walking, turned to face me and asked, "Do you have an alarm on this place?"

"No, I don't," I admitted.

"You should think about getting one. I'll text you the name of a guy who installs them. Obviously, it's up to you, but I would recommend it, at least for now," he suggested.

"It's probably not a bad idea to have one anyway, since I do live here alone. I just never had a reason to be worried before," I said.

"That's something police work does to you. There's always a reason to be worried. Bad things can happen. There are bad people in the world," he said and then paused. After a beat he continued, "There I go getting on my soapbox again. I don't want to scare you. Most of the time things are fine, people are fine, but that doesn't mean you shouldn't try to protect yourself, to make it harder for bad things to happen. That's all I'm trying to say."

"No, I understand. What you're saying makes perfect sense, and you're not scaring me, at least not any more than I already am with everything going on," I admitted.

"I'm sure you'll be fine, Kary, but before I head out, I'd like to do one more thing, if you'll let me," he said vaguely.

I felt a sense of nervous excitement. He was standing just a stride away from me. Was he going to ask to kiss me? Did I want him to kiss me? Was he feeling the same connection I was feeling? Was it even appropriate for him to do that? Was he technically on duty? My mind raced with questions but all I asked was, "What's that?"

"I'd like to do a quick walk-through of the house, make sure everything looks in order. I know you said Thomas was outside, so I'm sure everything is fine, but I'd feel better checking the place out before leaving you here," he suggested and looked at me expectantly.

I felt disappointment replace my excitement. I guess I had wanted him to kiss me. But I also felt grateful. He was looking out for me. He was doing his job. I needed to refocus on the reason he was here in the first place. I smiled and accepted his offer. "I would really appreciate that," I said.

"Good," he responded.

We spent the next five minutes walking through the house, checking closets and making sure all of the doors and windows were locked. It didn't take long. My house was small. The coziness of the space made me feel more secure. There really weren't many places to hide.

After we both felt satisfied that the house was clear, we walked to the front door. I unlocked it to let him out. He turned to face me once he was on the porch.

"Call me if you need anything," he reiterated.

"I will, and thanks again for coming tonight," I said again.

"You're welcome. Good night, Kary." He nodded his head and smiled.

"Good night, Ethan." I smiled back.

I watched him walk toward his car and get in. I closed the door and locked it. I heard him pull away. I leaned my back against the door and took a long, deep breath. What a day it had been. I felt exhausted, but I also felt a spark of exhilaration. There was no denying it now. I did like Ethan. And after tonight, I thought there was a good chance he liked me too.

CHAPTER 16

I woke up the next morning to a text from Ethan. It was the information he promised about the home security company. I sent a simple text back: *Thanks.*

He responded right away: *Did everything go okay last night? Sleep well?*

A rush of warmth ran through me. He wanted to know how I was. It felt good. I replied: *Yep, it was uneventful, in a good way. And I slept well. Thanks again for stopping by.*

Glad to hear it. Stay safe, he responded.

I will, I wrote back.

That seemed to end the conversation. I closed my eyes and did a full body stretch. I had slept well. I think having Ethan confirm the house was safe and secure allowed my brain to relax. I felt refreshed and rejuvenated.

As I lay in bed, I turned my thoughts to the day ahead, to what I had on my schedule. I realized it was Friday. Although I loved what I was doing now with my business, I still experienced a feeling of excitement as the weekend approached. I looked forward to the downtime Saturday and Sunday would bring. This may not be a usual weekend though.

When it came to Veronica's murder, I didn't have a next move in mind. Maybe that was a good thing. I had learned quite a bit over the last week, but none of it added up to more than just a lot of speculation. And all the potential suspects I had come up with were on the police's radar now. What had I really accomplished? What I had managed to do was put myself on the radar of a few possibly dangerous individuals. That didn't seem productive at all.

I realized it might be time to step away from the whole thing, allow the authorities to do their jobs. I decided right then, before getting out of bed, that's what I would do. I was going to take a break for the weekend, for the next three days. No phone calls, no interviews, no online research. I was bowing out for the time being. I needed a break. My mental and physical well-being depended on it. Making that decision felt like the responsible thing to do, and I was usually a very responsible person. I didn't know what had gotten into me this last week. I guess having the police consider you a person of interest in a murder, however ridiculous the idea, can make you do crazy things. I didn't want to do crazy things. I longed for some semblance of normalcy.

I hopped out of bed. Normalcy was what I was striving for, but I wasn't going to deny reality. I called the home security company before I even brushed my teeth and made an appointment for someone to come out the next day to install an alarm system.

I had four coaching sessions planned at the studio, one late morning and three in the afternoon. I decided to get there by 10 a.m. to prepare for the day. I would pack a lunch to take with me and either eat in my office or sit outside during the lunch hour. I appreciated the fact that my day ahead would be normal, and I knew coaching would get me back into a good headspace overall. It was the best part of my businesses. I loved helping people. I loved giving people ways to look at their thoughts about life differently. There was so much opportunity and so much authority we all had over our experiences. It was incredibly rewarding to help others realize that for themselves.

* * *

A few hours later, I was sitting across from my first client of the day. Her name was Samantha, and she was a quiet, slight woman in her mid-30s with beautiful red hair. Today she had it tied back away from her face. She was struggling with dating, and we had been working together for a few weeks. When we first spoke, her thoughts about dating were primarily, "I'll never find the right fit for me" and "Dating is miserable." Because of these thoughts, although she said she wanted to date to find a relationship, she wasn't doing much dating at all. I helped show her that it was her thoughts that were making her feel terrible about the whole concept of dating. This in turn was making her avoid it altogether or go into the handful of dates she did have with a defeatist attitude. Of course, she wasn't finding the right fit and of course dating felt miserable. I was working with her to challenge those thoughts and to find alternative ways of thinking that would help move her more in the direction of her goal.

"So, I did go on a date with a guy last weekend. He's someone I wouldn't normally have thought would be a good fit for me," Samantha shared.

"Why not?" I asked.

"Because he's a personal trainer and doesn't have a college degree. I just thought intellectually that we wouldn't be a match," she explained.

"And how did it go?" I asked.

"It was great! I had so much fun. I don't know that he's someone I'd want to date again, but I did realize that I have to give guys a chance, not just look at their profiles and dismiss them based on my preconceived thoughts about what they choose to share." Samantha lit up as she continued. "And showing up for the date without expecting him to be the love of my life, really took the pressure off. I was much more relaxed than usual. It made me want to go on more dates with other guys. I've never felt like I wanted to go on dates with anyone unless I knew it would result in a serious relationship. I was always putting on so much pressure before, on myself and I guess on the guys as well."

"And what thought have you been using to open yourself up to dating more broadly?" I asked.

"The one that seems to feel the truest to me right now is, 'Dating could be fun.' And I've also been working on the thought, 'I am open to new people and new experiences.' They both seem to lighten up the concept of dating overall, which is helping me take some chances with different types of guys. And it's helping me show up in a more open and accepting way. I'm a lot less judgmental. Honestly, the whole concept of dating and relationships is starting to shift completely in my mind. It's like everything I thought was true is up for consideration." Samantha spoke with excitement.

"Like we've discussed, you can decide to examine any thought or belief you have. You get to decide what you choose is true for you," I responded.

"My mind is really blown with all of this stuff," she said, and then admitted, "It's exciting but a little confusing, too."

"How is it confusing?" I asked.

Samantha looked thoughtful for a moment before replying. "Well, if I can believe whatever I want to believe about dating, then I can also believe whatever I want to believe about relationships, so technically I can decide to be with anyone. All I have to do is change my thoughts about them and about our connection. If that's true, then who do I decide to be with?"

"Whoever you choose to," I explained, feeling myself get animated. "That's the beauty of it. Once you know you can choose whatever you want to believe, you make the choice, but you know it's a choice. It puts you in the driver's seat. It gives you all of your power back. You decide what you want in a partner, and then you decide if someone is a fit. But you know that it all comes down to your thoughts and beliefs about you, about them and about your relationship. It doesn't have to be a passive thing. You can go out there, meet someone and then decide they are your perfect match."

Samantha looked like she was still confused. This often happened with new clients. Thought work was a foreign concept to most people, and although they seemed to understand it intellectually at first, starting to use it in their own lives in specific situations usually led to all kinds of questions. My role was to help guide them through it.

I continued explaining, "I know it's hard to wrap your head around it, even when you're starting to see how the shift in thoughts really does change your experience. Just keep working on it. Keep challenging your old beliefs and keep choosing what you want to believe moving forward. It's a process. The old beliefs won't immediately go away. They may never go away. The important thing is remembering they aren't true unless you decide they're true for you. Got it?"

"Yes and no," she said with a little laugh.

I smiled back and said, "We can continue working on it together. There's no rush on any of this. You just have to stay committed to working on creating the results you want by intentionally choosing thoughts that move you toward them. It will get easier over time. I promise."

"Okay, well I'm choosing to believe you," she said with a smirk.

"See, that's how it works," I said. She really was starting to get it.

"Can we schedule another session for the same time next week?" Samantha asked, glancing at her phone. "I have two dates in the next few days, and I'm sure I'll want to talk after them."

"Of course," I said and made an entry on my virtual calendar.

"Thank you so much, Kary! This coaching really is amazing," Samantha said.

"I'm glad you think so and I agree," I said. "Have fun on those dates!"

"I will," she said with a smile, and left the office.

I sat back in my chair and gave myself a few minutes to reflect on the session. I always like to take some time to review what had been discussed, how I had handled things, what I had offered and ways I could do things even better next time. After gathering my thoughts, I made some notes and closed my notebook.

I decided to grab my lunch and walk down the street to sit in front of the water. It would be a relaxing way to spend the hour, and I knew I would be in the office for three more sessions after that.

The afternoon was bound to fly by, and I was grateful to feel more like myself. I wasn't some gumshoe investigator. I was a life coach just trying to get my business off the ground. I didn't have to worry about my safety or the safety of others. I didn't have to worry about being followed or the police showing up. Things were going back to normal. I was going back to normal. Deciding not to continue investigating this weekend was the right thing to do.

About twenty minutes later, I had finished my sandwich and was enjoying watching the boats come and go from the dock. While sitting there, I started getting some thoughts about things to build into the coaching program I was working on. My mind was finally starting to turn to more productive and safer pursuits. In the midst of my brainstorm, my cell phone started buzzing, indicating a call. I had the ringer off, but I had placed it face up on the bench beside me. I glanced down and didn't recognize the number. For a second I thought about letting it go to voicemail. Then I reconsidered. Maybe it was important.

I picked it up and hit the accept button. "Hello."

"Is this Kary Flynn?" a woman's voice asked.

"Yes, it is. Who is this?" I asked.

"Kary, my name is Cheryl Barclay. You've left a few messages for me," she said.

"Cheryl, hi. Yes, I did. Thank you so much for calling me back. I had no idea if I was calling a number that would reach you. I'm glad it did," I said, feeling a rush of excitement. Despite my decision not to pursue more leads during the weekend, there was no harm in wrapping up the leads I had started to follow previously.

"On your messages, you didn't give me much information..." Cheryl let the phrase hang in the air, prompting a response.

"Sorry about that. I wasn't sure how much to say in the message," I explained. In fact, I wasn't sure how much I should say now. I decided full disclosure was probably my best bet. I had a feeling I may not be able to keep Cheryl on the phone very long. "I got your number from Phil Cranston."

She sighed audibly with apparent frustration. "So this is about Janet."

"Yes, it is. I'm not sure if you're aware, but Thomas' most recent wife was killed last weekend," I explained, rushing my words, trying to catch her interest before she had a chance to tell me she wouldn't talk to me.

"Oh my gosh! No, I hadn't heard about it. I try not to watch the news very much. It stresses me out." She paused and then asked, "When you say killed, what exactly happened?"

"Murdered. She was pushed off a ridge," I explained bluntly.

"How awful!" she replied.

"Yes, the whole thing is awful," I agreed.

"But wait, who are you exactly? You said you knew Phil? And this has something to do with Janet?" she asked, confused.

I didn't blame her. I would be confused too. "Sorry, let me explain. I just met Phil. I actually knew Veronica, Thomas' late wife, the one who was just killed. I'm not a detective or a private investigator or anything like that, but I did know her and I'm just looking into a few things."

"You think Thomas killed her," Cheryl stated.

"Well, I'm not sure about that but I have to admit that when I found out about what happened to Janet, it did seem suspicious. I reached out to Phil, and he shared what he knew. He suggested I try to talk to you," I explained.

Cheryl sighed audibly into the phone again, but this time it sounded more sad than frustrated. "It's been so long since I thought of Thomas and Janet and those days working for him. I was his assistant for ten years, a decade of my life. I loved the job, and he treated me well. I liked Janet a lot, but she had issues. She struggled with depression. I know it was hard on their relationship."

"Did you ever suspect that Thomas had something to do with what happened?" I asked, getting to the point.

"I was loyal to Thomas. He treated me well. I know Phil suspected him and he reached out to me numerous times, but I just couldn't get involved. I felt strongly that Janet had done it to herself," she shared, and then quickly added, "accidentally, of course."

"You said you felt strongly, as in past tense. Do you feel differently now?" I inquired.

Cheryl paused. There was silence. For a moment, I thought she may have hung up, but then she finally spoke. "I don't know anything for sure, but after I stopped working for Thomas, I guess the veil was lifted. I started hearing rumors about how he ran his business, even how he had treated Janet. I didn't witness any of those things myself, mind you, but they planted seeds of doubt in my mind. I started looking at things a little differently, more suspiciously than I had when I worked for him."

"And?" I prompted.

"And I remembered something. It's nothing really. It's such a small thing. It didn't occur to me at the time that it could be important," she said.

"What was it?" I asked with anticipation. I realized I was literally sitting on the edge of the park bench.

There was another pause. I wondered if Cheryl was debating how much to share with me. I didn't want to push too hard, but I was dying to hear what she had to say.

I was about to repeat my question when she started to speak again. "About a week before Janet died, I was running errands in town, and I stopped at the pharmacy to pick up their prescriptions. When I got there, the pharmacist told me there was nothing to pick up. I usually stopped by every month to pick up refills of various medications. It was odd that nothing was waiting. I checked with Janet to see if she had all her pills, and she said she did, so I just forgot about the whole thing. It didn't come back to me until years later, and by then, well you know, Janet's death had already been ruled an accident, and certainly a small memory like that isn't proof of wrongdoing by anyone."

"But you think there's a chance that Thomas picked up the meds himself and did something to them?" I conjectured. I wanted to make sure I understood what she was implying but not stating directly.

"I don't know," she said quickly. "Maybe Thomas picked them up or maybe Janet picked them up herself. Like I said, it's probably nothing, but it was the only time that ever happened in all the years I worked for him. I always did a pharmacy run for medications once a month, both before and after Janet's death. That's why looking back after the fact, the timing of it seems a little odd."

"Did you ever tell the police about this?" I asked.

"I've never told anyone about it," she said.

"Would you be willing to tell the police now?" I asked.

She responded with a question. "Do you think it would help?"

"Honestly, I have no idea," I said, shaking my head even though I knew she couldn't see me through the phone. "But if it's the truth, it can't hurt to make sure the police have all the facts."

"And you think maybe knowing this about Janet would help them figure out if Thomas killed your friend?" she asked, conjecturing now as well.

"I think it might," I admitted.

"Let me think about it," she said with another long sigh. "Thomas was such a good boss, and I didn't suspect anything at the time. I would hate to hurt him if he didn't do anything wrong."

"I completely understand. Thank you for sharing this information with me and for even considering talking to the police about it," I said.

"You're welcome. I'll let you know what I decide," she said, and I could sense she was ready to end our conversation.

"Thank you, Cheryl. I really appreciate it," I said.

"Good-bye," she said, and hung up.

I couldn't believe what I had just learned. It was small but potentially significant. Would it be enough to cast doubt on Janet's accidental death ruling? I didn't think so, not on its own, but it was a small piece of the puzzle. How many other pieces were still left to be uncovered? I wanted to be respectful of what Cheryl had told me. I decided not to share it with Ethan until I heard back from her. If she decided not to talk to the police, I would need to decide if I would share it anyway. I hoped I wouldn't have to make that decision.

* * *

My afternoon sessions flew by. I was able to stay focused while my clients were with me, but in-between, I found myself ruminating again on the case, going over all the things I'd learned and carefully considering each suspect. The call from Cheryl had sucked me right back in. Although there were three men in Veronica's life with motives, I felt strongly that Thomas was the one who hurt her. He was the one who made the most sense. He was the one who had a suspicious past. He was the one who showed up unexpectedly at my house. I hoped it was only a matter of time before Ethan arrested him, but I felt satisfied knowing I had information now that could help push suspicion over the edge if the arrest didn't come quickly.

It was after 5 p.m. when I left my office and walked into the main yoga studio. Zuri gave me a wave from the equipment room in the back. She was straightening up after the last class of the day, and a few women were chatting by the door. I felt a rush of familiarity and regret. This was exactly how things were just a week ago when Veronica came barging in and confronted me. I wished I had known what was coming. I wished I could turn back time to warn her. Unfortunately, turning back time wasn't an option.

I pushed my thoughts of regret aside, walked up to the equipment room and greeted my friend. "Hey there."

"Kary, hi. I'm almost done here. We're still grabbing dinner, right?" Zuri asked.

"Of course. There isn't anywhere else I'd rather be on a Friday night," I said with a smile.

"Cool. I wasn't sure. You've been so distracted this week with everything going on. I thought you might have something else planned," she said without looking at me, obviously taking a little dig.

"I would tell you if I did," I said defensively.

"Would you?" she asked, turning to look at me directly.

I realized she was still hurt about what happened earlier in the week. I needed to make things right between us. My defensiveness was unwarranted. I was the one in the wrong. I apologized again. "Zuri, like I said on the phone, I'm sorry about Wednesday night. I shouldn't have gone there alone, or I at least should have told you where I was going. I thought we were good."

Her body relaxed visibly, and her expression softened. She shook her head slightly and said, "We are good. I don't mean to be difficult. I'm just worried. I think this whole investigation is more dangerous than you realize."

"I agree. And that's why I'm bowing out," I said.

"You are?" she asked.

"I am for now. I'm taking a break this weekend. No interviewing, no researching, no checking out spots related to the crime. I'm leaving things to the police." Zuri was right to be worried. Things had gotten a little more real than I was comfortable with the last few days. I would take a break, just like I planned. The call from Cheryl didn't need to change that.

She gave me a skeptical look. "What spurred this decision on? Did something happen?"

I couldn't keep things from her. She knew me too well. And I didn't want to keep things from her. I had learned my lesson Wednesday night. So, I shared what happened the night before when Thomas showed up at my house. Zuri listened with a concerned look on her face.

"This is exactly what I was talking about, Kary. You don't need to put yourself in the middle of this. Let the police handle it," she said.

"I am. Well, I am now. And Ethan gave me the number of a home security company so they're coming tomorrow to install an alarm system for me," I explained.

"I think an alarm system is a really good idea," Zuri said seriously.

"I think so too," I agreed.

Silence filled the air between us as Zuri continued straightening up the equipment. I wasn't sure what else to say. After a few moments, Zuri broke the silence, turning toward me with a mischievous smile. "So tell me a little more about Detective Andrews coming to your rescue."

I felt my face flush, but I didn't say anything immediately.

"You like him," she taunted playfully.

"I do," I admitted.

"I knew it! This is awesome, Kary. At least something good may come out of this whole mess. We may finally be able to get you a boyfriend!" She grew animated as she spoke.

"Boyfriend? I never said anything about a boyfriend. We haven't even gone on one date," I said, not wanting to get too excited about things yet.

"But you will. I'm really excited for you," she said with a smile.

I smiled back and said, "Thanks. I promise, I'll tell you more about it but for now we should get over to the restaurant. Ben is probably already there. Is Dean coming?"

"Yep, his back is feeling a lot better today. And you know him, sitting around in the house is definitely not his favorite thing to do," she said.

"I'm glad it will be all four of us. I just want to have fun and forget about everything that's going on. I want to have a few drinks, have a few laughs, listen to some music. You know, the usual," I said, feeling a sense of calm flow through my body as I thought about what the next few hours would be like.

"The usual sounds really good to me," Zuri agreed.

* * *

Fifteen minutes later we were comfortably seated at an outdoor table at the Bluegill Grill with Dean and Ben. The band was setting up their equipment outside, and thanks to Dean, who had arrived two hours earlier, we had one of the best tables available. There was an energetic vibe flowing through the crowd, excitement for the weekend ahead. I looked around the table at my friends and felt warmth for all three of them. They made me feel safe.

"What are you thinking about?" Ben asked me. He was seated next to me with his arm draped across the back of my chair.

"What do you mean?" I asked.

"You just went somewhere. I could tell you were lost in thought," he said.

I shrugged lightly. "Nowhere really. I was just thinking about how happy I am to be here right now with all of you."

"That's so nice. I'm glad to be here too," he said.

"What are you glad for?" Zuri jumped into our conversation.

"For friends like you guys," I said, "and for Friday nights."

Dean raised his glass. "To Friday nights."

"To Friday nights," we all echoed, clinking glasses and each taking a sip.

I was committed to making sure the night ahead stayed as far away from the investigation as possible. I chose a subject completely unrelated and asked, "So tell us about the class you went to yesterday, Zuri. Was it worth it? Did you learn anything you can implement at the studio?"

"Oh my gosh, it was amazing! I'm so glad I decided to go." Zuri's excitement was palpable as she started to explain her experience.

For the next hour that's how it went. We enjoyed each other's company. We laughed. We ate and drank. It was a normal Friday night, and that felt good. Right after dinner, the band started to play. They were a band we'd seen before, and we liked them.

Dean was in the middle of cracking us up with a story about his unsuccessful attempt to get out of bed with his hurt back, when Zuri cut him off. "Hold on a second. Kary, I think there's a guy staring at you from a table on the other side of the band."

"There is?" I asked, suddenly alert.

As a reaction, we all started turning our heads to look in the direction of the patio Zuri was facing.

"Don't everyone look at once!" Zuri ordered and we froze. "Hold on, let me just make sure," she said, cautiously observing things for a bit, "Yep, he's definitely staring at you and not in a friendly way."

"You don't recognize him?" Ben asked.

"Nope," Zuri said. "Dean, you can see him from your angle. Do see the guy I'm talking about? Do you recognize him?"

"Oh yeah, I can see him and you're right, he's definitely not friendly," Dean said. "I don't recognize him either."

"I'm going to take a look," I said, and then added, "I'll be nonchalant about it." I repositioned myself so I was facing an angle and turned my head to glance in the direction Zuri had indicated. It took just a second for me to find the guy she was talking about, and when I did, I caught my breath. It was Steve Moretti.

CHAPTER 17

I locked eyes with Steve, and he gave me a wink and a sly smile, tipping his beer to me, as if we were old friends. My blood ran cold.

"Do you know who he is, Kary?" Zuri asked in a worried tone.

I turned back to face my friends, but before I could explain, Ben cut in angrily. "That's Steve Moretti. He's obviously here to intimidate Kary."

"He's the bartender from the Carriage House," Zuri said, understanding the situation.

Dean's expression grew serious. "We should go over and say something, Ben."

Ben nodded and they both started to get up.

"Stop! Wait!" I said this more loudly than I intended but it did get their attention. They both paused. "Please. Sit down. Do not go over there."

Ben looked down at me. "Come on, Kary. A guy like him needs to be put in his place. Let us stand up for you."

"Please sit down, Ben," I pleaded.

Ben slowly took his seat again. Dean did as well. They all looked at me expectantly.

I sighed deeply, "Look, you're right. He probably is here to intimidate me. If you guys go over there, he won. That's probably what he wants, to rile us up and ruin our night. Besides, I don't think the two of you saying anything to him directly will be productive. He doesn't seem like the kind of guy that will back down just because you ask him to."

"So, what do you think we should do?" Zuri asked.

"I think we should do nothing," I suggested. "We're going to continue on with our night as if he isn't here. We're going to ignore him. Let's not feed into any drama. That's exactly what he wants. Besides, the guy may be unstable. I don't want to drag any of you into this."

"Are you sure?" Ben asked.

"I'm sure," I said, nodding my head. "Let's just ignore him and see what happens. He's going to get bored and leave or he's going to try to start something. If he starts something, that's when we take action."

Ben shook his head, disagreeing with my approach, but he didn't say anything. His face was turning a light shade of red. I could tell he was angry.

Zuri accepted my suggestion, "Okay, that's fine. We'll do nothing for now." She turned to direct her next comment at Dean, who was still propped on the edge of his chair. "I don't think you're in any condition to get involved right now as it is."

"I'm more than okay to stand up to an asshole," Dean replied. He looked at me. "But if Kary wants us to hold off, we'll hold off. Right, Ben?"

Ben paused before responding with a single word. "Right." It didn't sound very convincing, but he made no attempt to stand up again.

"What's he doing now, Zuri?" I asked. I didn't have a good view of his table without turning around and staring at him.

"He's drinking his beer and watching the band now, or maybe just pretending to watch them. I can't tell. Wait. Okay, now he's looking over here again," she explained, giving us a play-by-play of his movements. "He's totally creeping me out."

"Well, just let us know if you see him get up or leave," I requested.

I barely finished my sentence when Zuri gasped, "He's standing up now. I think he's heading over here."

I turned in my chair so I could see the section of patio that Steve had been sitting in. As Zuri warned, he was walking toward our table, a beer in his hand and a fake smile on his face. I sensed Ben was about to stand up again, and I put my hand on his arm. The gesture stopped him. Within moments Steve was standing at the edge of our table, looking down at the four of us.

"Kary, fancy meeting you here," he said with a sneer.

"Steve," I said coldly.

"Funny how small a town this is," he continued. "I mean I hadn't even heard of you until a week ago and then you show up at my place of work and then we run into each other here. It's like the universe is trying to tell us something."

"Hey man. Back off," Ben cut in.

Steve waved the hand that wasn't holding a beer up in a gesture of surrender. "Kary, your friend here seems a little angry."

Ben popped up out of his chair and got right in Steve's face. "You haven't seen angry! Get away from our table."

Steve didn't flinch. He looked right at Ben and said, "I'm just saying hi to a friend. No need to get all pissed off about it. Kary, you better get a leash on this boyfriend of yours."

At that, I saw Ben's body tense up even more. It looked like he was going to throw a punch. Luckily, Dean jumped up and stepped between them before he could.

"Hold up Ben. Stop. This guy isn't worth it," Dean said, facing Ben, his back to Steve. Ben took a step back but stayed poised to move back in if necessary.

Steve laughed and took a sip of his beer. "Everybody's so sensitive these days."

"What do you want, Steve?" I asked.

"Like I said, I just thought I'd say hi. It's really nice to run into you, Kary. I hope you and your friends enjoy the band," he said, and then started to walk away. After a few steps, he stopped and turned around to look back at me. "Hey, maybe I'll see you around. Like I said, it's a small town."

After that, he did walk away. He didn't stop at his table. Instead, he continued past it to walk out of the patio area, leaving the restaurant completely. I watched him walk until he was out of my line of vision.

I turned back toward my friends and realized that both Ben and Dean were still standing. Ben's fists were balled up and Dean had both of his hands on Ben's chest, physically holding him in place. I had never seen Ben angry like this.

"It's over, man. Don't do something you'll regret." Dean tried to calm him down.

"Somebody has to stop him. You heard what he said. He just threatened her. What if he's the killer? What if he goes after Kary next?" Ben was nearly yelling now.

Most of the bar was staring in our direction, watching us instead of watching the band. I knew I was the only person who could really calm Ben down. I jumped up to stand with the guys and put my hand lightly on Ben's arm for the second time of the evening. "Ben, listen to Dean. He's right. And look." I paused to gesture to myself. "I'm right here. I'm fine. I'm safe."

Ben's demeanor shifted slowly. His tense stance relaxed, and I could see him start to breathe more normally. Dean removed his hands from Ben's chest and took a step back, looking relieved.

Ben's expression softened and he said, "I'm sorry. I guess I sort of lost it there for a minute. I've just been so worried about Kary during this whole situation and the guy is clearly bad news, maybe even dangerous."

"Ben, I know you're worried about me but I'm fine. I really am. Can you please sit down?" I asked.

Ben obliged. Dean and I took our seats again, too.

"Shows over, everyone!" Zuri called out, waving her hands in the air. Most people went back to their meals or to watching the band.

"I'm sorry to drag all of you into this mess," I apologized. "That's the last thing I wanted to do."

"If you're in this, we're in this," Zuri said. Both Ben and Dean nodded in agreement.

"I appreciate your support and love you for it, but I just don't want any of you to get hurt," I said.

"Well, we don't want you to get hurt either," Ben said. "I never understood this whole investigation thing from the beginning, but you have to admit now that things have gone too far. First you were followed that one night and now this Steve guy is showing up where he really shouldn't be."

"And Thomas showed up at your house last night," Zuri added.

Both Ben and Dean looked surprised.

"You're not helping, Zuri," I said to her.

"I'm just sharing what happened. I think it's better if we all know what's going on," she explained.

"Thomas showed up at your house?" Ben asked.

"He did," I admitted.

"What did he want?" Dean asked. "Was he trying to intimidate you too?"

I shrugged my shoulders because I wasn't sure what his intentions were. "I'm not sure. He told me to back off, to stop asking questions, to stop talking to people. Oh, and he told me he thinks I'm the one who killed Veronica. Apparently, he's made the police very aware of his feelings on the matter."

"Why didn't you call me?" Ben asked.

"Well, I did call the police as soon as he left," I said.

"Good. Did they go arrest him?" Dean asked.

I shook my head and explained. "He didn't really do anything to be arrested for, but the police did submit a formal complaint. And I know they were going to talk to him to tell him to stay away from me. So, hopefully I won't see Thomas unexpectedly anymore."

"It sounds like they need to have the same discussion with Steve," Dean offered.

I sat back in my chair, suddenly realizing the reality of the Steve situation.

"What, Kary? What are you thinking?" Zuri asked.

"I just remembered something that Fiona told me about what Steve would do to Veronica. He would show up unexpectedly in public places, always making it seem like a coincidence. He was trying to intimate her. I guess it's his M.O. What happened tonight is exactly the same thing, because even if I tell the police, what could they possibly do about it? He's allowed to go to a restaurant, even the same one as me." I said the thoughts out loud as they came. I felt a sense of desperation as the realization of the situation hit me.

"So, you're saying this is probably only the beginning with this guy, then," Ben scoffed. "That's exactly what I was afraid of."

"I still think you should tell the police," Zuri said. "They may not be able to do anything right now but at least they'll know about it."

Dean nodded, "I agree. It's worth reporting."

I looked around at my friends who all appeared to have made up their minds. I agreed it probably was best to let the authorities know. Steve could be the killer. Would he come after me next? He did appear to like intimidating women and I was on his radar now. My heart sank. This might be only the beginning with him.

"You're right," I told them, "I'm going to call Ethan right now to let him know what happened."

I saw Ben flinch slightly when I said Ethan's name. I knew he was jealous. I had hoped he wouldn't be. The whole just-being-friends thing wasn't what he really wanted. I didn't want to hurt him, but I didn't have the energy to worry about that tonight. I picked up my cell and gave Ethan a call. He answered on the first ring, and once I assured him everything was okay and gave him a quick overview of what happened, he agreed to stop by the Bluegill Grill to talk to us in person. I hung up the call.

"He's on his way," I told my friends.

"Good," Zuri said.

Dean smiled. Ben smiled too but it seemed a little forced.

Twenty minutes later, Ethan walked onto the patio in street clothes. He caught my eye, and I waved him over. I hadn't seen him in anything other than his more formal detective clothes before. He looked good in khaki shorts and a light blue button-down shirt.

Despite the casual attire, he walked up to our table with an air of authority. "Kary, thanks for calling me."

"Are you off duty?" I asked.

"I am, but that's okay. I want to stay close to this case. I'd rather take your statement myself than have you talk to anyone else," he explained.

"You remember my friends Zuri and Ben? And this is Dean," I said, gesturing to the rest of the table.

Everyone said their hellos. Dean grabbed another chair. Ethan settled in and pulled out a notebook. We explained what happened and he took a few notes. It didn't take long to tell the story. The whole thing had only taken a few minutes to transpire. When we finished recounting the events, Ethan thanked us and put his notebook back in his pocket.

Ben jumped in with a question. "So now that you heard what happened, is there anything you can do to protect Kary from this Steve guy?"

Ethan shook his head. "I have to be honest. He didn't break any laws here. This is a public place, and all comments are open to interpretation. From what you all told me, he never overtly threatened Kary or any of you for that matter. Unfortunately, it appears that he knows how to game the system."

"Based on what Fiona told me, it sounds like the same type of thing he was doing to Veronica," I suggested.

"It does," Ethan agreed. "According to our records Veronica never reported any of that to the police, but there were complaints made about Steve by two other women in the past. Both of them talked about the same type of stalking behavior."

"Who were the women? How did they know him?" Zuri asked.

"Well, one of them was a woman he dated briefly. By her account, it was just a handful of dates, nothing serious. When she told him she didn't want to continue to see him, that's when the behavior started. That was three years ago, I believe," Ethan shared.

"And what happened to her?" I asked.

"Luckily nothing. After a few months, Steve seemed to lose interest and the stalking stopped. After speaking with Steve Wednesday, I followed up and made sure she was okay, and she is. She lives two counties over and is married with a baby now. She hasn't heard from or seen Steve in years."

"And the other woman?" Dean asked.

"She worked with Steve at a local bar. She reported his behavior toward some of the female patrons to the bar owner. I guess she deemed it inappropriate. That got him fired, which is when the stalking started. It persisted for a few months, until she decided to leave town. I spoke to her yesterday. She lives down in the Outer Banks now and is doing fine. She didn't see or hear from Steve after she moved," Ethan shared.

"So, he does have a pattern of this type of behavior in the past, but it's never escalated to violence," I said, feeling some sense of relief.

"No, not that we know of, but it doesn't mean it won't or that it didn't with Veronica," Ethan said. "We should take it seriously. Although we can't do anything legally concerning his behavior right now, I want you to promise to be careful and to report anything at all that you experience. Maybe he'll do something stupid that we could charge him for. Nothing is too small to report. I'll make sure the information about tonight goes into your file."

"I have a file?" I said, feeling deflated again.

"I don't like this," Ben stated firmly.

"None of us do," Zuri added.

Ethan looked at me directly and asked, "Did you call that alarm guy I told you about?"

"Yep, he's coming tomorrow to install a security system," I said.

"Good. Just to err on the side of caution, I recommend you stay with a friend tonight. I'm not saying it's too dangerous to stay at your house, but I think it would be best if you try not to be alone for a while, just until we see how a few things shake out in the investigation. Once the alarm is installed, then you should at least be secure in your home."

"Well, obviously you're staying with us," Zuri said, motioning to herself and to Dean.

"I am?" I asked.

"Yep, and you can stay as long as you like, even if you want to stay after the alarm is installed. We just want you to be safe." Zuri glanced at her boyfriend. "Right Dean?"

"Right. The more, the merrier!" Dean agreed with a warm smile.

I looked at my friends. "Thanks guys. I really appreciate it."

"You're welcome," Zuri beamed.

"And you're always welcome at my place too," Ben chimed in a little awkwardly. Before I could respond he quickly added, "I mean, if you need a break from staying with those two."

"Hey, what are you implying?" Dean asked with a fake quizzical expression.

"Should I be offended?" Zuri added playfully.

"Thanks, Ben," I said and smiled at him.

Silence settled over the table.

After a beat, Ethan stood up. "Okay, so it looks like my work here is done."

"Thanks again, Ethan," I said.

"You're welcome," he replied.

"Actually, you said you were off-duty, right?" Zuri asked.

"Yes, I am," he confirmed.

"Why don't you join us for a drink?" she asked, followed by a sly wink in my direction.

"Unfortunately, I have plans," he said, showing what seemed to be genuine disappointment. "But thanks for the offer. Maybe another time?"

This last question was directed at me. "Definitely," I said.

"Well, until then," he said, his eyes meeting mine for a split second. I felt warmth rush through my system. He turned his focus to the rest of the table and said, "You all have a nice night."

"You too," both Zuri and I chorused back in unison.

The guys said their good-byes as well and Ethan left. I felt a little stab of disappointment. I would have liked him to stay. I wanted to spend time with him, to get to know him. Although Steve appearing here hadn't been the most pleasant experience, it did give me a chance to see Ethan. I stopped myself in mid-thought. I can't believe I was almost feeling grateful to that stalker for stopping by. The stress of this whole situation was clearly making me lose my mind.

"So, what now?" Zuri asked. Her words brought me out of my head and back to the table.

"I can't believe there's nothing they can do to protect you," Ben said with frustration.

I shrugged and said, "I know, but it makes sense. Steve really didn't technically do anything wrong."

"Except be a creeper," Zuri said.

"Except be a creeper," I echoed.

"Well, let's just hope that's all he is," Dean said.

Ben did not look mollified. "You know, I think I've had enough for tonight. I'm going to head home."

"I think I'm done too," Dean agreed. "Getting out of the house was fantastic, but I need to get myself back into a horizontal position for a while." He reached around to touch his lower back and flinched slightly. "This has been fun though, as usual, kids."

"Are you ready to go too?" Zuri asked me expectantly. Her expression told me she wasn't ready to go just yet.

"Let's stay for one more drink. That was a lot of drama. I think I need to calm down a bit before heading home." I corrected myself. "Well, heading to your home."

"Are you sure that's safe?" Ben asked.

"We just need to walk down the block to the studio, and we'll be together," I responded.

"I don't like it," Ben said.

"Neither do I," Dean agreed, and then suggested, "Why don't you give me a call when you're ready to head home and I'll come down and walk back with you?"

"That would be great. Thanks Dean!" I responded before Zuri could. "I would feel better if it were the three of us. Safety in numbers and all that."

"Good," Dean said.

"It's a plan," Zuri agreed.

Ben and Dean both stood up, said their good-byes and exited the patio together. Zuri and I watched them go.

Once they were out of eyesight, Zuri turned to me and said with a mischievous grin, "Now, we can finally talk."

"About what?" I wasn't sure what she was referring to.

"About you and Detective Andrews!" she smiled coyly.

"Oh my gosh." I felt my face flush again, just like earlier.

"You promised to tell me all about it. You admitted you like him, and he obviously likes you, too. Why else would he rush over here while he was off duty?" She looked incredibly smug as she spoke.

"I don't want to get ahead of myself. I just want to take things slowly. See what happens," I explained. I was trying to keep my expectations under control. I was attracted to him, yes. But also, I barely knew him at all. And he was in the middle of investigating a murder, a murder that involved someone I knew. The whole thing seemed very messy. I didn't like messy. Messiness made me nervous.

"Well, if you don't want to get excited about it, I'll get excited for you. You deserve to have some fun. Now tell me all about what happened when he stopped by last night. I'm dying to know." She smiled and settled in her seat conspiratorially.

"Okay, let me see if I can remember exactly what we talked about," I said. I was glad she was making me share the details. Thinking about Ethan and the possibilities of what could happen between us felt good. It was a highlight in the darkness of what this last week had been.

Two hours later, we were finally settling down in Zuri and Dean's apartment. We had our girl talk and even danced a bit. It felt good to think about something other than murder for a few hours. As planned, we called Dean, and he escorted us back to their place. Despite the Steve run-in, overall, it was a good night. I thanked Zuri and Dean profusely before they headed off to their bedroom, and I fell into a deep, dreamless sleep.

A persistent ringing woke me up. The room was still blanketed in darkness. I was confused at first. What time was it? What was that noise? Where was I? Then I realized I was on the couch in my friends' apartment and the ringing was my phone. It was still in my bag, which was on the floor next to me. I reached in and dug around, trying to find it in my sleepy haze. I didn't want to wake up Zuri and

Dean. After what seemed like an eternity, I finally found it at the bottom of my bag and pulled it out.

I checked the caller ID. It was Ethan. I accepted the call.

"Hello," I squeaked out, my voice was barely above a whisper.

"Kary, it's Ethan." He was almost shouting on his end. "Are you at Zuri and Dean's? Did you stay there last night like we discussed?"

"Um, yes," I said, confused by his questions.

"So, you were with them last night then. You weren't alone at all?" he asked.

"Yes. I mean no. I mean yes." I was having a hard time thinking straight. I was starting to feel alarmed. The fog of sleepiness was lifting. I pulled my thoughts together and tried to be clear. "I was with Zuri the whole night. I wasn't alone at all. We came right to their place together from the bar."

"Good," he said.

"What's going on?" I asked. "Why are you asking me these questions?"

There was a pause on the other end of the line. Ethan finally spoke. "Steve Moretti was found dead about an hour ago."

CHAPTER 18

"Oh my god!" I exclaimed, well above a whisper now.

"I just got to the scene," Ethan explained. "As soon as I realized who it was, I wanted to make sure you were okay."

"Was he murdered?" I asked.

"Honestly, it's too early to tell," he said.

"But he might have been murdered?" I asked again, prompting him for more information.

"Homicide is always considered a possibility until it's ruled out," Ethan said, not directly answering my question.

"And that's why you wanted to make sure I was with Zuri and Dean all night, right? You wanted to make sure I had an alibi?" I asked, my heart pounding.

"Like I said, first I wanted to make sure you were okay. But then, yes, I wanted to make sure you had an alibi. Not because I thought you did anything, but because it will be easier to rule you out as a potential suspect," he admitted.

I exhaled loudly into the phone, taking in the reality of the situation. I allowed myself to breathe in deeply, and then said, "I understand. The timing is suspicious. First, I have a fight with Veronica, and she's found dead the next day. Then I have a run in with Steve and he's found dead the next day."

"It could be interpreted as a pattern," Ethan suggested.

"I can see how someone might think that, but since I wasn't alone last night, it would be impossible for me to have done anything to Steve, unless Zuri was involved as well. Do you think I have anything to worry about?" I asked, my heart pounding. I couldn't believe this was happening. It seemed surreal.

The door to the bedroom behind the couch where I was lying opened, and Zuri walked into the living room with a worried expression on her face. I held up my finger giving her a just-wait signal and turned my focus back to the phone.

"I wouldn't worry at all. We need to identify Steve's cause of death first and go from there. If it's found that the death is suspicious, you will likely be questioned, along with your friends based on what happened last night," Ethan explained. "As long as you tell the truth, you should be fine."

"I hope you're right," I said, feeling a drum of anxiety start to move throughout my body.

"I'll make sure you're okay," Ethan said.

I realized I believed him. "Thank you," I said gratefully.

"Okay, I've got to go. I'll check in with you later today once I have more information," he offered.

"Okay, I'll talk to you later then," I said.

"Bye, Kary. Stay safe," he said.

I ended the call and looked at Zuri who had settled into an oversized armchair across from me. She had a blanket pulled tightly around her shoulders. It was still early, and the room was cool.

"What's going on?" she asked.

"That was Ethan. He said Steve Moretti was just found dead," I explained.

Zuri's hand flew up to cover her mouth. Her eyes grew wide, and she let out a surprised gasp. "Oh my god!"

"That was my exact reaction," I said. "I'm sorry I woke you up."

"No, it's fine. I want to be up. I can't believe this is happening," she said.

"What's happening?" Dean walked into the room in his boxer shorts and with a serious case of bed head.

"Steve Moretti is dead," I said one more time.

"Holy shit!" Dean said, stopping to stand at the edge of the couch.

"Was he murdered?" Zuri asked.

"All Ethan would tell me is that homicide is always a possibility until it's ruled out. And it was suspicious enough that he called to make sure I had been with you guys all night, that I hadn't been alone," I explained.

"So, he was checking to make sure we could vouch for your whereabouts," Dean said, shaking his head. "This is wild."

"Yeah, he was. Thank goodness I decided to stay here last night," I said with a sigh of relief.

"Thank goodness," Zuri agreed. "I hate to sound morbid, but you have to be feeling a little relief knowing that he's dead, right?

The guy was a creep, and after what happened last night, it was pretty clear he had his sights set on making your life miserable."

"You know, I didn't even have time to think about that yet, but you're right. I'm not unhappy that he's gone," I admitted, and then quickly added, "Although I wouldn't wish death on anyone."

"It's natural to feel that way, Kary. Don't feel bad about it. I'll say it for you. I'm glad the guy is dead so he can't hurt you. It sounds like from what we heard about him last night, he had it coming. Maybe he finally messed with someone who fought back." Zuri was getting animated as she spoke.

"Or it was an accident," I offered.

"Whatever it was, you lucked out, Kary. Zuri is right. The guy seemed to have it in for you. I think you just dodged a bullet," Dean said.

"Maybe. I just hate being surrounded by so much death. It's hard to know what to feel. I can't help but think, what's going to happen next?" The anxiety was thrumming as a light pulse throughout my body.

"Don't worry. It's going to be fine," Zuri said with a smile and what was probably forced optimism. "Maybe Steve's the one who killed Veronica and he killed himself out of guilt. Or maybe Thomas tracked him down and killed him for murdering his wife. Or maybe Thomas and Steve were in cahoots. We have no idea. Maybe there isn't another terrible next thing that's going to happen. Maybe this is the end of it."

I nodded my head in agreement. "You're right. I shouldn't get ahead of myself until we have more information. Any one of those options you just listed could be what really happened, so this could be the end of it."

"Hey, sorry to interrupt, but we should give Ben a call," Dean suggested. "Let him know what's going on."

"That's a really good idea," I said. "Do you want to tell him? I don't feel like explaining it again."

Dean nodded. "Sure. Let me put clothes on and I'll go grab us some coffees. I'll give him a call while I'm walking. I don't think any of us are going back to sleep at this point."

"Thanks Dean," I said. "Oh, and you both should know and let Ben know, the police may want to talk to all of us. With the situation at the bar last night happening just a few hours before he died, they may want to get our statements."

"Oh wow! Okay, thanks for the heads up," Zuri said.

"Makes sense," Dean said. "I'll let Ben know."

Dean walked back into the bedroom and Zuri and I made eye contact.

"I have a feeling this is going to be a crazy day," I said with a heavy sigh.

"I have a feeling you're right about that," Zuri replied.

* * *

A few hours later, I was sitting at a table in Stews & Brews with Zuri and Ben. The morning had flown by. After having our coffees, I showered and dressed at Zuri and Dean's. I was decked out in some flashy yoga clothes Zuri let me borrow. They were not my usual style. I felt uncomfortable and it wasn't just the clothes. I had been on edge all morning, feeling a combination of anxiety and excitement.

We believed Steve's death had to have something to do with Veronica's, but that was only speculation at this point. The death was covered in the local news, but there were few details divulged; however, we were hopefully about to get some information. Ethan agreed to meet me here to give me an update. Dean had a boat tour scheduled, but both Zuri and Ben jumped at the chance to join me. We were all hoping to learn that Steve's death would bring an end and closure to the events from the last week.

We had arrived early to grab lunch and were just finishing our sandwiches when Ethan walked in. He made a beeline for our table.

"Hi Ethan," I said, moving the chair next to me away from the table so he could sit down.

"Hi Kary," he said, and took the seat. He turned his focus to my friends. "Zuri. Ben."

"I hope you don't mind. Zuri and Ben are just here for moral support," I said, realizing I didn't check to see if he had intended this to be a private conversation.

"That's fine. They're involved in this whole situation now anyway," he said, and then continued. "I can't stay long, but I'll give you as much of an update as I can. And I want to talk candidly about what this might mean for Veronica's case and how that affects you, Kary. The incident at the bar last night with you all and Steve obviously comes into play if this becomes a murder investigation."

"So, you still aren't sure if he was murdered?" Zuri asked.

Ethan shook his head. "We still haven't confirmed it, but with what we know right now, it's highly suspicious."

"What makes it suspicious?" Ben asked.

We collectively leaned in closer as Ethan explained, "This morning, around 4:45 a.m., on her way to a morning workout class, a woman drove past a vehicle pulled over on the side of the road. It was an odd location to see a car, and she made note of it but didn't think it was anything to worry about. After the class, on her way home, she noticed the vehicle was still sitting there. This time she was on the same side of the road. She slowed down as she passed and realized there was someone in the vehicle, slumped back in the driver's seat. She went home, told her husband and he drove down to check it out. When her husband approached the vehicle and got a better look, he could tell the person was dead. He called 911 and once the first responders confirmed the death, I was called in. I took one look and recognized Steve immediately. And the location where he was found was just a few driveways down from Thomas' house. That's when I called you, Kary. It's too coincidental not to have something to do with Veronica's murder."

"How did he die?" Ben asked.

"We aren't sure yet. Our best guess is that it was an overdose," Ethan explained.

"So, he killed himself?" Zuri asked.

"That's one possibility," Ethan replied.

"Or someone killed him," I offered.

"That's a possibility as well," Ethan said. "We can't confirm anything until the medical examiner does an autopsy, but we are assuming foul play, unless we are told otherwise."

"Are you looking into Thomas?" Ben asked. "Steve was obviously on that road for a reason. Thomas has to be your main suspect."

Ethan nodded. "We spoke to Mr. Calhoun this morning, along with all of the residents on that street. We're just gathering information at this point."

"What does this mean for Kary?" Zuri asked. She put her hand on my forearm in a gesture of protection. I smiled in appreciation.

"That's why I'm here now, talking to you," Ethan explained. "I don't think it will be long for us to make some connections between the two cases, but we don't have enough information at this point to make an arrest." He turned to focus on me and asked, "Are you still planning to have that alarm system installed?"

"Yes, they're coming by this afternoon," I said.

"Good. Continue to be extra careful. I think we're probably twenty-four to forty-eight hours away from locking this all up, but there's no saying what someone who is desperate will do. I don't want you to take any unnecessary chances," Ethan said with a seriousness that felt a little alarming.

"Because you think Thomas killed Steve and he might come after Kary next?" Ben asked.

"I can't share what I believe from an investigative standpoint, but I can promise this will all be over soon. I just want to make sure you stay safe until then. Be cautious, use the alarm system. Maybe one of your friends can stay with you, just for the next few nights," Ethan suggested.

"I can stay with you, Kary, or you can stay with me and Dean again," Zuri offered.

"Thanks, Zuri," I said, grateful again to have such a supportive friend. "And I promise to be careful. I'll just be relieved when this whole thing is over."

"It almost is," Ethan said.

"Is there anything else you can tell us?" I asked.

"Unfortunately, not right now," Ethan said, glancing up at the clock on the wall above the counter. "And I really have to get back to the station, but I'll give you a call tonight, just to check in."

"Okay, I'd appreciate that," I said.

Ethan got up from the table and said, "Be safe."

"You too," I said.

Both Zuri and Ben said their good-byes as well. Ethan walked out and we sat in silence for a few seconds.

It was Ben who broke the silence. "So, what's your take on what he said?"

"That Thomas murdered Steve and maybe Steve murdered Veronica and that's why Thomas murdered him. I don't know. My head is spinning," I admitted.

"I think it's clear, though, that Ethan is basically telling you to be afraid of Thomas until he's arrested," Zuri offered. "He's the one you have to watch out for, but I don't think he can explicitly say it."

"I agree," Ben nodded. "It's Thomas who is the wild card here. He's the one that's dangerous."

"The two times I've seen him in person, he was so angry and there was something in his eyes, something dark," I said. "That's the only way I can describe it. It's not a stretch to believe he's dangerous."

"Good thing you're getting that alarm installed today and that I'm staying with you tonight," Zuri said.

"You want to stay at my place?" I asked.

"Sure, let's give Dean a night to himself. That way he can spread out on the bed. His back is still bothering him. Besides, then we can have girl time." Zuri smiled, trying to bring some lightness to the situation.

"That sounds amazing," I said, relieved I wouldn't be alone.

"Is there anything I can do?" Ben asked.

"Nope, we'll be fine," I said. I checked the time on my phone. "Actually, I have to head out, too. I'm meeting the alarm guy in like twenty minutes. After the alarm is installed, I'll turn it on and stay home until you can get there."

"I should be there around 6 p.m., Zuri said. I have one more class this afternoon and some odds and ends to take care of. Will you be okay until then?" she asked.

"Absolutely," I said. I looked back-and-forth between my two friends. "Thank you both for being here for me and supporting me through all of this. I'm so lucky to have you in my life. And Dean too."

"What are friends for?" Zuri said with a smile.

"Yep, what are friends for?" Ben echoed.

* * *

My afternoon flew by. The guy from the alarm company pulled up to my place right after I got home. His name was Gary. He was a nice, middle-aged man who owned and ran the company. Although technically he was a stranger, I felt comfortable knowing Ethan had recommended him. He wired up the system so alarms were set on both the front and back doors and all of the downstairs windows. He suggested installing some cameras, but I wasn't sure they were necessary. The idea of being watched, even if it was just by me, gave me the creeps. He suggested that even just putting up one facing the front door and looking out to the yard might be sufficient. I told him I would start with the alarm system and think about adding cameras next. I hated feeling like I had to live in fear in my own house. This

A-frame was my happy place, my comfort zone. I couldn't wait until this entire ordeal was over.

It took about two hours for Gary to do his thing. He gave me the bill and said his good-byes. I set the alarm after closing the door behind him. It was official. I was on lockdown, by my own choice, but that didn't make it feel good.

I checked the time. I still had a few hours before Zuri arrived. I sent her a text to see if she would be up for eating dinner in, and she agreed. I felt antsy. Maybe I would try to make something rather than ordering takeout. I checked the refrigerator. The bare shelves made my decision for me. Takeout it would be. We could decide what to order when she arrived.

I spent the next hour online, trying to find out any additional information I could about Steve's death. All I could find were the basics: a man in his late twenties was found dead in his car on the side of the road in the early hours of Saturday morning. His name hadn't been disclosed yet. One of the local news stations had already started correlating the death to Veronica's. Although Steve's death wasn't confirmed as a murder yet, it was unusual to find someone dead in their car on the side of the road without there being an obvious car accident. And the fact that he was found just a week after a confirmed murder—things like that didn't happen here. It wasn't surprising that the news outlets would try to draw some connection between the two, even without knowing if the two individuals had a connection when they were alive. Pineville was not usually this exciting—I thought of the alarm system I just had installed—or this dangerous. A chill ran up my spine. I looked around my house. Everything looked safe and secure. I was freaking myself out. I needed a distraction.

I decided to call my mom. We hadn't spoken since Tuesday night, and so much had happened since then. It would be good to get her perspective on it all.

"Kary, honey. I've been meaning to call you. Is everything okay?" she answered after a few rings, sounding a little breathless.

"I'm fine. You sound weird. What are you doing?" I asked.

"Oh, I'm on a ladder putting up decorations for a wedding we have here starting at seven o'clock. My wedding manager got food poisoning and now I'm stuck doing the rest of the setup," she explained.

"Wait, you're on a ladder and you answered your phone?" I asked, incredulous.

"Honey, I always answer when you call," she said.

"And normally I appreciate that," I said. "I was just calling to give you an update on everything going on, but it can wait. Besides, it's probably not a great idea for you to be balancing on a ladder, putting up decorations and talking on the phone. You're not the bionic woman, mom."

"I'm not?" She gave a little chuckle, clearly amusing herself. "Well, I'm glad it's nothing time sensitive. I suspect tonight is going to be a bit chaotic. Can I give you a call tomorrow?"

"Of course. Do you want my help? I could head over there now. I'm not doing anything. Zuri's coming over but that's not for like two hours," I offered.

"Oh, you're sweet, but it's not your job. I've got this. You just enjoy your Saturday, and we'll catch up tomorrow," she said.

"Okay, I will. Bye mom," I said.

"Bye honey."

The call clicked off and I was left alone with my thoughts. I needed to keep myself busy until Zuri arrived. I hated sitting around doing nothing, but I wasn't sure I could be focused enough to be productive. I also knew there was no way I could relax, so reading a book or watching TV wouldn't help. I still felt a low hum of anxiety pulsing throughout my body. It had remained with me all day, from the moment I woke up to Ethan's phone call. I had a sense that everything, this whole week, all that had happened, was coming to a head, and yet there was nothing I could do about it.

At that moment, my thoughts were interrupted by a knock at the front door. It startled me. I wasn't expecting anyone, and I immediately tensed up. Thank goodness the alarm was set. I got up and walked slowly through the hallway toward the door. It had taken me some time to get there and as I approached, there was another loud knock. I jumped back. Startled again. I didn't say or do anything. I just waited.

After a few seconds, I heard a muffled voice from the other side of the door. "Kary? Are you there?"

I recognized it immediately. "Ben?"

"Oh good. You are here. Are you okay? Can you open the door?" His voice gave away a hint of concern.

Relief flooded my system. I opened the door and the alarm started beeping immediately. I gestured him in, closed the door behind him and hit the code to reset it. I then turned to face him.

"What are you doing here?" I asked, both relieved and surprised.

"Well, I know you said you didn't need anything this afternoon, but with everything going on, I just thought I'd stop by to make sure you're okay. I know Zuri isn't getting here for a while. I thought you might want some company." He readjusted his glasses as he spoke.

"You don't have to be at the shop?" I asked.

"Nah, it's covered," he said.

"Well, then yes. I would love your company," I said gratefully, and gestured for him to walk farther into the house. "Honestly, I'm glad you're here. I was kind of going a little crazy on my own."

Ben stopped abruptly and turned around with a worried expression. "Why? Did something happen?"

"No, nothing. That's the problem. Nothing has happened and I'm going crazy just sitting around here, waiting for news." I sighed heavily.

"Well, Mr. Detective did say he would call you later, so I'm sure it's just a matter of time before you know what's going on." Ben said this with a flat tone.

It was a strange comment. "You mean Ethan?" I asked.

"Oh, that's right, Ethan. I forgot the two of you are on a first-name basis." Again, his tone was flat. He turned back around and continued walking toward the living room.

His comments caught me a little off guard. I decided not to respond but followed him into the heart of my house. When we got to the living room, he turned to face me again.

"There's something going on with you two, isn't there? Please, just be honest with me," he pleaded, and I could see sadness in his eyes.

"There's nothing, not really, not yet anyway." I was fumbling with my words.

He nodded his head knowingly. "Not yet."

"I'm sorry, Ben. I really am. I never meant to hurt you," I apologized.

His expression grew dark, and his face twisted in a way I had never seen before. "It's such a shame," Ben said. "After everything I've done. It's still not enough for you to see me that way, to see us together."

"What you've done?" I asked, suddenly knowing but at the same time dreading the answer.

"I killed for you Kary, and you don't care at all."

CHAPTER 19

At that moment everything grew clear in my mind.

"It was you," I whispered, fear flashing through my body.

"It was me," Ben confirmed.

"Veronica? Steve? Why?" I spoke slowly, my mind putting the pieces together.

"I was protecting you." Ben's face lit up with something like pride.

"But I didn't need that kind of protecting," I said.

"Well, I didn't think so at first either. I mean, it didn't start out that way, but that Veronica—what a bitch!" His face grew dark again.

I did a quick assessment based on memory of the distance I was from the front door. It was behind me, but I was closer than Ben. If I made a run for it, would he catch me? I had to keep him talking. "She could be. You're right. What happened though? It sounds like you didn't intend to kill her."

Ben's face softened. "Of course not. I'm not a monster, Kary."

"I know that. I just want to understand. Please, Ben. Will you tell me?" I didn't have to force interest. I really did want to understand what happened, but I also wanted to get out of here. I wasn't sure why he was suddenly admitting this to me. Was he still hoping for a happy ending between the two of us? I didn't think so. Something had changed.

"I'll tell you everything, but you have to sit down to hear it. It's a good story, I promise. With a hero and a heroine and some assholes trying to ruin their love story before it even began," he said dramatically.

Escape won out over interest. I spun around and ran as fast as I could toward the front door. I could sense his approach behind me.

"Bitch!" he called out.

My hand was almost within reach of the doorknob, when his body slammed into mine, shoving me forward toward the door. I hit my head, hard. I was in a daze.

"See, look what you made me do." Ben's words were registering but he sounded far away.

My eyes started to refocus, and I realized he was on top of me. Before I could respond, he started dragging me back toward the living room, into the heart of the house, into my cozy comfort zone, into my safe space. But there was nothing safe about it anymore.

He muttered under his breath the whole time. I couldn't understand what he was saying. When we got to the middle of the room, he stopped and looked down at me. He took a deep breath and his expression shifted to something softer. He reached down, picked me up and set me gently on the couch.

"I'm sorry about that. I really am. I didn't want to have to hurt you." He spoke with sincerity.

I realized his feelings for me, however warped, could be my saving grace. I had to play into them. "I know. I'm sorry too. I just wasn't prepared to hear what you were telling me. I guess I'm in shock."

"Look at you. I can't be mad at you. Even after all of this," he threw his hands up and chuckled lightly.

"Ben, I didn't realize you felt like this. If I'd known…" I left the phrase hanging for him to fill in whatever he wanted to.

A spark of excitement lit up his face. He started moving around the room animatedly as he explained, "I know. I was too weak to tell you. I've loved you all along, Kary. Even in high school, even when you had other boyfriends, I hoped. I dreamed that one day you would see me differently, but you never did. Then we graduated and you moved away. I gave up hope and moved on. But then when you moved back last year and we ran into each other, I thought this is my chance. This is the love story that's been meant to happen all along. Guy loves girl. Girl moves away. Girl moves back and realizes he was what she had always been looking for."

"I like the sound of that story," I offered. I was closer to the back door now. Would I get the opportunity to make another run for it? I forced myself to look at Ben, to pretend I was fully engaged. In reality, I was playing out escape scenarios in my mind.

Ben shook his head, "But that's not the story."

"It isn't?" I asked.

"You know it isn't. You didn't realize anything. It's been a year, and no matter what I did, you wouldn't look at me as anything more than a friend. I thought that kiss would change things, but it didn't." He caught what sounded like a sob in his throat.

"Ben…" I tried to speak.

"Don't!" he demanded. "You can't rewrite the story, Kary. You have to be truthful. You didn't see me differently and the kiss didn't mean anything. It wasn't a turning point. It wasn't the start of our great love. Admit that to me. It wasn't."

I thought briefly about lying but decided that would be worse than the truth. I needed to go along with the story as it was up to this point. Maybe I could change the ending, though.

"It wasn't," I admitted.

"Thank you for being honest. It wasn't, and it's okay. I get it. Because I wasn't showing up as the person you wanted me to be, the person you needed me to be. You didn't realize how much love I had for you and what I would do to protect you, to protect that love. What I had already done. You didn't know, but I couldn't tell you. Can you imagine how horrible this has been for me? I wanted to tell you everything, Kary, but I couldn't," he said.

"Can you tell me now, Ben? I want to hear what happened. I want to know. I want to understand what you did for me. Please, what happened with Veronica?" I asked.

I had to keep him talking. Maybe I could convince him that our love was still a possibility. Would he believe that enough to let me go? I couldn't be sure. It was worth a shot, though. My head was pounding, but I fought through the pain. I needed to stay clear. I needed to survive.

"Okay, I'll tell you and you'll see. I love you. I can take care of you," he said.

"Tell me, Ben," I prompted.

His expression softened, either with the hope of winning me over or with the pride of bragging about what he'd done. I couldn't be sure.

"I didn't intend to kill her. I just wanted to talk to her, to explain that you would never do the thing she was accusing you of. And there was that kiss. After all this time, all these years, especially the last few months, you kissed me, and I thought that everything was finally coming together. But there was the Veronica situation, and if she ruined your business here, you might leave town. I couldn't let that happen. I had to do something," he explained with an almost manic energy now, continuing to pace back and forth as he spoke.

I glanced around the room during the moments he wasn't focused on me, desperately trying to find some way to escape. It was useless. He was blocking my path to every exit. I had to buy more time. I prompted him to continue. "So how did you find her? How did you get her out on that ledge?"

Ben stopped pacing and looked right at me. His eyes were wide with an expression I could only describe as insane. He said, "It was meant to be. The timing was impeccable. It was the universe working in my favor, working for our love."

"It was?" I asked, trying to sound as excited as possible. I could tell he wanted me to be excited. In truth, I was terrified.

"Oh, it was!" he exclaimed loudly, throwing his hands upward in a gesture of reverence. He paused for a moment; then he dropped his hands back down and started pacing again as he continued his story. "After I dropped you off here, I drove out to her house. I knew where she lived. I stopped at the end of the street, debating what my next move would be. I didn't have to debate long, though. Before I knew it, I saw her car pull out of the driveway. At that time of night? Where could she possibly be going?"

"So, you followed her," I concluded.

"I did," he confirmed, "and she ended up pulling into the lookout parking lot. I couldn't believe my luck. She was obviously meeting someone, alone in the dark at night. I figured it was a secret I could use against her. I parked further up the road where she wouldn't see me and snuck back down to the lookout in the woods from a different path. I watched her waiting and checking her cell phone. After a while, it became clear that whoever she was meeting wasn't coming. But I knew I had to act quickly. I couldn't wait to find out her secret. I could lose you. So, I decided to confront her. I thought maybe she'd listen to reason."

"Wasn't she freaked out when she saw you?" I asked. I could only imagine Veronica's fear being confronted in the middle of nowhere by a strange man.

"Oh, I startled her for sure." He chuckled, clearly proud of himself. "That was part of the beauty. I caught her off guard. I explained who I was and my relation to you and how I had known you pretty much forever and could completely vouch for your honesty. It was all so logical and clear. I just had to get the truth through to her. And you know what she did when I was done?"

I shook my head but didn't say a word. I could sense a swell of anger beginning to rise up in him.

"She laughed. She laughed right in my face." He said this with venom.

I wasn't sure how to respond. He seemed to be waiting. I managed to pull some words together. "I'm sorry, Ben. She wasn't a very nice person."

"No, she wasn't. And you wouldn't believe what she said about you," he said.

Again, he was waiting for a response. "What did she say?" I asked.

"That you were a coward, relying on a lovesick puppy to fight your battles for you. I knew right then and there she wouldn't stop. There was no talking sense into her. She was a miserable human being, and she was going to ruin you. And she was going to ruin me, everything I had looked forward to for so long. It all happened so fast. I grabbed her neck. She was shocked. I don't think she thought I had it in me. I just wanted her to shut up and to go away and leave us alone. She pushed back but she was no match for me. We were so close to the edge. It was just a few steps away and then it was done," he explained and then paused as if visualizing the incident, playing it over in his mind.

"It sounds like it was a terrible accident. She pushed you to do it. She provoked you," I offered, trying to downplay what happened, trying to make him think I understood.

Ben looked me straight in the eyes, that insane look even more intense than earlier. He spoke quietly but firmly. "It wasn't an accident. You know it wasn't, and I'm not sorry I did it. I saved you."

I gulped deeply. He looked so serious, so sincere and so scary. I felt my body begin to shake with fear. All I could think to do was to agree. "You did save me."

He suddenly became animated, emboldened by my response. He started pacing again and continued to explain. "But then it all went wrong. First, those detectives came in and started considering you a suspect. I never intended that. Then you just wouldn't stop looking into it. And then Thomas and that Steve guy both started threatening you. The whole thing just went out of control. By trying to protect you, I put you on the radar of two dangerous men and of the police. You have no idea how worried I've been all week. I've been trying to keep an eye on you, follow you, make sure you're okay."

The realization hit me, and I said it out loud: "It was you that followed me home from my parents that night and you've been watching the house."

He nodded. "I had to make sure you were safe."

"Thank you, Ben. You have kept me safe," I said, trying to sound sincere. I had to try to make him believe I was on his side, and I had to keep buying more time. "And what about Steve? What happened to him?"

His expression lit up and he explained. "Steve was a gift. I didn't think so at first. He made the situation so much worse. He was a bad guy, and I knew after what happened last night at the bar, he was never going to leave you alone. I had to do something. And then it came to me. Two birds. One stone. I could kill Steve, make sure he was found near Thomas' house and the only explanation is that he killed Veronica and then Thomas killed him. Situation resolved. I didn't realize how good at this I could be."

"But how did you kill Steve? How did you manage to get close to him?" I asked, glancing at the clock on the wall. Zuri was still a few hours from arriving, and although I longed for someone to save me, I didn't want her to walk into this. I couldn't be sure Ben wouldn't hurt her. I was on my own.

"Steve was creep and a stalker, but he was an opportunist. After what happened at the Carriage House on Wednesday, I looked him up, learned everything I could about him, including where he lived. After I left you guys last night, I made my way over to his place, knocked on the front door and talked my way in. Of course, he was suspicious at first, but after I convinced him that I had a way to get

Thomas to offer a huge payday, in exchange for him staying away from you, it was an offer he couldn't refuse. During our little chat, we had a few beers. I doused his with pain meds, the ones I never used for that neck injury. I never got rid of them for some reason, and if Dean hadn't had his back injury a few days ago, I wouldn't have remembered I had them stashed in the back of the medicine cabinet. See, the universe really is working in my favor!"

His crazed excitement was almost as scary as his anger. I didn't recognize the person in front of me. He had hidden his true self so completely. I prompted him to continue. "But how did you get him in the car and parked near Thomas' house?"

"I just suggested we drive out there together. He tried to be cautious by driving his car separately, but that worked in my favor too. I instructed him to follow me there and pull over to the side of the road. My only concern was that he wasn't going to make it there before passing out. He did though. After we stopped, I got into his car, and he was just about asleep. I couldn't be sure the pills would kill him though. It was taking too long, so I suffocated him." Ben said this without emotion, without regret. "I know that sounds harsh, Kary. Like I said before, I'm not a monster but I did what had to be done. You see it now, right? You see how I am the only one who has protected you this whole time?"

I nodded my head and agreed. "I see it now, Ben. I do. I didn't see it before, but now I see it. Now I know. You saved me."

"Do you think you could ever love me, now that you know the real me? Now that you know what I would do for you?" He looked at me expectantly.

I had to try to convince him. "I know I could. I already love you so much as a friend and now that I know all of this, of course I could."

His expression turned sad, and he sighed deeply. "I wish that were true."

"It is true," I pleaded.

"Don't lie to me!" he shouted with rage and took a few steps toward me.

I curled my body up, bracing for a blow, trying to protect myself. But he didn't touch me. He towered over me and repeated in a softer tone, "Don't lie to me, Kary. I deserve the truth, just like I was truthful with you. I told you everything. Could you love me like I want you to? After everything I've done, could you love me now?"

I looked up at his hope-filled eyes. If I lied, it didn't seem like he would believe me. If I told the truth, he might explode with anger. I decided something non-committal was best. "Ben, you're scaring me, and this is a lot to take in all at once. I just need some time to process everything. I mean, it's amazing, all these things that you've done. I just need to figure out how I feel about it all. Please, if you love me, will you give me a little time?"

He took a step back and looked at me, really looked at me. It was the longest pause of my life. I held my breath, waiting for his response. He reached toward me and pulled me up into a standing position. He leaned his face toward mine and kissed me, gently at first and then harder. It was all I could do not to recoil from his touch. I felt disgusted. Bile filled my throat, but I choked it down.

He finally pulled his face back and looked at me again. Sadness filled his eyes. "Time's up, Kary. It's too late."

Before I had a chance to react, he spun me around and pulled me tight against his body, my back against him now. His arm moved up around my neck. He had me in some kind of chokehold. I couldn't breathe. I punched and kicked and scratched but nothing caused him to loosen his grip. My lungs cried for air. My mind raced. This was it. I was going to die. He was going to kill me.

And the whole time he was whispering in my ear how much he loved me, how much he wished we had been able to be together, how grateful he was that I forced this side of him to awaken, how grateful he would always be to me, how much stronger he was now.

The room was spinning, and darkness seeped in from the edges. I started to let go. There was relief in letting go. Flashes of scenes from my life swirled through my mind. I started moving toward the darkness.

CHAPTER 20

All at once, I was being pulled strongly toward the light. I felt a surge of energy flow through me and then I was back in the room, on the floor, coughing. My head was pounding. My eyesight was blurry. My ears were ringing. There was a voice. It sounded far away. No wait. It was right here. The room stopped spinning and my coughing started to slow. My vision finally came into focus, and I registered the reality of the scene.

I was in my living room, on the floor. Ethan was kneeling over me. He was saying words, but the sound was muffled. I felt confused. I didn't know what had happened. I realized we weren't alone. Ben was lying on the floor next to me, blood flowing from a wound I couldn't identify. His eyes were closed. His face was white.

At the sight of him, memories flooded to the surface—Ben coming over, admitting what he'd done, pushing me into the door, trying to kill me.

I scrambled to move away from him. "It was him! It was him!" I cried out, but my voice was barely above a whisper. My throat screamed with pain at every word.

Ethan put his hands on my arms to keep me in place. His grip was firm but gentle. "Kary, he can't hurt you. Don't move. I need to make sure you're okay," he said with concern.

"Ben's the killer," I managed to whisper and then started coughing uncontrollably again.

"Don't talk," Ethan told me. "They'll be plenty of time for that. Just breathe. Are you okay? Nod if you're okay."

I nodded.

"Good," he said, looking relieved. "I'm going to check on Ben now. Don't move. The ambulance is coming."

He turned his attention to Ben and started to perform CPR. It was like being in a nightmare. My head was pounding. I felt dazed. I moved my hand to my throat. The pain was almost unbearable. I watched as Ethan worked on Ben, trying to get him to breathe again.

I focused on my own breathing, trying to stay calm and trying to get as much air into my lungs as possible. They were still burning. I realized how close to death I had come.

Ethan continued working on Ben, pumping his chest. Up and down. Up and down. Counting out loud.

My front door flew open, and people rushed in. Police. Emergency Services. Everything seemed to be moving in slow motion. I was escorted from the house and put in the back of an ambulance. They were asking me questions. I was trying to answer them. My head pounded. My throat burned. Exhaustion took over and darkness overcame me once again.

* * *

It was Friday night, almost a week later, and I was sitting on the outside patio at Bluegill Grill with Zuri and Dean. From any outside observer, we were three friends having a drink after a week of work, just like we had done every Friday night for so many months before. But from the inside, this wasn't a normal Friday night at all. It was my first time out in public after spending the last week recovering. First, I was in a hospital bed, and then in the spare room of my parents' house and finally back in my own bed last night. It was my first time out after nearly dying at the hands of someone I thought I knew and trusted. I was consumed with competing feelings—joy, relief, gratitude, appreciation but also sadness, betrayal, confusion, guilt. Although my body had come quite a way healing itself in the last six days, I knew my mental and emotional healing would take longer. I was okay with that. I was willing to be patient with myself. I understood that my thoughts were causing my emotions and I was doing my daily self-coaching sessions, which were helping a lot. I had also started to see a therapist to help me process the trauma. I knew with my coaching skills, the guidance of a therapist and the support of my friends and family, I would overcome this. It would take time, but at least I was alive to experience it.

"Kary, are you sure you want to do this tonight? We can go somewhere else if this is too much for you?" Zuri said with a concerned expression on her face.

"Yeah, we can order pizza and hang at our place, or go hang at yours," Dean suggested.

I shook my head and replied, "No, I want to be here. I need to get back into normal routines. I can't stay holed up forever. I have to start living again." My voice wasn't completely back to normal, but my throat no longer stabbed with pain when I spoke, and I no longer had to whisper.

"Do you feel okay, though? Being here?" Zuri asked.

"Yes and no," I said honestly. "It feels good, normal but not totally normal. It feels a little off. It's hard to explain."

"It feels a little off for me, too," Dean agreed. "I just keep waiting for Ben to walk through the door to join us."

"Dean!" Zuri scolded him.

"No, it's fine," I said. "We can talk about him. I think it's better if we do, just get everything out in the open."

"You sure?" Zuri asked.

"Yeah, I'm sure," I nodded.

Zuri and Dean glanced at each other. Then Zuri spoke. "So, we know he survived his gunshot wound and is still recovering in the hospital and he's obviously under arrest, but do you have any other information?"

"I do have a little more," I said. "Although he confessed everything to me, he's not talking now. He has a lawyer, and Ethan expects that he'll probably plead not guilty. You know Ben. He's smart. He knows that they don't have any physical evidence at this point tying him to either murder."

"Does that mean you'll have to testify?" Dean asked.

"If it goes to trial, yes," I answered.

"That's horrible, and he's horrible!" Zuri exclaimed loudly, and then lowered her voice after noticing she had drawn the attention of the nearby tables. "I can't believe he fooled us for so long. Everything I thought I knew about him was a lie. I'd be happy to never see him again."

"Honestly, in some ways, I look forward to facing him," I admitted. "I want to show him that he has no hold over me and that he can't just mess with people's lives. He deserves everything he's going to get.

Veronica and Steve may not have been the best people, but he had no right to take their lives. I agree, though, Ben wasn't who we thought he was. He was able to hide who he truly was for years."

"It almost makes you hesitant to trust anyone," Dean said.

"I'm trying not to think about it that way. If I go down that path, I really will end up holed up hiding in my house. I have to believe that most people are good. They're doing the best they can. And most people won't hurt others—not intentionally, anyway," I said.

"And most people aren't psycho stalker killers," Zuri added.

For some reason that made all of us bust out laughing. The reality of the situation was just another thing to be conflicted about. If I wasn't laughing, I might be crying. So, for now, I was choosing to laugh.

"Speaking of psycho stalker killers, is anything going on with Thomas now?" Dean asked.

"I heard from Cheryl, Thomas' old assistant," I said. "She did end up sharing some information with the police. It isn't much, but because of that, and because of the insistence of the family, Ethan told me they're planning to reopen the investigation of his first wife's death."

"Do you think he did it?" Zuri asked.

"We'll see if the police can discover anything new this time around, but I don't think we'll ever know for sure."

We sat in silence for a few minutes, sipping our beers, listening to the band and soaking in the warm weather. I felt blessed to be alive to enjoy it.

"So, speaking of Ethan…" Zuri prompted with a hopeful tone. "What's going on there? It sounds like you've been in touch with him this week?"

I felt my face flush. "Actually, I invited him to come tonight," I said, and checked the time on my cellphone. "He should be here any minute."

Zuri smiled and said, "Awesome! He's a good guy, Kary. You deserve a good guy."

"Well, he does get points for saving my life. That's not a terrible way to start a relationship," I said.

"Wait, now we're calling this a relationship?" Zuri asked expectantly.

"I think it is. At least it's the start of one," I admitted. I had come too close to death to continue to hide from my feelings. I liked Ethan. He liked me. That was the truth of it, and I was going to jump into this relationship with my heart open.

Zuri squealed with excitement.

"Hey, speaking of Ethan, how did he end up saving you, anyway?" Dean asked. "Zuri gave me a quick rundown of what happened, but why was he at your house in the first place?"

"When we met with him earlier in the day, he said he would call to check in on me, but for some reason, instead of calling, he decided to stop by in person," I said. "He said he just had a feeling that he should come to my house instead of calling. When he got there, he was about to knock on the front door when he heard a loud bang against it. He knew right away something wasn't right. He decided not to knock. Instead, he called for backup but didn't want to wait for them to arrive. So, he circled around to the back door and was able to see what was going on inside. He tried to get in without

Ben noticing, but the situation escalated. As soon as he saw Ben start to choke me, he decided stealth wasn't an option anymore. He ended up firing his gun through the sliding glass door and barging in. Ben wouldn't let me go, so he shot him."

"And you don't remember any of that?" Dean asked.

I shook my head. "Just the end when Ethan revived me and then started trying to revive Ben."

"Amazing!" Dean said.

"I know, right? I owe him my life," I said.

"Well, he may have saved you this time, but I have no doubt that you're more than capable of saving yourself next time," Zuri said.

"Wait, next time? There's going to be a next time?" I said, my eyes widening.

"What I mean is that you can do anything you put your mind to," Zuri said. "I've always known that you can, and I just hope this whole situation doesn't make you think otherwise." She gave me a pointed look.

I took a deep breath and smiled. "Actually, I've been thinking about that a lot over the last week. I realize that although I've taken some risks in this last year by moving here and starting my coaching business, I've still been playing small. I've been hesitant to put myself out there, both professionally and personally. I've been allowing my fear of failure or of heartache to hold me back. But after this, after what happened, I realize that I want to put myself out there. I want to get myself out of my comfort zone. I want to take risks. Life is just too short not to."

A swell of excitement raced through me as I spoke. This last week had been a struggle to heal, but it had also ignited in me a desire to live, and I was going to take a hold of that desire and see where it took me.

Zuri smiled proudly and brought both her hands to her heart. "That's my girl," she said.

Dean nodded in support and tipped his beer to me. I took a sip of my beer as well.

Zuri turned her head toward the entrance of the patio. "Speaking of putting yourself out there, it looks like your boyfriend is here."

I looked over and caught Ethan's eye as he approached our table. He smiled and I felt a rush of warmth flow through me. Yep, I repeated to myself. I was ready to start living.

ABOUT THE AUTHOR

Kristen Dougherty is a lifelong mystery lover and a self-development addict. When she isn't consuming mysteries or coaching herself, she enjoys time with her fiancé and her dog. *Coaching Can Kill* is her first novel.